ALICE BLACKMOOR

Drowning in Venom

"Serpent's Nest" Book 2

First edition

Editing by Chelsea Anders
Cover art by Youness Elh

This book was professionally typeset on Reedsy.
Find out more at reedsy.com

For the women who are more interested in joining the monsters than fixing them.

Preface

When I first sat down to write *A Tangle of Serpents*, I never intended it to be part of a series. However, the characters (and my editor) had other ideas. I was more than halfway through the first draft when I realized that the most dynamic, interesting, and attractive character was not the brooding mafia don but his charming, sadistic, dramatic best friend. I'm sure many curses were yelled in my direction as you read the ending of the first book, but I hope you agree that it was worth it by the time you finish this second (and final, sorry Chels) installment of the *Serpent's Nest* series.

Content Warnings:

Drowning in Venom features dark themes. Throughout the story, the characters experience, enact, or witness grief, violence, torture, assault, murder, references to child abuse, and sexual assault. The romance is spicier and darker than *A Tangle of Serpents*, exploring themes of dominance, fear kinks, and knife play, to name just a few things. However, all of this takes place fully within the bounds of consent.

Everyone's boundaries for spice and violence are different, so I won't attempt a numerical rating for either. Just make the decisions that feel right for you and feel free to DNF at any moment if things get uncomfy.

Recap of "A Tangle of Serpents"

Newly divorced single mom Elizabeth is just trying to enjoy a quiet night out with her thoughts and some entertaining people-watching when she first meets the Marchetti men. Vincenzo is charming, almost boyishly so, and a stark contrast to his dark and intimidating friend, Damien. She doesn't think much of their initial interactions, but when Damien attempts to save her from a would-be rapist, they both realize there's more to one another than they'd assumed. Damien is intrigued by the woman who didn't need him to save her after all, and Elizabeth is shaken by her instinctual reaction to the coiled, simmering danger pouring from every aspect of Damien's being.

The three frequent the same haunts over the next few weeks, although they don't interact directly. Liz particularly notices the company Damien and Vince keep and a disturbing pattern of people tending to disappear soon after Vincenzo focuses on them. She starts to suspect there's more to the duo than they'd like the world to believe. One night, Damien finds Liz dancing with an off-duty bouncer at his club. His interest in her has only grown since the night they met, and it's more than he can stand to watch her grinding against another man. He intervenes, earning an earful from an angry Elizabeth for daring to tell her what she can and can't do. When he buys her a drink to apologize, she proves to be even more of an enigma by voicing her suspicions that Damien and Vince are involved in illegal activities. Though he brushes off her concerns, Damien resolves to keep a closer eye on her until he's sure she won't become a problem.

The two are thrown together again when Liz discovers that one of her clients is attempting to launch a cyber attack on Damien's company. She's certain by now that Damien is involved in criminal activity and struggles to decide whether she should warn him or stay as far away from him as possible. Luckily, he has no such hesitation, so his men are nearby when the client attempts to kidnap her to keep her from spilling his secrets. After a heated conversation where she confesses everything, and Damien berates her for disregarding her safety, the sexual tension between the two boils over.

Liz demands to be included in the plan to take down the attackers and is paired with Damien's younger brother, Alonzo, for the operation. She realizes too late that Alonzo is working with the attackers in an attempt to seize control of the Marchetti family, and she ends up imprisoned and used as leverage against Damien. Damien's instinct is to rush to her rescue, but Vince holds him off, and they form a more strategic plan that has Damien meeting with Alonzo. Meanwhile, Vince breaks into the warehouse where Liz is being held and kills everyone.

After the dust has settled, Damien and Liz decide to give their relationship a real chance, but it's not long before his overbearing and possessive nature has him interfering in her life and career to "keep her safe." Liz confides in a newly formed acquaintance, Maria, and the women begin spending more and more time together as they bond over their relationship troubles. Though her friend encourages her to give Damien another chance, it turns out that she simply doesn't want the two to break up before she can use Liz as a tool for revenge against Damien. During a movie night, Maria drugs Liz and is preparing to kill her when Damien bursts through the door. Damien kills Maria before she can harm Liz but isn't fast enough to dodge her shot at the same time. He bleeds out on the floor while Liz screams and confesses her love for him. Vincenzo arrives moments later, freeing Liz and immediately jumping into action to assume the role his late friend has left behind.

After Damien's funeral, Vince swears on his grave that he'll take care of the Marchetti family as well as Elizabeth. He vows to finish the quest of vengeance that he and Damien were on against the man who killed Damien's mother.

Chapter 1

Elizabeth

Mid-August – One Month After the Funeral

It feels like drowning, and yet you never die.

That's what life is like now. You know those scenes in movies where the character is drowning, but they're so out of it that they aren't even fighting back? They're just suspended underwater, eyes blinking slowly as they accept their fate. I'm stuck in that moment. No energy to fight, but unable to fully close my eyes and find peace. Suspended. Waiting.

The slam of a laptop lid breaks me out of my haze. As the other department heads and project managers file out of the conference room, I slowly gather my things. The notes doc I created is still blank, save for the date and attendees. I jot down what little I can remember from before I dazed off and shove the laptop into my bag.

It's not like it matters anyway. No one expects much from the internal projects team, and thanks to Damien's earlier influence, the execs are too afraid to suggest that I'm not putting forth my best effort. I mean, I'm *not*. But they'll let me get away with just about anything now.

My phone chimes as I near my desk. I consider ignoring it, but as I take it out of my pocket to set it on the charger, I realize it's a message from Vince. I've let a lot of relationships die in the wake of Damien's death, but Vince is one of the few that I can't let go of. Maybe it's guilt. I am the reason his best friend is dead, after all. I don't know why he even wants to hear my name, let alone keep in touch. But if keeping some thread of connection between us helps him cope, who am I to deny him that?

> Vince: Hey there, Copperhead. How's my favorite spicy danger noodle? You get all settled into the apartment, okay?

Not for the first time, I feel a bite of envy at Vince's acting skills. His mask slid into place mere moments after Damien's death, and it hasn't budged since. He's moved smoothly into his role as the new, unflappable leader of the largest organized crime family in the Southeast. At the same time, he keeps up a steady stream of good-natured banter anytime we speak. I wish I had the compartmentalization skills necessary to do that. I can barely drum up enough energy and willpower to pretend to be okay in front of Sam. I can't imagine the effort it must take to do it in absolutely every interaction.

> Me: Yeah, the move was smooth, and we're all settled. Thanks again for arranging the movers!

Maybe I should give myself more credit in the "pretending to be okay" department, at least when it comes to lying over text message. The move was uneventful from a logistical standpoint, but I'll bet the movers wouldn't say that having a client who breaks down in tears every 30 minutes because of her dead ex-boyfriend is their idea of an easy day.

Hell, I'm still shocked myself. I mean, I knew when I finally made the decision to move into the apartment Damien had left me that I would have to face a lot of memories. I just didn't realize my subconscious would decide I needed to face them all on Day One. Though perhaps that's what I get for bottling everything up until that point.

2

Oh well, it's not like they'll report back to him. Unless... aww, hell, he is technically the one who hired them.

"Ughhhh."

My forehead hits my desk with a thud, and I plead with the universe to grant me mercy in this one instance. I really don't want to talk about my lack of emotional stability with anyone, least of all the man who has every right to resent me yet refuses to do so. Oh well. There's no taking any of it back now. All I can do is distract myself and hope that I get lucky this time.

Aiming to do just that, I spend the rest of the afternoon trudging through emails and project plans, making updates as needed, and trying to keep my responses professional. All I actually want to do is tell Josh from accounting that he can shove his "preferred resource budget" up his ass. No matter how much Big Daddy CEO may want it, there's not a developer in the whole company who could get that project done in three weeks.

When my calendar finally chimes to tell me they day is over and it's time to go pick up Sam, I let out a heavy breath. *Thank god.* Gathering my things with the speed and precision of an MI6 agent, I'm in the elevator, heading toward the lobby before anyone else has even risen from their desks.

The new private school I've transferred Sam to, also thanks to Damien's will and the "education fund" set up for him, is just a few blocks from my job. I arrive just in time to see him exiting the front door with a couple of other boys. He smiles when he sees me, turning to say something to his friends before waving and running over. I was anxious that the move would be rough on him, but it seems like I needn't have worried.

Sam talks animatedly about the school, his new friends, and his teachers as we walk the rest of the way home. Apparently, the high points are that his science teacher has an actual robot assistant in his class, the playground includes a ninja course, and the cafeteria has a fruit buffet complete with a variety of seasoning options during lunch. *Jesus, maybe this place is worth the $20,000 tuition they're charging per semester.*

After dinner, I drag out Sam's bedtime routine as long as possible. When I catch my own consciousness fading to the sound of his soft, rhythmic breaths, I force myself up and back into the living room. This is the worst part of every night. The wandering. I shuffle through the empty space, turning on the fireplace even though it's summer. I just like to get lost in the flames sometimes. But I'm not ready to settle in yet, so I pad over to the open kitchen, making laps around the island as my fingers drag along the marble countertop. There's nothing to clean, nothing to prep, nothing that needs *doing*. But if I stop moving, that's when the torture starts. And so I wander instead, pacing through the apartment like an extra filming the latest zombie thriller.

My cruel subconscious is the most active at night and has grown resistant to the many forms of distraction I've applied over the last several weeks. Not even a gripping drama, a foolproof escape in my past life, can hold my attention long enough to keep me from replaying every naive, stubborn, selfish choice I made that led to Damien's death.

It's not that I think I don't deserve the punishment because I *know*, with every fiber of my being, that I have earned this. But I'm just so empty. So drained of energy, strength, and tears that it's starting to feel like I don't even care anymore. The numbness that's taken over every other aspect of my life is starting to creep into this, too. And honestly, that feels worse than anything.

*How fucking **dare** you? You think you can just file this away as something shitty that happened and move on with your life? Is that really how you think this works? Because Vince doesn't get that option, and Damien sure as hell didn't. So, who the hell are you to think that you should get special treatment?*

4

And she's right, whoever the "she" is that lives in my head. Maybe I should give her a name. Or maybe that's veering a bit too close to padded room territory. But either way, she's right, so I finally sit down in the living room, curling up in Damien's favorite leather armchair to stare absently at the fireplace as I accept my daily flogging with whatever scraps are left of my dignity and grace.

Chapter 2

Vincenzo

One Week Later

"...and then we'll take the elephant carcasses and send them to Albania for processing so that they'll be ready for..."

Gah, kill me now. I'm not cut out for desk jockey life. I've practically worn out the lock on my newest pocketknife trying to focus, but Gabriel has been talking for what feels like hours about these damn elephant carcasses. *Wait. What?!*

"Stop. What the fuck did you just say?"

Gabriel reaches down to tap the face of his phone before replying.

"Hmm, I think that's a new record." He smirks. "I made it through almost 18 minutes of bullshit before you tuned back in."

"*Fuck.*"

I sigh, running my hands through my hair. My Marchetti family ring snags on a curl, and I barely, just *barely*, resist the urge to rip it off and chuck it across the room. *Fucking ball and chain.*

I wince the second the thought crosses my mind. Being welcomed into the Marchetti family saved my life. All I've *ever* wanted was to serve this family in any way possible. It was my desperate, futile attempt to repay Federico Marchetti for taking me in, even when I was a constant reminder of his wife's death and his friend's betrayal. Yet now, just because the service the family needs from me is not of my choosing,

I'm ready to pack it in? To turn my back on the entire organization? Fuck that. *And fuck you, Caputo. Quit acting like such a princess and make your family, the only family that's ever really mattered, proud.*

"Alright. Run me through that last bit again. I tuned out after the briefing on the new production partnership."

Gabriel shoots me a searching look but doesn't comment any further on my lapse.

"Right. You've got dinner with the new chairman of Rockport Group next week. It's meant to just be a meet and greet, but it would be ideal if you could pique his interest in the Blackbird project. Gaining access to their raw materials network would help reduce production costs by at least 15%..."

It takes every ounce of willpower I possess, but I manage to stay focused as he continues, taking mental notes on the new chairman and resolving to do a bit of digging on my own before our meeting. *Never hurts to have a bit of leverage, after all.* Thankfully, that's the last report, so I don't have to hold out for too long.

Gabe stands to leave, tucking his tablet into his side. I move back to my desk, dropping into the charcoal desk chair with all the grace of a beleaguered day laborer, and snap open the forecast report that's waiting on my desk for final approval. When I notice his feet still rooted in place after a few seconds, I glance up at him without raising my head. He's got that look on his face again, eyes narrowed on me in scrutiny.

"If you've something to say, just spit it out, Martoza."

"It's just, well..." he starts uncertainly.

His hesitance is enough for me to close the report and focus fully on him. Gabriel is only a few years younger than me, in his late 20s, and one of the sharpest men I've ever worked with. Hell, if he hadn't kept things afloat during the early days of my transition, there's a solid chance my leadership would have been questioned a lot more than it was. I may hold a majority stake in the company, but I still wouldn't

7

have the level of trust that I currently do with the executive staff if not for Gabe's uncanny ability to anticipate what information I'll need before I even know I need it. After having spent the last month working closely together, I know that one thing Gabriel Martoza does *not* do is waffle. Until now, that is. I wait, fixing my eyes on him and making sure my face is open, inviting him to continue.

"Right."

He clears his throat.

"Well, to put it plainly, I'm getting married in a couple of months. Before his...passing, Mr. Marchetti had approved an extended leave of absence for the wedding and honeymoon on the basis that Ronaldo would take over my duties while I was gone. However, as you know, Ronaldo recently took a job outside the company. And, well, I know things have been chaotic due to the transition, and you're still being read in on some of the more obscure parts of the organization, but I wanted to talk with you about what to do regarding my leave."

I run a hand down my face, no easy solutions jumping out at me. But this is my problem to solve, not Gabriel's. He should be focusing on preparing for his wedding and making sure his work is organized enough to smooth the handover. The rest is on me.

"First of all, any arrangement you had with Damien still stands. The least this company can do to reward your dedicated service is to give you a few months off to settle into married life. So don't worry about that part."

Gabe gives me a tentative nod and expresses his thanks, watching me closely as if he expects a "but" to follow that statement.

"As for who that replacement will be now that Ronaldo is gone, just leave that part to me. I'm sure the staffing team can find someone suitable in the next few weeks. I'll let you know when I have a solid lead."

He thanks me again and tells me to just let him know if he can help facilitate interviews, but I wave him off.

"You just worry about keeping this well-oiled machine going until then. Oh, and I'll be out of the office after lunch. I've got some outside business to attend to."

Gabe just nods and heads back to his desk, used to that excuse from Damien, and likely well aware of what it actually means. He's a smart kid. I just hope we can find someone half as decent as him while he's gone.

* * *

Stepping into my home office isn't much better than being at Marchetti International, given that it is still, well, an office, but it does have its perks - the freedom to shed my tie and undo the top few buttons of my shirt being two of them. I drop into the charcoal desk chair, identical to the one I had installed at MI, and kick my feet onto the desk. Leaning my head against the seat, I steal a second to close my eyes and *think*. Not that I don't spend most of the day "thinking" now that I'm at the helm of not one but two multi-million dollar organizations, but that's all surface-level bullshit.

> There are the cookie-cutter decisions for MI:
>
> "Should we invest in this project or that one? Will the company focus on physical or digital customer outreach in the upcoming year?"
>
> "This one because it'll turn a more steady profit long term. And digital, but personalized. We want real people responding to customers, not AI."

And then there are the more *clandestine* decisions for the Marchetti family.

"The Colombians are raising their price by 20%. What should we do?"

"Tell them to go fuck themselves and shift the orders over to the Saltero Cartel. Yes, I am *aware* that their previous leadership betrayed us, captain fucking obvious. Their new regime runs a much different operation with a higher quality product than we've ever seen. Plus, Adrian Nuñez and I have come to a solid understanding. They won't be a problem again."

Like I said, boring, everyday *bullshit.* But that's what being the don of a criminal empire, as well as the chairman and CEO of an international conglomerate, entails. It's not a role I ever envisioned or desired for myself, but it's one that I fill dutifully as a successor to the Marchetti empire. I owe Damien and his father this much, at least.

That doesn't mean I don't still crave time to do what I'm best at, what I did every day for the past five years as consigliere to my best friend and the previous don, Damien Marchetti. I crave time to *think.* To puzzle out the larger, more complex threats and opportunities on our horizon. To stay two steps ahead of anyone who thinks they can encroach on what we've built, or in this particular case, to get revenge on someone who thinks they got away with murder two decades ago. *Let's just hope you're more on your game for this one than you were when Damien's future killer was sitting right under your nose, Caputo.*

Shaking away the true but unnecessary reminder – as if I could ever forget the failure that led to my best friend's murder – I open my eyes and sit up in my chair, feet dropping to the floor.

My man in Madrid thinks he's close to gaining the trust of one of the capos[1] in my sperm donor's operation. The bastard has set up a whole new identity, calling himself Marco Colombo these days, but to me, he'll always be Raphael Caputo, the gutter trash who cursed not only me but Damien to a cold, motherless existence when we were just children. Once we have a man inside his operation, it'll be time to kick things into high gear, which means setting up our own base of operations in the city.

If I'm being honest, that's what I really crave. Getting out from behind these damn desks that have become a special sort of prison and back into the field, dispatching the unique brand of justice that's earned me more than a few sordid nicknames over the years.

And while Damien's murder isn't directly related to this particular mission, it is adding an exponential amount of fuel to the fire that's driving my hunt. I swore on Damien's grave that I would carry out the vengeance that he never got the chance to deliver.

A swift knock at the door ends my rumination. At my call, several Marchetti capos file into the room. They stand before my desk, hands crossed, and await my invitation to sit before settling themselves into the wingbacked leather chairs that face my desk. Looking around the room at my most trusted men, I find myself resonating with the space's ambiance particularly strongly today. The stormy blue walls match my stormy mood, and the stoic expressions of the men seated within mirror that of my empty soul.

Yet, even on a day like today, I can't suppress a smirk as my eyes land on the decorative accents on the far wall. The thin strips of wood are painted to match the room and set in a repeating horizontal S pattern. I don't remember there being a point to the design when it was first installed. The designer even referred to it as "abstract." But since Elizabeth pointed out how fitting it was that one of her favorite

---

[1] generals

snakes had a slithering serpent embedded on his wall, I can't ignore the resemblance.

Thinking about Elizabeth makes me think about Damien all over again, though it takes a few seconds longer for my brain to make that connection than it used to. But to be frank, I don't have any more time to spend suffocating in rage and regret at the moment. Even more important than the persona I wear at MI is the one I project here in front of three of the most dangerous men on the Gulf Coast. They won't follow someone who's too weak to put aside emotions and focus on the business at hand, nor would I ever want them to. Locking away every human shortcoming I possess, I turn to face the nearest man, once again the embodiment of a carefully leashed and cunning monster.

"Roberto..." I drawl, fixing the man with an icy glare. "What the *fuck* happened at the lounge last night?"

Chapter 3

Vincenzo

Later That Evening

Blurry vision is the first clue that I've worked well into the evening again. I look up from the real estate report I was studying and rub my eyes, trying to blink them back into focus. A glance at my watch confirms that it's already 8:30 p.m. I've been working nonstop since I walked into the office, and my body is clearly over it. As soon as my vision clears, my stomach chimes in to remind me that I also haven't had anything to eat or drink since noon.

I pick up my phone to order takeout, too drained to bother with cooking. *Yet another night of the lone wolf special, I suppose.* Sigh. While I normally don't mind being alone, today that prospect feels particularly pathetic. *What if...*

As the call connects, I make a snap decision. Placing my order, I spring from my chair with renewed vigor. I skip the suit jacket, opting instead for Kevlar and leather. I need to let off some restless energy, and my newest shiny toy presents the perfect opportunity to do so. As I secure my helmet and kick up the stand, a true smile crosses my face for the first time all day.

Traffic is a beast, making me appreciate my choice of transportation even more. I fly through the streets with relative ease, senses heightened as I weave through the lanes. When I finally reach my destination,

I'm almost disappointed that the ride is over. But what, or who rather, awaits at the top of the building I'm currently parked beneath promises to be far better company than my own abrasive inner voice. *Assuming she lets me through the front door, of course.* But I came prepared. I shake my hair loose from the helmet, hoping it's at least somewhat presentable, and pull two takeout bags and a bottle of wine from the side pouch. *Surely, she can't turn down a guy bearing snacks and booze.*

I take the first elevator to the lobby, calling out a greeting to the concierge.

"Heya, Cliff. Think you could badge me up? My hands are a bit full." Raising my arms as a show of proof, I shoot him a pleading grin.

"Certainly, Mr. Caputo," Cliff nods as he meets me at the penthouse elevator. "Is Ms. Greystone expecting you?"

"Not exactly, but there's no need to call ahead. I'm aiming for surprise."

Cliff gives me an assessing look, probably trying to determine if Elizabeth will be reigning hellfire on him later for the lack of warning. Perhaps he's getting soft in his old age, because he eventually nods and swipes his badge to open the elevator.

"I hope your visit is just the pick-me-up Ms. Greystone needs," he tells me solemnly as I step inside. "She's lost her spark since Mr. Marchetti's passing. Perhaps going toe-to-toe with a troublemaker like yourself will reignite a bit of it."

"Troublemaker?!" I gasp. "Cliff, you've got me all wrong. I'm a trouble-solver, not a maker. If anyone should be accused of such mischief, it's the vixen 30 stories up who's got you believing her innocent act."

The sly smile on my face doesn't exactly support my case, but Cliff just shakes his head and chuckles as the elevator doors close. As soon as I'm alone, my smile drops, and I think about what Cliff said. I'd thought Elizabeth was coming back into herself lately. Sure, I was a bit concerned by the report I got from the moving company last week, but I thought maybe her moving day breakdown was a sort of final release for her since she seemed so much more upbeat this week. I even got a few emojis in her last couple of messages. *Maybe she's simply masking just as hard as you are, Rattles.*

If that's the case, that shit stops tonight on *both* sides. I know I sure as hell need at least *one* person that I can be real with, and I'm willing to bet she could use the same. The elevator doors open into Liz's entryway, but I don't step out right away. I call out, loud enough for her to hear me but hopefully not loud enough to wake Sam, assuming he's already asleep at this hour.

"Oh, Coooopperheaddd! Your favorite person has arrived bearing goodies. May I come in?"

I hear footsteps, and a beat later, Elizabeth's head pops around the corner from the living room, eyes narrowed in suspicion. She doesn't say anything, and for a fleeting moment, I think I'm going to be refused. But then I see her eyes spark as she realizes what's in the bags, and I know that I've won her over.

"Glass noodles?" She questions.

I answer with a nod.

"I even had them add extra sauce."

"Alright. Come on in."

Her head disappears back around the corner, and I follow her into the living room. I reach the seating area just as she's curling back into her cocoon on the couch, snug within at least two blankets despite the fact that she's already wearing sweats and fuzzy blue socks.

"You do know it's August, right?" I question as I lay out the food on the coffee table.

"Tell that to my anemia," she snarks, swiping a container and a pair of chopsticks.

Did I know she was anemic? I rack my brain but come up empty and

15

tell her as much.

"Yeah, well, I had a good handle on it for a while, but my eating habits have been less than ideal lately, I suppose, so here we are."

And there it is. That one sentence is all the confirmation I need to know that I put way too much trust in the fabricated chipper energy she's been feeding me through her messages. One thing Elizabeth Greystone does not have a problem with, or at least she never used to, is a solid eating schedule. Hell, I can recall several occasions where we had to rearrange our plans mid-day because Copperhead over here was "starving" and needed to be fed before her hangry side emerged.

Looking at her more closely now, I can see subtle signs that she's lost some weight, mainly in the sharpness of her jaw and a bit of hollowness around her eyes. Though that could also be a trick of the light, thanks to the dark circles she's sporting. To be fair, my own eyes aren't looking much different these days. Sleep is a fickle thing when your mind is determined to play your greatest failings on repeat for all of eternity.

At least she's tucking into her food with gusto now. I move to do the same, sliding a glass of wine over to her side of the table before settling back on the couch. It's only once we've both made a significant dent in our food that she speaks.

"So, to what do I owe the pleasure of a personal visit from Houston's most notorious crime lord?"

I debate cutting a joke about her forgetting my more respectable new titles, but realize that I just don't have the energy.

"Honestly? Today just sucked. Nothing out of the ordinary happened, but I was just feeling so...alone? Overwhelmed? Hell, I don't know what to call it. But I can't let anyone else see me struggling. I mean, you know who I have to be. I just needed to spend time with someone who would allow me to just be...real, I suppose. I needed to take off the mask, at least for a little bit."

She nods, trading her takeout container for a wine glass.

"I can understand that," she says quietly.

It looks like she's about to say more but stops. I wait for a few seconds, but she still doesn't continue.

"Where did you go just then? What are you thinking?"

She sighs, looking up from the wine glass she's been tracing with her finger and shoots glassy eyes in my direction.

"I'm thinking that I've only just this moment realized what a shitty friend I've been to you, yet again. I'm glad you came here when you needed someone, but I'm sorry you had to be the one to finally break down and force it. I should have been there for you more. I mean, you and Damien always used to be each other's safe space where you could just be yourselves. And now, not only have you taken on an insane amount of responsibility and power, but you're grieving the loss of the one person who could be that outlet for you. I should have realized you'd need someone to be there for you. But I was so wrapped up in what I'd lost that I didn't even bother to care about what anyone else was dealing with."

The dam finally breaks as she finishes her speech, a single tear tracking down her cheek. The sight snaps me out of my shock at her wholly undeserved self-flagellation, and I slide over to her side of the couch. Grabbing her face with both hands, I force her to hold my gaze.

"Listen to me very carefully. My current mental and emotional state is neither your fault nor your responsibility. I haven't been any better about seeing through the facade you were feeding me to realize that you're struggling just as much as I am. We are both just trying to keep our heads above water right now, and that's okay. I didn't tell you any of that to make you feel guilty. I told you that so you'd know how much I value your friendship, especially now. Because I didn't lose the one person I had that would allow me to be real. You're still here. I have you. And I hope that you realize that you have me, too."

I don't so much as blink as I wait for her to respond. This is important.

She needs to understand how completely serious I am right now. We were both destroyed by Damien's death, but if we have any hope of putting ourselves back together in a way that even remotely resembles the people we once were, we're going to need to do it together. I know that now. *I should have known it a month ago, but just add it to the ever-growing list of things I figured out too late.*

Finally, after what feels like forever, she nods and shoots me a soft smile. It's not much, but it's enough. I pull her into an embrace, her face buried somewhere between my neck and my chest, and squeeze tight. She frees one arm to wrap around my back, the other still clutching her wine glass between our chests. As I let go and she sits back up, wiping the remnants of her tears from her face, I'm suddenly unsure of what to do next. Heavy displays of emotion are not familiar ground for me unless that emotion is rage. At a loss for other options, I can't help but fall back on my trusty, old, dark humor crutch.

"You know, I'm pretty sure the last time I made you cry, Damien threatened to make my remaining time on Earth very short. Do you think ghosts are still capable of wielding a handgun?"

She barely manages to keep the wine she was sipping in her mouth, her cough turning into a laugh as she swallows.

"What the fuck, Vince?! You've got to warn a girl before you dive straight into ghost jokes. Jesus!"

But she's still laughing, so...mission accomplished, even if my timing was a bit off.

"And I'll have you know," she snarks as her laugh dies down, "all he did was tell you to stop making me cry. That threat was actually a warning to me about what would happen to any other man if I ever called him 'baby'...save for teasing you, of course."

"Ah, you're right. I was confusing the two. Well, that's a relief. But just in case, do you have some table salt I could take home with me tonight?"

It seems that was just the conversation starter we needed, and we spend the next several hours drinking and trading our favorite memories of Damien. Knowing that I need to be steady enough to get home on my bike, I stay away from the whiskey and stick to just a few glasses of wine.

"Wait a damn minute," Liz says when I mention it. "You bought a *motorcycle?!*"

"Yes. And?"

"And? And I don't know whether to be excited or anxious over that decision. I mean, I kind of want a ride, but also, *you are not allowed to die on me, too!*"

"Woah, calm down there, Copperhead. No one is dying on anyone. I am the picture of safety, I swear it. Helmet, armored gear, the whole nine yards."

"And your driving?"

"I am always in complete control of the situation."

Elizabeth's narrow gaze tells me she sees through my dodgy answer, but she doesn't press. Instead, she reminds me yet again just how shrewd she really is.

"Feeling a bit cooped up, are we?"

"Umm, what? Change of subject, much?"

"No, same subject. I'm just saying that you're probably going crazy stuck behind a desk or in meetings most days, so I guess I can understand why you bought the bike. Needed to feel some adrenaline again, right?"

Elizabeth is a living picture of the cat that got the cream, an arrogant smirk spreading slowly across her face. *It's slow blinks to assert dominance around a feline, right? Or is it no blinks?* Whichever one it is, I doubt it even matters. She's too busy being proud of herself to even notice, let alone be cowed by any displays of power on my part. *Ah, let her have this one, Caputo. You know she's earned it.*

"Well, hot damn. Am I that transparent?"

"Don't worry. I doubt your *soldiers* will think of it that way if that's what you're worried about. Hell, in their eyes, it probably just makes you even more worthy of following. I mean, it's basically a big 'fuck you' to mortality. Pulling something like that after everything that's happened? They're probably more afraid of you than ever. The most dangerous people are the ones who don't fear their own death."

The crackle of fire is the only sound as I process what she's said. *God, I've missed this.* This real, insightful, no-holds-barred kind of conversation with someone who knows me, the real me. Or at least as much of the real me as anyone does. Liz may not know me as well as Damien did, but the shit we've been through in our short acquaintance, plus her uncanny ability to see beneath the surface, means she knows me a hell of a lot better than any of the men that work for me, even Mono.

The smile that had crept onto my face at the thought is muted as I respond, reality charging back into my thoughts. My short reprieve is apparently over.

"Well, I may not fear dying, but I do fear meeting that fate before I've had time to fulfill my promises to Damien. I've stepped into Damien's shoes, but no one has stepped into mine, and everything is just taking too damn long."

A frustrated growl escapes my throat as my head drops into my hands. I hear Liz shuffle on the seat next to me and the soft thunk of her glass landing on the coffee table.

"Huh, I guess I'd never thought about it before, but how does one replace the head of intelligence for an underground organization? I mean, it's not like you can just solicit resumes. And how would you even know if they were qualified? I imagine that's something you'd need to see in live action, isn't it?"

I raise my head just enough to peer at her through the few errant curls that have dropped over my face. I expect to see a teasing grin on her face, but she looks dead serious. She's really sitting there thinking through the logistics of hiring a right-hand man for the head of a criminal enterprise as if it were one of her projects. Even my caustic thoughts are no match for the sheer absurdity of this conversation, and I catch an indulgent smile snaking its way across my face in their absence.

"Hold on there, Copperhead, before your head starts smoking from how fast you've got those gears spinning. I don't think another me is really what I need. I am still the best person to handle that side of things. It's just taking longer than I'd hoped for things move into maintenance mode between Marchetti International and the family business. It'll all even out in time, I'm sure."

I'm not entirely sure I believe that, but either way, she doesn't need to spend her time worrying about it. She mumbles something that I don't quite catch but nods as she stands up, grabbing our wine glasses and the empty bottle.

"Should I open another bottle?" she asks as she pads into the kitchen.

After checking my watch, I tell her not to bother. We'll probably both be cursing our lack of responsible choices as it is when our alarms blare in just a few short hours. I stand and stretch, shaking life back into my drowsy muscles as I grab my jacket off the back of a chair. Liz meets me at the entryway hall, a contemplative look on her face.

"I'm glad you stopped by tonight, Vince," she says plainly. "I thought I needed space to get over my grief alone, but now I think that talking about him helps more than anything. My soul just feels lighter, you know?"

"I know exactly what you mean. And just to make sure there are no misunderstandings between us, our days of respectful distance and fake positivity via text are over. If you're having a shitty day, not only do I want you to just say that, but you should also be prepared to have me show up on your doorstep with snacks no more than a few hours later. Capisce[2]?"

"Capisce. As long as you know that applies to you, too. And I know you have everything under control, but if there's anything I can do to help ease some of your burdens with *either* Marchetti organization, you sure as hell better let me help."

I give her my signature charming smile.

"It's a deal, Copperhead. Just remember this conversation and that you offered first in the future."

"Yeah, yeah," she mumbles. "Now get over here, you big oaf. Let me hug you one last time before you're a crespelle[3] on the side of 610."

A low chuckle rumbles through my chest as I wrap her in a firm hug. *Someone's been studying up on their Italian culture. I wonder if Damien took her to Nona's. Her crespelle with spinach and ricotta has always been the best.*

I let her pull away first, and when she does, I snag my helmet off the sideboard and step toward the elevator. Just before the elevator doors close, I call out.

"Oh, and Elizabeth? You owe me dinner sometime soon. I had to tip those movers extravagantly to cover the emotional damage they sustained thanks to your repeated mental breakdowns."

I can't see her face as the doors close, but her groan is loud enough to be heard through the steel doors. Seconds later, my phone chimes.

> Liz: I refuse to acknowledge anything you just said. You must be mistaken. Also, this is why I always say you should never trust a snake.

I chuckle and slide the phone back into my pocket before donning my

---

[2] Understand?

[3] thin Tuscan crepes, often used in place of pasta

22

helmet. *Yeah, she's going to be just fine.*

Chapter 4

Elizabeth

The Following Day

No part of me has any intention of waking up when my alarm chimes the next morning. Running on only a few hours of sleep has never been something I'm naturally good at, and it takes less than a second to decide that I'm turning the alarm off and rolling over. I'm sure Sam wouldn't mind a mental health day, right? *Wrong.* It's that exact moment that I'm accosted by a small banshee in swim trunks yelling something about "aquasports day."

Once my brain catches up, I remember that Sam's school has dedicated the day to all things water. Apparently, everything from math to language arts and even music will be taught outside using water as a base. Realizing there's zero chance he'll take me up on my offer of playing hooky, I channel all the energy I can muster to wrestle his wriggling body off of me and tickle him into submission.

"Okay, wild boy. Go grab a yogurt and a granola bar for breakfast and give Mom some time to get dressed."

As he bounds off down the hallway, I drop my feet onto the floor and trudge over to my closet. *Stupid, expensive, overachieving private school. How dare they make children excited to go to school! Where's the angst? The melancholy? What kinds of monsters are these people?!*

I grab the first suitable thing I see, and before long, Sam is skipping backward down the sidewalk, chattering animatedly about all the things he's going to do today.

Once he's safely inside the school gates, I finally have a moment to reflect on my own upcoming day. There's certainly nothing exciting on the docket. Hell, there hasn't been anything exciting on the docket in the entire time I've been in the internal projects department. Not that I expected there would be. It's a big part of the reason I fought so hard when Damien's well-intentioned but poorly thought-out meddling landed me there in the first place. But despite the lack of excitement, I still feel...brighter about the day than normal. Hmm. Yeah, I think that's the only way to describe it. For the first time in a long time, I'm feeling optimistic and much more like the old go-getter Liz. I'm sure I have Vince and his late-night therapy session to thank for that, so I suppose dark circles and a bit of fatigue are a small price to pay for reclaiming a piece of myself.

As I ride the elevator up to the Cerberus floor, I decide that I'm going to use my newfound motivation to restart the job search I was in the midst of when Damien died. I need to get out of the suffocating Hell that I'm now stuck in, and leaving Cerberus is the only way to do it. But in the meantime, I'll also do my best to leave the department in better shape than I found it. It's the least I can do, considering all the leeway the team has given me lately.

By mid-afternoon, my motivation is still holding strong but the energy needed to actually accomplish anything has almost completely evaporated. Dire circumstances call for dire measures, and I break my self-inflicted "no coffee after lunch" rule to run down to the cafe in the building lobby. I need a boost to get through the end of the work day and the start of the mom day, and I'm pretty sure I'm tired enough that this afternoon jolt won't keep me counting sheep into eternity later tonight. Fingers crossed, at least.

I'm at the condiment bar, methodically seasoning my drink in a way that's been perfected over years of caffeine addiction when a masculine voice sounds to my right.

"You know, the baristas will do all that for you if you just mention it at the register. They are the experts, after all."

Looking up, I see the voice belongs to an attractive man in a fitted grey suit. He's shooting me a charming smile full of gleaming white teeth. Carefully styled salt and pepper hair makes him look distinguished but doesn't age him the way it would me if I let mine grow so freely. *Rude-ass beauty double standards.* By my quick glance, I'm guessing he's around 40 and not someone I've seen around before, despite years working in the building. I turn back to finish doctoring my coffee as I reply.

"Experts they may be, but they are also constantly swamped, and mastering my personal idiosyncrasies is most definitely not in their job description. I'm happy to do it myself."

"Spoken like someone who knows what's what. I'm guessing you've done time in the service industry."

"Mmmm," is the only reply I can offer as I lick the leftover spices and foam off my stir stick before throwing it away. "All throughout high school and college, in fact. Learned early on never to trust someone who hasn't spent at least a year working retail or food service of some sort."

The look I give him is pointed. Based on his initial commentary, I'm assuming he hasn't spent any time in the industry, and I'm not in the mood to withstand inane chatter from an entitled executive who got where he is by simply being a man who knows other men. His response is not what I expected, and I have to work to hide my surprise.

"Ah, so true. I, myself, spent five years as a barista during college. I had the beanie and everything. Though I always liked it when pretty women trusted me with their complicated coffee orders. I made sure to take extra care with those. Show them they were in capable hands."

I swear his blue eyes twinkle as he shoots me another grin. *What is happening right now? Is he...flirting with me?* Oh no, this won't do.

"Right, well, it's been...interesting chatting with you, but I need to get going. Enjoy the rest of your day!"

"Wait, before you go, could you point me in the right direction? It's my first time in the building, and I'm headed to a client meeting. Do you know where the ARC offices are?"

"ARC? Oh, right, I think they're on five. You'll want the elevator bank on the left-hand side."

"Ah, thank you so much. I'm Lance, by the way. And you are...?"

He extends his hand, and my people-pleasing nature won't let me ignore it. I meet it with my own and give a firm shake.

"Elizabeth."

"Well, thank you again, Elizabeth. Perhaps I'll see you around on a future visit."

I doubt the likelihood of that since I usually spend the entire day holed up on the Cerberus floor, save for the occasional lunch out. But he doesn't need to know that.

"Yeah, sure. Maybe."

With a small wave, I head toward the right-hand bank of elevators. I turn over the conversation in my head as I wait. I'm not usually so quick to judge, and it's even rarer that I'm so far off base. Looking back, it seems like Lance was just trying to make friendly conversation with a woman he may or may not find attractive. There's nothing wrong with that. It's not like he could know that I'm so far off the market right now that not a single man in existence could catch my eye. And it's not like he's unattractive. In another life, I'd probably be all over that. *Ugh, pull it together, Liz. We're going to have to be more graceful than this if we don't want to end up with Vince as our only friend for eternity. No shade to Vince, of course, but still...*

Oh well, nothing I can do about it right this second. *Deficiency noted and filed away next to the rest for future examination. Now, on to what we can change more immediately.* By the time I sit down at my computer, I've put the entire exchange out of my head and I fully immerse myself back into my improvement plan for the department.

* * *

As I'm packing up my things later, I feel like I've got a solid plan for how to make some real impact on the department. Of course, it's not likely to fully relocate the team from the land of forgotten toys, but it should at least bring some structure and respectability to the work they do every day.

I've also decided that it's time I started working out, mostly thanks to a ream of copy paper that almost murdered me when I was moving things around in the supply room earlier. I'm not getting any younger, and if I'm going to have any hope of keeping a budding teenager in check over the coming years, I'll need a lot more strength and stamina than my neglected frame currently offers. It's good for sons to know that Mom can still put them into a headlock if they get too crazy.

That's not to say I'm going to become a fitness guru, but a bit of running and some light weights won't be unwelcome. And thanks to the swanky gym on the 10th floor of our new building, I can safely sneak away to work out while Sam sleeps at night and still keep an eye on him through the camera feeds in the apartment security system.

I do just that after post-bedtime cleanup, despite my lingering fatigue from my late night with Vince. I know myself well enough to know that I need to seize this momentary motivation now or risk losing it altogether by the time I wake up tomorrow. Snagging a treadmill on the far end of the row, I pop in my earbuds and crank up the volume on my phone. Before long, I'm fully immersed in the act of keeping my breathing steady, and my mind clears almost entirely, granting me the type of mental reprieve I've been dying for but have been wholly unable to obtain over the past few weeks.

Ugh, are you freaking kidding me? This whole time I could have just been working out?! Not a fan of the implication that the solution was right in front of my face, or rather just a few floors beneath my feet, I instead decide that it's only the combination of my cathartic conversation with Vince alongside the exercise that has allowed this level of release.

Trudging back into my apartment later that evening, I'm exhausted but feeling content. After the quickest shower known to man, I decide to damn the consequences and flop onto my pillow with wet hair. *Worst case, I can always wet it again in the morning, right? As if that's not the personal hygiene equivalent of "I'll stop for gas before work."* C'est la vie[4], though, because sleep overtakes me mere seconds later, and I drop blissfully into her arms.

---

[4] That's life

Chapter 5

Early September

I meet Andre's eyes over the video connection as he briefs me on his progress in setting up our foothold in Spain. Things seem to be close to finalized in Madrid, but I've also asked him to set up a satellite base in the port city of Valencia. What started as just a cover story to get access to Raphael has evolved into a legitimate expansion operation. Once Raphael's organization is wiped out, the Marchetti family will be ready to swoop in and assume the territory.

"It's been a bit more difficult to source suitable properties in Valencia, given the heavy cartel influence near the docks, but I've just emailed over two properties that look like good options."

Pulling up the file, I don't see any obvious deficiencies with either property.

"Which will be easier to adapt for security?" I ask, partly to test Andre's aptitude and partly because I truly don't feel like making yet another decision at the moment.

"The traditional villa has the benefit of the concrete surround and proximity to both the airport and the port, but truly, the newer property on Del Rio has a much more strategic interior layout and a better defensive position. It sits at the end of an isolated street and backs up to a cliff, so it would be difficult to approach from most sides. It also

30

wouldn't be too much effort to put up a high privacy fence."

His words are confident, but I can see the uncertainty in his eyes as he waits for my response. His gaze darts between his camera and his screen as if he's afraid he's overlooked some detail that might nullify his assertion. My answering smirk is enough to have him breathing out a subtle sigh.

"Bravo, apprendista[5]. I agree. Let's secure the property on Del Rio, and make sure to outfit it similarly to what we've discussed for the Madrid property."

After assuring me that the other preparations are progressing smoothly, Andre promises that he'll have the final paperwork for all of the properties and vehicles on my desk by the end of the week. Of course, officially, everything belongs to Impuente, a Marchetti subsidiary based in Spain that's buried under several layers of corporate shell companies to avoid Raphael catching wind of our plans. But that's for the lawyers and accountants to work out. All I need to know is that when I ultimately land in Spain, I'll have a secure base of operations, plenty of tools to carry out my mission, and the element of surprise on my hands.

The rest of my meetings for the day are for the legitimate businesses, and it is thriving. We've several upcoming acquisitions, one merger, and a handful of new product launches planned for the next six months. Which is fantastic. Truly it is. But how in the ever-loving hell am I supposed to maintain momentum on all of this while at the same time spending the majority of my time in Spain hunting down the devil?

It doesn't help that Gabriel is due to start his leave in a little less than four weeks. *Seriously. What the actual fuck am I going to do? There's no way in Hell that I can do all of this without Gabe, even with Spain off the table.*

---

[5] Well done, apprentice.

He must be thinking the same thing, because Gabriel interrupts my brooding to mention that the last several candidates he interviewed to temporarily assume his role weren't quite up to par.

"I think we need to find a new headhunter," he tells me flatly. "I mean, I know they're temps, but one of the last candidates they sent over asked me what a board of directors was."

The disgusted look on his face is enough to make me laugh, even though the situation is anything but funny at this late stage in the game.

"Honestly, Gabriel, at this point, I'm not even sure bringing in just one replacement will cut it. I feel like I'm going to need a whole fucking army to cover for you while you're out."

"Hey, there's an idea!" he chuckles. "Maybe we *should* recruit someone with a military background. An ex-drill sergeant would be perfect. Someone who's good at whipping things into shape and keeping them that way. Yeah, maybe I should call..."

As Gabe paces around the office, talking mostly to himself about the different feelers he could put out on that particular idea, I have a rogue thought of my own. *What if I don't need an actual drill sergeant but just one militant and highly detail-oriented project manager who's not afraid to go toe to toe with monsters, let alone insipid businessmen...*

I shoot to my feet, decision made almost before the thought has finished forming.

"Stand down, Gabe. I've got it handled."

I ignore his sputter and questioning look as I throw on my suit jacket and swipe my phone from my desk before striding toward the door.

"Hold my calls and reschedule any meetings I've got for the rest of the afternoon. I need to go see a snake about a job."

* * *

Unfortunately for my enthusiasm, she doesn't agree to meet with me until later that evening. But that's for the best. I use the extra time to solidify my case, knowing that this won't be an easy sell, no matter how generous the compensation package.

I'm the first to arrive at Vic's, securing our usual semi-secluded booth in the corner. A subtle nod to Marlo at the bar ensures a strong drink isn't far behind. Reclining against the booth, I run my gaze across the restaurant. It's a normal Friday night crowd - politicians, businessmen, and a table of moronic finance bros half-drunk along the back wall. I've already lost interest in them when the one at the head of the table loudly proclaims his lack of fear of those "limp-dicked Marchetti assholes."

Oh, you've got my attention now, frat boy.

I'm too far away to catch everything that's being said, but I hear enough to conclude that he owes us a fair bit of money after a recent bender that involved both gambling and what I'm guessing was enough cocaine to kill an elephant. I'm about to call in one of my men to interrupt his night out when he makes the biggest mistake of his life.

"Oh, come off it. How scary can they be? The way I heard it, their boss got offed by some chick just a few weeks ago. If some bitch can take out their top dog, they can't be all that tough to start with. I'm sure I can handle myself."

Oh, fuck that. Quella fica è mio[6]. But that will have to wait until later. I slide my phone back into my pocket just as Elizabeth walks up, shooting me a wide smile. Given her expression, I'm assuming she didn't hear the bastard's comments. And thank God for that. I'm not sure I could jump over the table quick enough to stop her if she'd caught wind of what that little maggot was saying.

I stand at her approach, stepping out from behind the table to give her a hug before sliding back into my seat as she joins me in the curved

---

[6] That cunt is mine.

booth. *That used to be Damien's seat. Neither one of us ever liked sitting with our backs to the room.* I smile a little as I contemplate the unexpected thought. It suits her. If anyone is worthy of sitting in Damien's place, it's Elizabeth.

The waiter approaches to take Liz's drink order, and I use the time to survey my target. She seems to be in a good mood, and a genuine one, too, considering her smiles are actually reaching her eyes tonight. That's an encouraging sign, but I'm not fool enough to think that it guarantees my success. We should with food first, just to ensure there's no trace of her hangry gremlin sabotaging things before I even get started. We're about a quarter of the way through our main courses when she gives me a knowing look.

"Okay, enough buttering me up with food and drinks. What are you up to, and what do I have to do with it?"

Forfeiting the bite of steak I was preparing, I set down my utensils and pick up my napkin to brush across my mouth. Shooting her an amused smirk, I lean back against the wall before I reply, earning a glare in return for making her wait. *Patience never has been among her virtues.*

"Nothing gets past you, does it, Copperhead?"

All I get are raised eyebrows and a head tilt in reply, so I decide to cut the flowery speech I'd drafted in my head in favor of just hitting her with it straight.

"I want you to quit your job," I state flatly. "And before you get all up in arms, it has nothing to do with trying to keep you locked away in a bubble for your safety. Quite the opposite, actually. I want you to come work for me."

I watch her shift tactics in real time as she squashes the urge to punch me for undermining her independence and instead enters detective mode, likely convinced there's something else at play that she's missing.

"You want me to come work for you."

"Yes."

"Work for you *how*?"

"Doing exactly what you do now, except the projects you'll be managing will be much more varied, fast-paced, and frankly far worthier of your skills and expertise. You'd report directly to me. Your official title will be the Senior Director of Special Projects for Marchetti International."

Her eyes narrow, and though she takes a few moments to consider my offer, I can see her rejection in them before she speaks it.

"Absolutely not."

Her tone is firm, and she's looking at me like a disappointed mother, but I'm not that easily dissuaded.

"May I ask why? Have you suddenly developed a tendre for the soul-sucking black hole that is your current job?"

"No," she grits out. "But my keen self-preservation instincts are telling me that working for you is far more dangerous to my soul, especially since I can hear the drum of the 'unofficial' title that accompanies the flashy official one as loud as if you were banging it in my ear."

"Ah, I see."

I sit forward, tilting my head knowingly as I lean closer to her.

"You don't think you have what it takes to make it in the underworld. That's disappointing. I suppose you were all bark and no bite all those times you spent telling Damien and me how we should be running the business."

"Stop trying to bait me, Vince. It won't work."

"Ah, but it's working a little bit, isn't it Copperhead? I can see you biting your lip to keep from telling me that you could run things better with one hand behind your back than I could with two extra hands. It's interesting that your moral code seems to have shifted now that you

35

might have to get your own hands dirty. Oh, careful, I think you're starting to draw blood."

"Dammit, Vincenzo!" She finally explodes, hands landing on the table with a smack. "You know damn well I don't give two shits about the morally grey bullshit that comes along with what you do. Hell, I grew up being let down by the traditional justice system enough times that I much prefer having a more direct path to evening the scales when needed. But what I *do* care about is that type of life affecting Sam, and there's a hell of a lot stronger chance of that happening if I start actively participating instead of simply offering moral support from the sidelines."

A valid point, I suppose. But not a strong one. And I've already prepared my rebuttal for that anyway.

"I understand your concern. Truly, I do. But it's not like I'm proposing you both move into the family mansion and start training him on advanced torture tactics. I mean, be honest. Does Sam even know the type of work you do now beyond some vague concept based on what you've explained to him?"

I pause and raise my eyebrows at her, waiting for a response. At her reluctant head shake, I reiterate the point.

"Okay, so why does coming to work for me have to change that? As far as Sam is concerned, you still go to work to pay the bills, and nothing about Mom at home has to change. It wouldn't even change anything from a safety perspective. The role I'm proposing is strictly an advisory one. You'll work in an office with me or my trusted employees. You won't be out roughing up rivals or conducting interrogations. No one outside the family even needs to know that you exist. And besides, you're already under Marchetti protection since you insist on continuing to associate with a psychopath like me. So, it'll just be more of the same in that regard."

I've almost got her. I can see it in her posture and how she's working her jaw as if she's fighting her last thread of control. She's trying so hard to keep from agreeing to do this thing that she actually really wants to do, but her ingrained sense of societal expectations is refusing to allow it. Luckily, I know just what will nudge her over the line. Perhaps it's a dirty trick, but I've never claimed to fight fair.

"If for nothing else, do this so that together we can find the bastard who killed Damien's mom and put a bullet in his brain. It's something Damien never got to finish, and I swore on his grave that I would see it through on his behalf. It'd be a hell of a lot easier with a partner at my side."

There she is. Liz's eyes shoot to mine, all trace of hesitation lost. She's in.

"Jesus, Vince. Talk about burying the lede. You couldn't have started with that?!"

"Hey, look, it isn't *all* about that. I'm drowning, woman, and I need your help with both sides of the business if I have any hope of keeping them afloat without losing my fucking mind. The last part is just a bonus project, really."

"Alright," she says, shaking her head as if even she can't believe she's agreeing to this. "I'll do it. But I have to ask. Why me specifically? I'm sure you could afford to hire just about anyone for the MI business, and you have no shortage of loyal soldiers who'd be ready to step up for the family business at any moment. So why bring in an outsider?"

Her teal eyes are softer now, curiosity and the slightest hint of self-doubt sparkling within them. *Ah, you silly woman.*

"Frankly, Elizabeth, I don't know that anyone else could possibly be better suited for this role than you. You're more than qualified for the MI role, judging by everything I've seen you do with Cerberus. And yes, I do mean everything. Remember that my background checks are thorough."

I shoot her a wink as she grumbles something about wondering what a girl's got to do to get some privacy around here. *Not jumping headfirst into a nest of serpents would be a good step one, darlin'.*

"And as for the family business, you have one of the sharpest natural inclinations for observation and analysis that I've ever seen. Not to mention your spine is tougher than adamantium, and you don't take any shit from anyone, not even me. That's exactly the kind of person I need working alongside me, helping me to pull together the big picture from a thousand loose threads, and speaking on my behalf when I'm not around. I have plenty of soldiers and employees, but the biggest thing I lost when Damien died was a partner."

She has never been good at taking a compliment, and it seems that's still true, given that she's now refusing to meet my eyes and squirming with discomfort at my assessment. I've always wondered why that is. She certainly has no problem biting back at anyone who demeans her ability or the accuracy of her statements, so she seems to have plenty of confidence. What's so different about someone recognizing her worth that she can't seem to stomach? Whatever it is, we'll have to work on that. She deserves to see herself the way that I see her, and I'm making it my personal mission right now to make sure that happens.

But I've pushed my luck far enough tonight already, so instead of questioning her lack of self-esteem, I redirect her attention to the food in front of her. Promising to have the full employment contract in her inbox this evening, we put aside any further talk of work and spend the rest of the evening as simply two friends catching up over dinner.

* * *

Later that night, long after I bid goodnight to Liz at the restaurant, I'm seated at the bar inside Rain, another one of the Marchetti nightclubs. I've been keeping a close eye on Mr. Justin Liverworth, III. *Even his name is so utterly predictable. Just as pretentious as the man himself is moronic.* Douchebag McGee is still holding court as if he's the fucking king, though thankfully, one of his less idiotic friends cut him off and started handing him tonic water a couple of hours ago. It wouldn't do for him to be too drunk for our little chat, after all.

When he finally breaks away from the group and heads toward the bathrooms, I'm so tightly wound that it's a wonder I haven't snapped my pocketknife in half with the force of my grip. Few things test the limits of my self-control, but disrespecting Damien's memory is absolutely one of them. It's taken everything I have to avoid shooting him point-blank and being done with it. But that wouldn't do. Not really. A quick death like that is far too generous, all things considered. And while what I have in mind won't do anything to bring Damien back, I'm hoping that avenging his honor will provide temporary relief from the venomous thoughts I'm constantly drowning in these days.

I stalk after him, grabbing an abandoned broom from a corner of the back hallway and snapping it in half on my thigh before striding into the dingy bathroom. After a quick visual inspection confirms that no one else is inside, I use the bottom half of the broom to secure the door, wedging it into the handle.

Liverworth still hasn't noticed me, or if he has, he hasn't registered the threat I present. Too busy playing with his pecker at the urinal, I'm sure. I wait until he zips up and moves to the sink before I make my move. I don't feel like having to bleach my eyeballs tonight. My footfalls echo in the tiled space as I saunter towards him, the broken broomstick resting on my shoulder and a hand tucked into my pocket for dramatic effect.

"Justin, Justin, Justin. It's a shame dear old Dad never thought to teach you manners. Do you think he'll regret that? You know, when you're gone?"

He doesn't have time to do more than turn his head and mutter a confused "Huh?" before the broomstick connects with the side of his face.

"Shit! What the fuck?! Who the fuck are you?!" he growls, one hand gripping the side of his face as he staggers back several steps.

"Ah, how rude of me. I'm Vincenzo Caputo, of course."

I punctuate the introduction with a sardonic bow, twirling the broomstick in my hands as I come back to my full height.

"Though you probably know me better as the, what did you call it? Oh, right, the 'top dog' of the Marchetti family."

Normally, seeing his face pale and listening to him begin to stammer as he realizes what's happening would bring me great satisfaction. But tonight, I'm just annoyed. Annoyed that I'm here, purging the world of insignificant trash like him instead of relaxing at home with a glass of wine to celebrate my success with Elizabeth earlier. But someone's got to leave a strong message for any other swine like him, and I *am* the perfect man for the job. *Let's see if anyone dares disrespect Damien or the Marchetti name after word of poor Justin's horrific death gets around.*

"P, please. I promise I'm going to pay up. I can have the money in your account in less than two hours if you just let me go."

I use the jagged end of the broomstick to poke him in the chest as I stalk forward until he's pressed against the grimy wall.

"Oh, Justin. It's far too late for that. In case your whiskey-muddled mind hasn't yet made the connection, I heard what you said. I was at Vic's earlier tonight, and I couldn't *not* hear your rather obnoxious comments about my brother and the Marchetti family as a whole, considering how loudly you were proclaiming them."

There we go. His face shifts from white to sickly green, the gravity of the situation finally clear in his no doubt pea-sized brain. Rearing back, I swing again for his face and relish the sickening crunch as his cheekbone shatters under the force. He curses and covers the spot with his hands again but makes no move to fight back. *Spineless coward.* Jabbing the broomstick under his chin, I lift up until he looks me in the eye.

"I'm not here to collect on your debts, though rest assured I will make sure those accounts are settled with your father after we're done here. But from you directly, well, I'm here to collect a rather different type of payment..."

I don't bother clarifying. Surely by now he knows what I mean. And if he doesn't, the sick grin spreading across my face is sure to give it away. Besides, I'm tired of talking, and my monster is positively howling to be set free.

Discarding the broomstick, my fist finds purchase in his stomach, and a sharp knee to the face breaks his nose when he instinctively bends over. He staggers to the side, nearly falling onto the filthy toilet in the nearest stall. Prowling after him, I aim a flat-footed kick at his knee, dislocating it and causing him to crumple to the floor. I'm on him like a starved beast, blow after blow connecting with his head and torso. He's full-on begging now, his words barely escaping his swollen and bloody mouth between the whimpers and screams that surface with each new strike.

"Please, please! I'll do *anything*. Please d-don't kill me. I'm s-s-sorry. I was drunk. I didn't mean any of it. I swear. I didn't mean it."

"Ugh! Shut. The fuck. Up!" I snarl, wrapping both hands around his throat. "I can't stand the sound of your insipid voice any longer, you sniveling little *cunt!*"

I squeeze harder with every word until the veins in my arms are near to bursting with the effort. I can feel his windpipe crumbling beneath my thumbs, and he gets quieter and quieter until even his strangled gasps cease, and his head lolls to the side. *Finally. Peace and fucking quiet.*

Pushing his lifeless body roughly away from me, I take stock of the scene as I work to cool my blood and get my breathing under control.

41

There's blood everywhere in this corner of the room, pooled in the toilet and on the floor, splattered on the tiles and stall, and, most prominently, covering my hands, face, and clothing.

It's a grim picture for sure, but it doesn't really communicate the specific message I'm aiming to send. *Well, let's fix that, shall we?* I grab one of Liverworth's ankles and drag him from the stall into the middle of the room before positioning him on his knees in a pleading position. I slide the tie from around my neck and wrap it around his wrists with his palms pressed together and fingers interlocked, bringing them to his chest. The broomstick is just the right height to wedge beneath them, holding his limp body upright and in place. Running my fingers through the blood pooled in the corner, I draw an M with a set of demon horns on the floor next to him, my own personal version of the Marchetti calling card.

Stepping back to assess the image, I'm satisfied with what I see. He's precariously balanced but should hold long enough for someone to find him and snap a photograph, at the very least. I take the time to wash my hands at the sink but don't bother trying to clean my face or clothing. This is my club, after all, and anyone on the police force who matters is in my pocket.

Wrenching the makeshift lock from the door handle, I exit the room and head for the back alley where my car is parked. The horrified looks on the faces of the nearby partygoers, darting between me and the bathroom, reassure me that it won't take long for everyone to be starkly reminded of what happens when you disrespect the Marchetti family.

Chapter 6

Elizabeth

Two Weeks Later

"Excuse me, everyone! I need just a few moments of your time." Vince's voice carries throughout the office floor, and all the typical sounds of business cease as everyone stops to turn and give him their full attention.

"As you all know, Gabriel is getting married in several weeks and will be taking an extended leave of absence to bask in newlywed bliss."

Polite applause and a few well-humored catcalls sound through the space as Gabriel nods his acknowledgment, a bashful smile on his face.

"My sentiments exactly, Wilson," Vince says to one of the catcallers. "And though things will certainly not be as seamless while he's gone, I am very pleased to share that his shoes will be partially filled by our new Senior Director of Special Projects, Elizabeth Greystone."

I smile and nod to the crowd as Vince gestures to me, trying my hardest to keep any nervous fidgeting in check. I'm sure the MI employees are all very nice people, but just in case, it's best to come off as confident and steady, especially considering the political weight and level of responsibility Vince is granting me on day one.

"Elizabeth is a tenured project manager and strategic advisor, coming to us from Cerberus Security. For those of you who were involved with mitigation efforts against the recent cyber threat we faced, Elizabeth

43

was single-handedly responsible for identifying that pending attack and alerting us to its imminence. She will report directly to me, and though her role will extend far past Gabriel's typical duties, she will act as a support arm for a handful of those items until he returns. I expect each of you to welcome her warmly and to candidly answer any questions she may have during her onboarding period."

Stepping forward during another round of polite applause, this one meant for me, I shoot Vince a grateful smile for making me sound like such a badass. He answers my look with a self-satisfied smirk of his own and a cheeky wink for good measure. I resist the urge to roll my eyes and instead scan the faces of the people in front of me.

"Thank you, Mr. Caputo, for those warm words of welcome. I look forward to working with each and every one of you in the coming months. I've always had the highest respect for the work done by Marchetti International, and while I'm sure Mr. Caputo and the late Mr. Marchetti are both extremely talented businessmen, I know that the people who really make MI shine every day are those of you in front of me and your colleagues. I'm excited to join your ranks and continue to show the rest of the business world how it's done!"

I step back next to Vince as the group breaks into applause once more, this time with a bit more gusto. I even earn a smattering of cheers from the louder personalities. Vince aims an exasperated but affectionate eye roll in my direction before turning his back to where the staff can see him.

"Alright, alright," Vince soothes. "I appreciate the enthusiasm, but party's over. Back to work, everyone!"

As the sounds of keyboards and conversation resume around us, Vince turns and gestures toward his absolutely gargantuan glassed-in office. Once the door is shut behind us, he turns and fixes me with an amused smirk.

"So it's 'Mr. Caputo' now? After all we've been through?"

Giving in to the urge to roll my eyes this time, I head toward the emerald-green sofa in the center of the room.

"I've decided it's best to keep up formalities at work," I state matter-of-factly. "No one here knows of our friendship, and I'd rather not have anyone find out. The last thing I need is for my authority to be undermined over rumors that I got this job because of that relationship instead of my own merit, even if that is partially true."

"Like hell, it is," Vince growls as he joins me, taking up one of the matching leather armchairs. "The only thing our friendship has to do with you getting this job is the fact that it allowed me to know you exist. Anyone who suggests otherwise will answer to me."

"Oh, reign it in, Rattles," I tease. "I know you're a stickler for chain of command anyway, so there's no use pretending otherwise. Plus, I'm going to enjoy it all the more, knowing that it gets under your skin. Just consider it part of my benefits package."

He scoffs.

"Well, as long as you're happy, then I suppose that's all that matters, isn't it, Copperhead?"

His sarcasm isn't lost on me, but I choose to ignore it in favor of being facetious a while longer.

"My thoughts exactly. I'm so glad you agree, *sir*."

His eyes snap to mine, a spark flaring in them. *Oh, this really is rankling him, isn't it?* I'm sure he's plotting some form of revenge, but I'm not too concerned. It's been too long since someone was audacious enough to cut him down a few notches, so really I'm doing him a favor. You know, keeping him humble and whatnot. *Plus, it's going to be so much fun.*

Our tête-à-tête is interrupted by a knock at the door. Vince waves Gabriel inside and rises from his chair.

"I'm assuming that's my cue," he says, buttoning his jacket.

"Yes, sir," Gabriel confirms. "They're waiting for you in conference room B."

With a clap on Gabriel's shoulder, Vince tells us to feel free to stay here for my crash course in all things Marchetti International. Promising to pop in when he can to add color to Gabriel's lessons, he strides through the door and down the hall.

Snagging my notebook and favorite pen from my bag, I settle into a comfortable writing position.

"Alright, Sensei," I joke. "Hit me with it."

* * *

After lunch, Vince and I are in his car, heading toward his penthouse for a meeting with the Marchetti generals. My fingers brush absently across the soft leather as I admire the sleek interior. Wiggling further into the cloud-like comfort of my seat, I turn my gaze instead to Vince himself. Close as we are, he's still a bit of an enigma, and in the back of my mind, I'm always trying to uncover a bit more of the puzzle.

Damien was certainly more predictable. He wasn't an asshole by any means, but he definitely maintained more of a distinct separation between himself and those who worked for him, save for Vince, of course. He was almost stereotypical in his actions, the traditional mob boss to a T. He never drove himself anywhere. There were always bodyguards at his flank. And he was certainly never quite so personal with his employees, maintaining more of an aloof demeanor at all times. At least, that's the picture Gabriel painted when I asked him how life had changed working under Vince. It's clear that Gabriel respected Damien, but it was more of a distant awe than the comfortable camaraderie he seems to share with Vince.

Vince, though, he's an interesting mix of privilege and humility, and I'm trying to figure out what exactly determines when he acts like a mob boss versus when he prefers to cosplay as a normal (or normal for him, at least) man. As Vince downshifts and steps on the gas to get around a city bus, I can see the allure in at least this small act of self-reliance. I never learned to drive a standard transmission myself, but even I feel powerful just sitting next to him while he commands the steel beast beneath us.

"Dollar for your thoughts?"

Vince's voice catches me off guard. I was so busy ruminating on his quirks that I failed to realize his attention had shifted in my direction.

"Don't you mean, 'penny for your thoughts'?"

"Nope."

He shakes his head, enunciating the word with a distinctive pop.

"Your thoughts are worth far more than a penny, Copperhead."

Hah. Silver-tongued punk. But if he really wants to know...

"Why is don-mode something you seem to turn on and off?"

His wide-eyed confusion has me cheering inwardly. I love catching the unflappable Vincenzo Caputo off guard.

"I'm sorry. What?"

"Oh, you know what I mean. Like right now, for example. Why are you driving us yourself instead of having one of your men chauffeur us? Why do you interact so closely with the employees at MI? Why do you clean your own apartment, *and* buy your own groceries, *and* refuse to have bodyguards *and*, well, you get the picture?"

He doesn't say anything, but I can see the wheels turning behind his eyes, even focused on the road as they are. I decide I should maybe clarify the reason for my questions, lest he think I'm doubting his ability or finding fault with him as a person.

"I don't mean that any of that is wrong, by the way. It's just... unexpected. Granted, I don't have a ton of experience with mafia dons, but Damien was always so serious. He only ever dropped his don persona around us, and even that was never a given, depending on what was going on that day. But you seem to move much more fluidly between Vince the don and Vince the man. I'm just curious why that is."

We roll to a stop at a red light, and Vince turns his head to shoot me a contemplative look.

"I guess the best answer I can give you is that being don is never something I expected to have to do. In my mind, Damien was and always would be the don, so I was free to be Vince the man, at least until I needed to deliver my special brand of justice to someone who'd crossed us. But even that role was one I was meant to slip in and out of. I couldn't be that version of myself forever, so I guess I just developed a knack for moving in and out of the different roles that were expected of me. Taking control of the family is no different. When I'm around the family or dealing with family business, I slip into that role, but it would be far too draining to keep up that persona forever when my natural state is so different."

I hum my understanding as I turn over what he's said. It makes sense. After all, aren't I already planning to do something similar in my new roles at MI and within the family? *Speaking of the family...* Vince pulls smoothly into his parking spot in the underground garage and cuts the engine. It's time to meet the generals. I have a feeling this meeting won't be quite as pleasant as the one at MI, and I steel my spine in preparation. *They don't have to respect you right off the bat. That's not how they're wired. With enough time, you'll earn it, one way or the other.* When my door opens, I tuck my resolve firmly in place and take Vince's offered hand to step out of the car.

Unfortunately, my bravado upon exiting the car is short-lived and my nerves ratchet back into high gear on the elevator ride up. But I don't want Vince to see my uncertainty. I duck past him when he opens the office door and immediately focus my attention on admiring, or at least trying to admire, the space properly. I was too high-strung to appreciate it the last time I was here, planning the failed operation to take out Armando. Really, I just end up staring unseeingly at the paintings and reminding myself to move from one to the next periodically to seem natural. *Is this what it's like to be a vampire pretending to breathe?*

Despite my inability to truly focus, I can safely say that Vince's office is my favorite room in his apartment. Not that I've seen his entire apartment, but it's hard to imagine anything beating this. Floor-to-ceiling windows stand sentry behind an imposing yet minimalistic desk made of black steel and smoke-grey glass. The space is further enhanced by the stormy blue color of the walls and the artwork displayed throughout the space. Vince seems to lean toward a mix of surrealism and expressionism, so the pieces are colorful, varied, and endlessly thought-provoking.

Vince seems content to let me peruse the space, and I assume he's using the time to catch up on emails or messages. I'm trying so hard to appear nonchalant and not draw his attention that I fail to pay attention to what he's doing at all. I don't realize he's stalked up behind me until I feel the heat of him at my back and see his arms come up to brace on either side of the piece I'm currently pretending to admire, effectively caging me in.

"Elizabeth..." he drawls. "Is there a particular reason you're refusing to look at me while blasphemously *pretending* to admire the priceless artwork I've spent my lifetime acquiring?"

I turn around slowly in the small space he's left me, trying to muster up my best poker face before I look him in the eye. I fail. He's so close that I can feel his breath ghosting across my ear as I turn, and the sensation releases an involuntary shiver throughout my body. And, well, now that the shivering has started, my nervous trembling has taken that as its cue to resume operations. There's no point avoiding his gaze now. It's not my eyes that will give me away anymore.

I raise my eyes to meet his, and I'm thrown off balance once again

49

by how close we are. I can practically count the darker freckles in his honey-brown eyes. I get lost in doing just that, some of the tension leaving my muscles as I count until he speaks again.

"You've got to give me something here, Copperhead. Did I do something, say something to upset you?"

Oh, hell. What am I doing? Get a grip, Elizabeth!

"Oh, Vince, no," I stammer. "You didn't do anything. I just, well, I was trying to get my nerves under control before the meeting, and I didn't want you to see how uncertain I was, er, am..."

Vince drops one arm and uses that hand to raise my eyes from where they've landed on the carpet back to his. His warm smile is reassuring, as always, and he laughs softly as he looks at me.

"Oh, Copperhead. You are the strangest mix of confident badass and modest mouse that I've ever seen. Do you remember when you looked dead into a camera and screamed for Damien and me to seek vengeance on your behalf instead of begging us to save you like you were supposed to, even knowing you'd likely be beaten or worse for doing so? If you can handle that, you can handle a few underworld generals who are on the same side as you."

Scoffing, I kick my chin up and lean my head against Vince's hand on the wall.

"That was different. I didn't care what Alonzo and Armando thought of me. Hell, I preferred they didn't think of me at all."

"Exactly!" He snaps his fingers. "This is no different. You shouldn't care what these men *think* of you, either. All you should care about is what they know to be true. And one of those things needs to be that you are not easily intimidated."

He steps back, dislodging my head from its resting place, and points toward the set of low-backed charcoal armchairs facing his desk.

"The best thing you can do right now is to go sit in one of those chairs and paste a look on your face that says you think you're doing us all a favor just by being here. No matter what happens, you keep that look. The more relaxed you are, the more off-balance they'll be."

He's right. Stop being a chicken, and let's grey rock[7] *the shit out of these macho men.* I take the armchair furthest from the door and try to settle into a relaxed yet confident posture. Vince activates the electronic tint on the windows, shielding my eyes from the afternoon sun, before assuming his throne behind the desk. He keeps up a steady stream of thoughts and light conversation related to everything that happened at MI this morning, which helps to keep me from spiraling back into self-doubt. *It's a shame he's so cynical about romantic relationships. He's so intuitive and attentive. I'm sure there are a thousand women who would kill to be by his side, morally grey lifestyle and all.* Before long, there's a sharp knock at the door. *Two o'clock on the dot. Points for punctuality.*

Three men stride into the room, eyes raking over me carefully as they settle into position around the space. None of them speak, but their surprise at my presence is written plainly across their faces. *So, Vince didn't tell them what this meeting was about. Interesting.*

The dark-haired one takes the seat closest to me and offers a subtle nod in greeting. He seems to be the youngest of the three - maybe in his late 30s. Next to him in the final armchair is the eldest, or at least I presume so by his looks. His medium brown locks have almost entirely given way to grey, and he's sporting a pompadour haircut that I'm willing to bet has been his go-to style since he was a teenager. There's no greeting from him, just a calculating look before he turns his attention to Vince. *He's going to be the hardest to win over. I can already tell.* The last man remains standing, anchored between the

---

[7] Acting neutral or disengaged to make the other person lose interest. Often done by using one-word answers, failing to react to intentionally explosive or triggering statements or actions, and minimizing opportunities for interaction. (Author's Note: It is extremely satisfying to watch insecure men scramble in search of a reaction that they're never going to get, isn't it?)

shoulders of the other two. He's a beefy brute with his arms crossed, but it's more of a comfortable posture than a menacing one. His face is blank. I can't get a good read on how he'll respond to my induction, but I'll find out soon enough.

Vince thanks the men for their time and wastes no breath on flowery speeches. When he flatly tells the three of my appointment as his strategic advisor, the grey-haired man shoots from his chair in protest.

"Capo, you can't be serious! I get that you want to do right by Mr. Marchetti, but bringing his mistress into the family is taking things a bit too far. What does she even know about our world? She'll be a liability!"

I keep my emotions from playing across my face, Vince's words repeating in my head. But damn, if he didn't just hit on every single insecurity I have about taking on this role. *You knew this wouldn't be easy, Elizabeth. Buck up and let your actions show your worth later.*

The beefy man isn't verbalizing his displeasure, but the look of disbelief he's sending my way makes his feelings clear enough. Only the dark-haired man seems unfazed by Vince's announcement. Either he trusts Vince's judgment far more than the other two, or he saw this coming and has decided to roll with the punches, which would make him both a potential ally but also the biggest threat. I meet his eyes with a steady expression of my own until Vince speaks.

"Roberto..." he drawls, his tone as cold as ice. His gaze is equally frigid, and I see each man shift slightly as Vince cuts his gaze between the three of them.

"What part of my statement sounded like this decision was up for discussion?"

Roberto is at least smart enough to keep his mouth shut now, so he's got that going for him.

"Let me make one thing crystal clear. Elizabeth is not here because of her relationship with Damien, God rest his soul. She is *here* because she has the particular combination of both skill and instinct that I need in an advisor to help me carry the load of both the Marchetti family and the Marchetti International business. She has proven herself to be trustworthy, loyal, and steady under pressure, even when facing the likelihood of her own death. That being said, I don't expect any of you to trust her right away. In fact, I'd be pretty fucking disappointed if you did. But you *will* treat her respectfully for no reason other than I am personally vouching for her. Though, I'm sure it won't take long for her to earn your true respect on her own. Am I understood?"

All three men nod solemnly. That's not good enough for Vince.

"I said, am I fucking *understood*?!"

"Sì, Capo![8]"

"Bene[9]. Now get the fuck out of my office."

Once we're alone, I ignore Vince's apologetic look and rise from my chair. Stuffing my hands in my pockets to hide the residual shaking from working to keep my emotions contained, I aim for distraction.

"Well, that went about as well as I'd expected. You mentioned we have one final introduction to make before the day is over?"

Vince looks as though he wants to say something, likely a pep talk about not letting them get to me, but he stops himself. Good. That's honestly the last thing I want to hear right now anyway. He leads me down the hall and back to the elevator to the parking garage. Our last meeting is with the infamous Mono, the Marchetti family's hacker extraordinaire.

* * *

"Wow, it's like the CIA in here."

---

[8] Yes, Boss!

[9] Good.

When Vince pulled into the garage of the 1970s-era bungalow, I thought we'd had a change of plans. I never imagined that hidden inside the nondescript house was a veritable treasure trove of technology. Once inside the daunting steel door, I note that the residential layout has been adapted for privacy and security. The windows all boast thick metal shutters, and the front door has even more locks and latches securing it than the garage, including a mechanical steel barricade.

It's once we step into what used to be the living room that I see the reason for all of the security. Twirling around slowly, I take in the overwhelming number of screens along the walls. Many are video feeds, but several seem to be running independent programs, with images, text searches, or even raw code running across them. One in particular shows a map of the city covered in colored dots. Most are static, but a handful seem to be moving at a steady pace throughout town.

Off to the edge of the city, away from most of the other dots, three are clustered together in one spot in the middle of a residential area.

"Is that us?"

I gasp when Vince nods, realizing that three dots means Mono has already been tracking my every move, though in hindsight, that probably shouldn't be quite so surprising.

"How did you? What? How long have you been...? Actually, you know what? I don't want to know. Forget I even asked."

Chuckling, Vince turns to the man seated in the center of the room behind a massive desk that boasts several keyboards, tablets, monitors, and who knows what else. As the man stands, I'm struck by how different he appears from what I expected. Granted, my expectation was fueled purely by the stereotypical Hollywood hacker archetype, so it wasn't exactly a solid foundation to begin with. Even so, the man approaching me now is lean but not lanky, with tattoos covering most of the tan skin on his arms and neck, and I'm willing to bet there are more that I can't see. His shaggy black hair hangs in front of his eyes, but he's not even the slightest bit greasy. To be honest, he's got more of an alt-kid vibe going, complete with at least two facial piercings, several visible neck tattoos, and a pair of black studs in his ears.

The room is also not what I expected. I don't see a single chip bag or discarded takeout cup in sight. Everything is meticulously organized, making the room feel spacious despite the menagerie of equipment crammed into it.

"It's nice to finally meet you in person, Elizabeth. I'm Mono."

Despite the slight gravel from disuse, the soothing baritone of his voice and his friendly dark brown eyes remove any lingering nerves I had about meeting the second most dangerous man in the Marchetti family. I grasp his outstretched hand and give it a firm shake, offering him a warm smile.

"Same to you, Mono. Thanks for keeping such a good eye on me during that whole mess a few months ago. I know I likely wouldn't be standing here today if not for your intel."

He ducks his head in humble acknowledgment, and I decide on the spot that I like him. I have a feeling he and I will get along extremely well. Deciding to test that theory, I let my inner geek take over.

"Okay, I don't want to overwhelm you, but I have about a thousand questions."

I'm already bouncing on my feet, and I have to clasp my hands together to keep from touching anything before I've been given permission. Mono chuckles warmly and runs his tongue across his bottom lip, playing with the hoop pierced through the end.

"Fire away, princess. Boss man made sure I cleared my schedule to fill you in on anything you want to know, plus a few things you'd probably rather not."

"Okay, first, eww. Let's not call me princess again in this lifetime. Or any other for that matter. Second, how long did it take you to lay out your cord management system? It's an absolute work of art! And is your nickname Mono because you like to be alone, or is it really 'mono' like 'monkey' in Spanish, and you're just letting us bolillos[10] mispronounce it? Oh, and is that a Morataki surveillance system? I've never had access to one in real life before. This must have cost a fortune!"

"Okay there, Copperhead. Take a breath," Vince teases as he throws an arm around my shoulders and steers me back toward the center of the room and away from the wildly expensive equipment. "Why don't you grab a cup of coffee from the kitchen and let Mono start from the beginning? You can take a tour later, but only if you promise *not* to touch unless Mono says it's okay."

I catch Mono's eye and throw an exaggerated eye roll in Vince's direction for his benefit. *Talk about a buzzkill, right?* His returning expression is very obviously one of agreement, and I know then that I was right about us becoming fast friends. Turning to Vince at my side, I bat my eyelashes and answer him in the only way that feels right.

"Of course, *sir*. I *promise* to be a good girl."

The syrupy, sarcastic quality of my smile and tone is not lost on Vince. His arm goes rigid against my back, and I can feel the tension in his grip, though he doesn't squeeze hard enough to hurt. His pupils dilate, and I can see the battle raging inside them. I'm sure he wants to rise to the bait I've set but is far less likely to do so with an audience. After a few beats, his posture loosens and he steps back toward the door, eyes still on mine.

"I've got some business to take care of. I'll be back in a few hours to pick you up, minaccia[11]."

Shooting his gaze to Mono, he tells him plainly to hold nothing back.

"When I'm not here, she's me as far as you're concerned."

At Mono's nod, he turns and continues back toward the garage. As the

---

[10] white bread rolls, but meaning white people in this case

[11] menace

heavy interior door shuts, a lengthy series of beeps and clicks indicates that we are once again safely sealed inside the Marchetti family's best-kept secret. Already having moved to the kitchen, Mono makes quick work of brewing a pot of coffee. I settle in at the table, and before long, he's deep into an explanation of the inner workings of the Marchetti family intelligence arm.

When Vince returns a little over two hours later, I'm peering over Mono's shoulder, watching him pull up data on one of his six primary monitors. Rising from my hunched position, I ask him to send the files to me once he's finished digging up what he can and raise my arms overhead to stretch out the tension in my shoulders.

"Have you got a project brewing already, Copperhead? That was fast."

"Just a little bit of background research is all. Context is everything when making strategic decisions, you know."

This particular bit of background might just be the thing to help me prove myself to the Marchetti generals. But I don't want Vince to know just yet what Mono and I were working on. This is one battle I need to win on my own.

After Vince and I say our farewells to Mono and undo the thousand various locks and latches to exit the suburban house turned intelligence center, I settle into the lush interior of Vince's black money mobile and allow my brain a much-needed chance to wander during the ride home.

Chapter 7

Vincenzo

Later That Evening

I get back to Liz's place around 9:00 that night, takeout bags in tow. I didn't have anywhere else to be after dropping her off following our meeting with Mono, but part of our agreement when Liz came to work for me was that we'd keep Sam away from it all. That means there's no reason for him and me to meet or for him to even know my name. Given the school he now attends, I'm sure at least a few of the tiny heirs in attendance have overheard a thing or two about me from their parents. It's best if he's kept fully in the dark so he doesn't make any connections on his own.

I ended up heading home to work out, even though I'd already done my usual routine before work that morning. An hour spent on my agility course was enough to reveal that I may have gotten a bit stale with that usual routine. I'd stopped spending so much time there in favor of traditional cardio and weight training, seeing as how I rarely leave my desk these days. Stealth and infiltration skills aren't commonly used in the boardroom, but I didn't think they would start to wane quite so quickly. *Shit, am I getting old or what? I can't show up for a full-scale operation in Madrid in this condition.*

After a quick shower, I change into grey joggers and a black t-shirt before jumping on the bike and swinging through my favorite Indian restaurant. Liz mentioned she hadn't tried this particular place just yet, and I can't wait to see the look on her face when she gets a bite of their makhani.

She told me to let myself in when I arrived, so I do, setting out the food on the dining table and grabbing plates and utensils from the kitchen. There's no sign of Liz, and I figure she must still be putting Sam to bed. It's admirable, the way she's able to compartmentalize work and being a mother, managing to be incredibly successful at both and still maintain a general "take things as they come" attitude. It's exactly why I have no doubt that she'll have most of the men in the organization bowing at her feet in no time. You'd have to try pretty hard, or just be in complete denial, to not be impressed with someone who's on top of their game all the time like that.

I hear her footsteps approaching from down the hall right as I'm setting out the last of the side dishes. I turn to tell her that she's barely avoided me stealing all the samosas for myself, but my brain short circuits before I can get the words out. Her hair is damp from the shower, forming loose waves around her face. That's not what distracted me, but I'm trying my hardest to keep my focus there, on her face, because the instinctual reaction I had to the rest of her is completely out of line. I'm seriously debating faking an urgent phone call so I can escape before I do something stupid.

What the fuck, Vincenzo? Are you a hormonal teenager now? One glimpse of a female's legs and you lose all of your self-control?

But they're not just legs. And she's not just some random woman. It's *Liz*, for Christ's sake, and the high-waisted black bike shorts she's wearing are showing off thighs that any self-respecting man would be chomping at the bit to dig his fingers into. The royal blue cropped tee she's wearing isn't helping either. All that does is highlight the contrast between her slim waist and ample hips.

I blink to blur my vision and use the visual break to force my thoughts back into neutral territory. *No. Absolutely not. This is* **Elizabeth.** *She's your best friend and your brother's widow. You are* **not** *fucking this up just because it's been too long since you got laid. Nope. Not going to happen. It's just been a while, something we will be rectifying as soon as possible after tonight.*

"Oh my gosh, that all smells amazing," Liz croons as she approaches the table.

She claims a seat facing the kitchen, and I quickly drop into the one across from her, extolling the virtues of each dish I brought in a bid to distract my carnal appetite with my gastric one. She listens intently, snagging a bit of everything in the end. Soon, scraping utensils and clinking glassware are the only sounds in the entire apartment.

"So, be honest," I tell her, breaking the silence once I'm full enough to focus on something other than food, "are you regretting your decision yet?"

"Ha! As-if, boss man. All things considered, I thought today went pretty well. Sure, the generals hate the idea, but I never expected they'd be jumping for joy. Bringing me into the fold does go against every one of the traditional ways of running the organization from what I can tell. But the MI team and Mono were all fantastic, and I'm eager to fully sink my teeth into everything tomorrow."

"Excellent. Then the wine I brought for after dinner can be a celebratory drink instead of a conciliatory one."

Liz rolls her eyes and scoffs.

"Thanks for the vote of confidence, friend."

"Hey, I've always been confident that you could do this. I just also happen to pride myself on being prepared for every possibility."

The wink I shoot her earns me a snarky look and a stuck-out tongue in response. I laugh as I stand up to start clearing empty containers and plates from the table. Liz grabs the last few, and soon we're lounging in the living room, glasses of wine in hand. Liz is curled up on the couch under a blanket, as per usual. I forgo my normal chair in favor of snagging the other end of the couch. It still feels too weird to sit there with Damien's empty chair between us.

We talk about the nuances of the day, Liz sharing her initial impressions of most of the team and me chiming in with helpful tidbits or funny anecdotes where I can. And as everything tends to do these days, the conversation eventually makes its way around to Damien.

"No way," Liz sputters, trying not to spew her wine at what I've just revealed. "You mean to tell me that little old Mary in accounting had the guts to tell Damien off in front of everyone?"

"Oh, she didn't just tell him off. She straight tore him a new one, yelling on about how just because he was the boss didn't mean the rules didn't apply to him, and if they were to fail an audit because he couldn't be bothered to turn in expenses, she'd make sure he never heard the end of it."

Her laughs ring throughout the living room, and I smile at the memory.

"Oh my god," Liz finally breathes out. "She's my hero. I cannot *wait* to take her to coffee and ask about it in person."

Wondering if I've just accidentally created my own worst nightmare by ensuring the two of them become friends, I take a long drink of my wine before I tell her anything else that could make my life harder.

"You know, that's the only thing that keeps me from being absolutely flipping ecstatic about this job," Liz says quietly, and I glance her way only to see that the light from her laughter has entirely disappeared from her eyes, replaced instead by a hollow look. "It's my literal dream role, but I only have it because he's gone. And even worse, he's only gone because I was too stubborn to listen to reason."

"Excuse you, but I'm pretty sure we've had this conversation, and I made it very clear that what happened to Damien was not your fault."

"Yes, Vince, it fucking *was*. Just because you say it wasn't doesn't

61

make that true. You and I both know that if I had just listened to him and not pushed against his protective measures so hard, Maria never would have been able to corner me the way that she did. Damien would never have rushed in to save me, and he'd still be sitting here, right there in that chair, telling both of us off for bickering like he used to."

I open my mouth to argue back, but she leans forward and covers it with her hand before I can. Her voice is low, tired even, and she sighs as she speaks.

"Vince, just admit it. There's no point in pretending otherwise, and I need to be able to talk about this with someone so I can work through it and eventually come to terms with everything. You're the only person I have. So just...accept reality, and let's move forward."

Fuck. I can't argue with her after she's said something like that. Not to mention she could give the ASPCA commercials a run for their money with those damn puppy dog eyes she's shooting my way. And maybe...maybe she's got a point. I will never agree with the idea that what happened to Damien is 100% her fault, but I am reasonable enough to acknowledge that it was a perfect storm of bad choices and shortcomings on all three sides: hers, mine, and even Damien's himself. I nudge her hand away from my mouth with a press of my nose and take a deep breath before looking her square in the eyes.

"Alright, Copperhead. I can admit that we all fell short in ways that ultimately led to Damien's death, and that does include your own choices. But it *also* includes my failure to identify Maria before it was too late, as well as Damien's failure to treat you like an equal instead of a pet. If he hadn't dictated your protection and instead involved you in it, you wouldn't have felt so compelled to push back, and you also would have been better prepared to fight off Maria even if you were still captured. Can you agree that we're all a bit at fault instead of shouldering the entirety of the blame yourself?"

Her nod is slight, but combined with the resignation in her eyes, I know I'm getting through to her.

"And while we're on the subject..." I tell her with a pointed look. "To avoid repeating the mistakes of our past, I'd like to propose something. I want you to let me train you to defend yourself. While your role at MI is completely above board, you'll still be linked to me publicly. No one will really know the depth of our relationship, but Marchetti family enemies may still target you in the future on the mere hope that you'll have information that can help them. I want to make sure that you can defend yourself in case that happens. What do you think?"

I've phrased it as a question, and of course it *is*, but I hope she agrees with me on this. I'm not sure what I'd do otherwise. All I know is that leaving her completely unprotected is unacceptable, but I also won't override her autonomy by velcroing bodyguards to her side the way Damien did.

"I'd like that," she says with a nod. "I've actually started working out more on my own recently, cardio mostly so I can run if needed, but being able to hold my own if running isn't an option would make me feel a lot better."

I already know about her new workout routine, of course, but no reason to remind her that she's still got eyes on her every move. My eyes are much more discreet than Damien's, and even if she knows they're there, she doesn't owe them any consideration, nor does she need to gain permission to do anything she damn well feels like.

Checking my watch, I realize it's almost midnight. Now that we've resolved the major issues of the night, it's time I head out so we can both get some sleep. I down the rest of my wine and pick up Liz's empty glass as I rise.

"Alright, Copperhead. I'll text you once I set a time for our first training session. But for now, we should both get to bed or we'll be zombies in the office tomorrow."

She walks me to the door, lecturing me again on bike safety and defensive driving as she hands me my helmet and jacket.

"Yes, Moooom. I promise to be safe. Scout's honor."

I raise my right hand to underscore my statement.

"Pssh, as if you were ever a scout."

As the doors close, she yells out, "And don't forget to text me when you get home so I know you're not dead!"

I shake my head in exasperation, but honestly, I don't mind. It's kind of nice having someone worry over me for once. Not that I need it, of course. But still. I don my helmet and stride out towards my bike, wondering a bit what Damien and I might have been like if we'd had a woman like Liz around to fuss over us as kids. *Sam has no idea how lucky he is.*

Chapter 8

Elizabeth

Several Weeks Later

Oh my god. I think I'm dying. When Vince said he was going to train me to defend myself, I thought he'd teach me how to break out of zip ties or elbow someone in the nose to loosen their grip. I never imagined I'd be training to be a freaking sniper or practicing slipping knives out of concealed body holsters. And that's not even the worst of it. The man has me learning full hand-to-hand combat techniques like I'm a damn UFC fighter or something.

I slouch against the wall of Vince's home gym/torture chamber, pouring water down my throat as I try to catch my breath. I'll admit that I'm in much better shape now than I was a few months ago, but Vince is still a wicked taskmaster with seemingly endless stamina.

"Break time's over, Copperhead. Get back over here and try that again. Act like you mean it this time."

Oh, I'm about to mean it, you coldhearted despot. I push off the wall, groaning at the ache in my already overworked muscles. We've been running the same drill for close to an hour. I'm supposed to slip a knife from my pocket and find a way to get it to Vince's throat before he can block me. No rules, just a variety of moves and tactics that Vince has taught me over the last few weeks, along with permission to try something scrappy of my own if I see the right opportunity. I've yet to succeed a single time. No matter how erratic and unpredictable I try to be, he always seems to sense my movements a split second before I make them.

At his nod, I crouch into a fighting stance. I palm the knife success-fully and feint to the right before ducking back to the left and rolling low. I manage to come up behind Vince for the first time all day, and I'm momentarily convinced I've finally got him. My internal celebration is premature, though, because even though I lash out my hand as quickly as I can toward his neck, he's still faster. His left hand reaches around to grab mine over his shoulder, and he pulls some crazy duck-and-spin maneuver that ends with him facing me, my knife hand firmly in his grasp. I'm not even sure what he does next. All I know is that I blink, and suddenly, my back is against the wall, my hand is empty, and the knife is tight against my throat with the entirety of Vince's body pressed against mine to hold me in place.

Dammit! I let out a frustrated growl, pissed at myself for not being able to even lay a finger on him after *weeks* of training. I test his hold, trying to fight back against his grip enough to get just the slightest leverage to hit him with a knee, or an elbow, or hell, even a foot, but nothing budges. Vince smirks down at me, looking so pleased with himself that I want to smack him right in his smug mouth. If only I had autonomy over my limbs at the moment. He must be able to read the murderous intent in my eyes because his flame in challenge. Mere inches apart as we are, I wonder if I could bite him. He shifts his weight against me and flexes his grip on the knife as if daring me to try.

Originally, I wasn't worried, despite the weapon at my throat, because I know Vince would never intentionally harm me. But some instinctual part of me seems to be waking up the longer Vince has me pinned like this. I'm suddenly very aware of the thin strip of metal pressed against my vulnerable skin and of every single place on my body where I am trapped by his overwhelming strength. Though my skin starts to pebble with the first hints of actual fear, I keep my gaze locked with his. One thing I will not do is let him get inside my head. That's probably exactly his goal, and I'll be damned if I grant him that victory in addition to this one.

Our silent sparring match lasts for several minutes, both of us too stubborn to give up first. He tries a few subtle threats to get me to cave, things like gripping a bit harder on my wrists or the knife and shifting his position to remind me just how firmly stuck I am. And it works to a certain degree. The longer we stay locked in this predator/prey scenario, the more adrenaline starts to flood my veins, ratcheting my pulse enough that I'm sure he can feel it. That's fine, though. That's a normal human reaction, and there's nothing I can do about it.

What is *not* fine is what happens when he slides the knife across my throat, not pressing hard enough to cut but definitely enough that I can imagine the scene in my head. What should serve to further terrify me, perhaps enough to finally let go of my pride and end this fucked up standoff, instead sends a frisson of heat through my stomach, landing at my core. I instinctively press my legs together at the sensation but end up practically grinding against Vince's thigh instead, wedged as it is between my own. His eyes go wide, and I watch his pupils dilate as he realizes what's happening.

But I guess I can count it as a win because he backs up lightning fast, putting a foot of space between us as if I had actually zapped him.

"Holy shit, Copperhead, you filthy little freak. You're taking fighting dirty to a whole other level. I didn't realize you were harboring a fear kink."

Oh my god. Kill me now. He looks both shocked and a little impressed that my tastes aren't quite as vanilla as he probably assumed. *You and me both, pal.* No one is more surprised than me at whatever the hell I just felt.

I open my mouth to say something, anything, but nothing comes out. Instead, I just pantomime a dying fish as I rack my brain for any way to explain away what just happened. I've got nothing, so I opt for changing the subject instead.

"Don't get distracted, Caputo. The real question of the day is, how the fuck did you get that knife out of my hand so fast?"

He looks at me for a long moment, and I'm almost certain he's not going to let this go that easily. Thankfully, he still seems to possess a shred of mercy because he takes the bait, and the conversation steers fully into a technical discussion on the specific move he used to disarm me in the literal blink of an eye.

* * *

"Good work today, everyone," I tell the group as I close my laptop and rise from the dark wood conference table. "We'll regroup tomorrow morning to review the final draft with the changes we've discussed."

We've been working on this acquisition proposal for the past few weeks, and it's the largest project I've completed to date at Marchetti International. I'm feeling much more in my element this afternoon, this particular milestone is a welcome boost to my confidence after my fruitless and embarrassing training session this morning. I walk down the hall towards Vince's office to give him the latest updates, stopping by a few different desks on my way to answer questions or provide guidance on several of the other projects currently in flight.

At his wave through the glass, I let myself into what I've dubbed the terrarium. I think it's fitting, considering the serpent king himself is on display for the entire office to see all day. Vince is on the phone speaking in rapid-fire Italian, so all I know is that it's family business. He doesn't seem upset though, merely animated, so it's likely nothing to worry about.

I set a stack of folios on his desk with a sharp rap on the top and a set of raised eyebrows to make sure he notices them. His look of despair confirms that he does, so I move to the sofa to wait while he finishes his call. I use the time to sort through emails on my phone, firing off simple responses where I can and flagging the rest for lengthier review on the big internet when I'm back at my desk.

"Wasn't hiring you supposed to lighten my workload?" Vince whines as he rises from his desk to join me in the seating area. "So why does it feel like every time you come in here, you give me more work to do?"

"Oh, my goodness. And the award for most dramatic performance goes to Vincenzo Caputo, ladies and gentlemen."

I mime my applause, and he sticks his tongue out at me in true man-child fashion. *At least it's safe to say we're firmly back in familiar territory.*

"Seriously, though. All you have to do is read and sign. I assure you all the actual work has been taken care of. Sir."

He narrows his eyes at me but doesn't argue. And I know he's not really complaining. He knows better than anyone what goes into getting those proposals and contracts onto his desk, and he shows his appreciation regularly, most notably through the very generous salary that's deposited into my bank account twice a month. Though to be fair, that same salary also covers my work for the Marchetti family. One of my firmest stipulations was that I wanted every cent paid to me to be 100% clean. If Hell ever does freeze over and the Marchettis go down for tax evasion or some nonsense like that, I wanted reassurance that Sam and I wouldn't end up destitute on the street thanks to frozen bank accounts.

"Of course, Your Majesty," he snarks. "Run me through the high points first, and I promise I'll have it all reviewed with either notes or a signature by the end of the day."

Wasting no time, I launch into my brief, probably more excited about the conversation than is normal or healthy. But I can't help it. I've spent almost my entire career sort of floating in mediocrity, able to excel

69

in my own work but without anyone to work alongside or challenge me. Vince's insightful comments, quick-witted suggestions, and his tendency to play devil's advocate make these briefs some of the best parts of my week. It still amazes me that he thinks he's not cut out to be the leader of the Marchetti empire. Sure, his style is different than Damien's and maybe he doesn't like it as much as Damien did, but his mind is formidable, as are his business instincts.

I watch his expression animate as those instincts kick in, and he has a flash of inspiration regarding a pending deal that's been a bit difficult to negotiate. It's all I can do to keep my chuckle under my breath. *Maybe, just maybe, I'll eventually be able to get him to see himself the way I do.*

Chapter 9

Vincenzo

The Following Day

I check my watch and sigh. *It'll be a miracle if she hasn't already ordered without me. Though, her getting a head start might be preferable to her hangry side biting my head off when I arrive.* I'm meeting Liz for lunch near the office, but my last appointment ran dangerously late. Or so I thought. I'm surprised and fairly suspicious when I spot her looking downright serene as she sips on her drink and rakes her gaze across the other diners, a casual lean to her posture.

She spots me as I approach and shoots me a bright smile, further heightening my unease. When I lean down to greet her with a kiss on the cheek, my senses are overwhelmed by the scent of peppermint. *Devil help me, she smells like a fucking candy cane.* Not that I mind. It's one of my favorite scents, thanks to my insatiable sweet tooth. My mouth is already watering at the smell, despite the lack of something sweet to actually sink my teeth into. But it's not her signature Earl Grey and honey scent, and I can't help but wonder what spurred the change.

"This place better have dessert," I say, sliding into the chair across from her. "Because that new perfume you're sporting has my sweet tooth in overdrive, and we haven't even had lunch yet."

She looks confused for a second before recognition sparks.

"Oh! That's not perfume. It must be the oils from my massage. The building was offering free 15-minute chair massages in the lobby, so when you texted that you were running late, I decided to treat myself. Best decision I've made all week, too. I'm sorry to say that you've been replaced. Kevin's magic fingers have earned him the honor of being my new best friend. It might even be love."

She bats her eyelashes at me sweetly, clearly enjoying her little joke. I, however, am less amused. She absolutely deserves to unwind, but my instincts have flared right the hell up at the image she's painting. The thought of some stranger putting his hands on her makes me want to break his "magic" fingers. Which I realize is irrational, considering the circumstances, but if I've learned anything in life it's that no one is ever quite what they seem. *It's Mafia Survival 101.* For all I know, one of my many enemies could have set the whole thing up just to get close to Marchetti employees in the hopes of learning something useful. And I'm responsible for Liz's safety first and foremost, especially since she'd only be a target because of me and the Marchetti family in the first place.

Except you've got eyes on her at all times, there has been zero chatter about any such operation, and she's sitting in front of you healthy and whole at this very moment. So let's put the fangs away for now and enjoy lunch. You can grill the men later to see if anything feels off about the situation.

Moving the conversation into safer territory, I brief Liz on the progress in Spain. Andre, the man I sent out to Madrid several months ago, has finally worked his way high enough in the ranks of Raphael's organization to be useful, and intel is coming in steadily now. All of the property and supply purchases are in place as well. There are just some final security modifications being made to the villa in Valencia, but realistically, we could head to Spain at any time to start playing our hand.

It's a given that I'll be on the ground for the duration of the operation, but what I haven't fully decided upon is the best way to lure Raphael into my palm. It's not like I can waltz in and demand a meeting. I'd be dead before I hit the driveway. No, for this to work, I need to get him isolated, or at least with no more than two guards on him, before he even knows I'm in town. The odds get too unpredictable with any more than that, and I'm not taking any chances with something this important.

As I explain the parts of the plan that I have fleshed out and highlight the gaps, Liz offers ideas and also calls out potential roadblocks I hadn't thought of yet. With operations like these, it's the little details that can blow your cover, and I'm damn thankful that I have her at my side to catch those exact details so keenly. It's as I'm marveling at how lucky I am that she walked into Damien and I's lives all those months ago when she says something that almost makes me spit out the bite of key lime pie I'm savoring.

"The simplest solution is to have me pose as a broker working for the Salteros and whatever alias we give ourselves under the guise of expanding our business into Spain. I can meet with Raphael's men, and with the right strategy, work my way up to meeting with the man himself."

"Woah, hard stop. You're going to need to take at least three gigantic steps back and start from the beginning. Since when is involving the Salteros and putting you directly in contact with the monster who murdered Damien's mother the *simplest* solution?"

I swear this woman is going to be the death of me, and not in the heroic martyr way like Damien went out. No, I'm more likely to break my neck while whipping my head around to process the latest insane thing out of her mouth. Or maybe I'll suffocate from the force of her audacity because the way she's rolling her eyes at me right now is so full of attitude that I think even the waitstaff are avoiding us.

"We need a legitimate business reason to approach Raphael's organization, right? Well, the simplest partnerships are those that deal with the trade of physical goods. Spain is known for being a distribution hub for cocaine into Europe, and now that things have smoothed over with the Salteros, it would be an easy negotiation to convince them to expand. They don't seem to have the resources to do something like that themselves, so we could offer our logistical services and form a solid partnership on this side that we then take to Raphael. You and I both know that Adrian's product is the cleanest in the entire U.S. and I'd be willing to bet it beats anything Raphael is sourcing currently. It'd be easy to entice him with the right deal. Plus, the Salteros will grant us the cover we need. We can't exactly tell Raphael that the Marchetti family wants to do business, now can we?"

"Okay..." I'm damn impressed with the plan she's just laid out. There's no issue there. But that's not the part that almost made me waste a perfectly good dessert.

"I'm not too proud to admit that your idea has merit. I see the logic and agree that we likely won't have too much trouble convincing Adrian or Raphael of the benefits. But what I'm still confused about is how you acting as the broker is the most logical choice, considering you've never brokered a drug deal in your life, and you've also been adamant about staying away from involvement in family business beyond your current advisory role."

My attention is fully locked on her, so it doesn't escape my notice that multiple reactions cross her face in the span of a second. On one hand, I can tell she's feeling defensive about my questioning of her capabilities, but on the other, she seems to be battling with herself over the idea as well. I can almost see the ideas waging war behind her eyes as she struggles to verbalize her thought process. *I bet at least one of those little bastards is a honey badger. It's probably the one ready to bite my head off for pointing out her lack of related experience.*

When I can see she's coming to a decision on how to respond, I school my face to remove any lingering humor at the fictional boxing ring I'd been picturing in my head. Her expression is subdued, almost somber. I don't understand why at first, but then she finally speaks.

"I know what I said before about staying out of family business. But this isn't 'family' business. This is for my *actual* family. This is for Damien. And for you."

I'm taken aback by her including me in that category, but I don't have a chance to dig into it before she continues.

"To be frank, there's very little I wouldn't do to make sure that you both get the vengeance you deserve for what that bastard did to you. As for my lack of experience negotiating drug deals, I hardly think that signifies. Negotiations are the same, no matter the terms. What's important is that the negotiator has a solid poker face, backbone, and the ability to think on their feet. While I'll admit I need to work on the first a bit, I know I don't need to waste my breath convincing you that I have the last two in spades. You acknowledged them yourself when you outright begged me to work for you."

Oh, begged, did I? This infuriatingly smug, capable woman... The simultaneous urges to strangle her and applaud her are strong, and I find myself momentarily locked in my own internal battle.

Her idea has serious merit, but if this is going to happen, we're going to need to kick her training into high gear. *And maybe add a few additional skills to the repertoire...* Decision made, I fix her with my most no-nonsense stare. If we're doing this, I'm not taking any chances. This means that she's going to have to tamp down her penchant for debating with me just for the fun of it and take orders like a soldier.

"Alright, Copperhead. You want to take a hands-on approach with this? I'll support you. But we're going to play by my rules. This is my world, and though you are capable, you don't have a lifetime of experience dealing with men like Raphael. So you'll do *exactly* as I say, both in preparation and during the operation itself. Can you handle that?"

"Absolutely." Her response is immediate, her face dead serious. "I'm not too cocky to realize when I'm jumping in over my head. I'll be the most obedient soldier you've ever had. In fact, I'll start right now. Just tell me what you need from me, *master*."

Oh, of all the... Nevermind, I take it all back. This is the worst idea ever, and we're completely fucked.

* * *

I've just dropped Liz back at the Marchetti offices after lunch and am checking a message from Mono on my phone before pulling back out. Now that Liz is firmly entrenched in the business, my schedule has cleared up enough that I can spend some time putting my boots on the ground for a while. I'm planning to visit a few of our most loyal partners just to check in and reassure them that the Marchetti family is still completely stable and fully in control of things in the area.

I look up one final time before putting the car in drive and notice Liz chatting with an unfamiliar man at the elevator bank. He's tall, around my height, judging by the way he has to dip his chin to look her in the eyes, with salt and pepper hair and a well-cut navy suit. As the elevator doors open, Liz is laughing at something he's said and doesn't notice a young woman exiting in a hurry. The man reaches out to grab Liz's forearm, moving her to the side just in time to avoid being bowled over by the frantic woman.

I don't realize how tense I am until I hear a pop and look down at my hand to see a crack in the side of my phone case. Turning my self-awareness back on, I process just how tightly coiled I've become, my every muscle poised for attack. *Man, my protective instincts are in serious overdrive lately.* It's probably because I just agreed to let her step into the ring with the other monsters who call the underworld home. It's only natural that I'd be more on edge than usual, and with good reason.

Rolling with the feeling in my veins, I snap a picture of the mystery man before he boards the elevator and shoot it over to Mono. I know he probably won't find much on the guy until I can get at least some cursory details out of Liz, but maybe he'll get lucky. Either way, better safe than sorry. I learned that lesson all too well with Maria.

Pulling away from the sidewalk, I head toward my first stop of the day, reveling in the excitement that's already starting to fill my blood. It's the first chance I've had in months to dust off my recon skills, and I'm buzzing with pent up energy.

* * *

Things go smoothly during my first few visits. Everyone is surprised to see me, but thanks to our long-running relationships, they're gracious about my lack of personal attention these past few months. My generals seem to have held things together flawlessly. *I should commend them personally at our next meeting.* I make a mental note to set up a nice bonus for each of them as well as a physical token of my appreciation for their hard work these past few months.

Overall, things seem relatively quiet. Not that I necessarily expected anything different, but it's nice to confirm it in person. That just means I'll have plenty of time to focus on Raphael. It's not until I'm seated in Vic's office with a glass of single malt in hand that I realize I've jinxed myself.

"It's good to see you out and about again, Nipotino[12]."

Despite my reputation, Vic is old school. He respects the Marchetti reign and sticks to formalities in public but refuses to treat me as anything other than an honorary grandson when it's just the two of us.

"I won't say I was worried because I know you have things well in

---

[12] Grandson

hand, but I know how close you and Damien were. I'm glad to see you're doin' alright."

"Thanks, old man. It was Hell at first, but things are better these days. I mean, look, I even managed to step away from desk duty for an entire afternoon. I almost feel like my old self again."

I flash him my signature charming smile, though it has little effect on him other than to make him chuckle indulgently.

"Well, your timing couldn't be better, honestly. There have been some new faces sniffing around in recent weeks, and I don't like the look of 'em."

Oh, really?

"Sniffing around how?"

"There's one guy in particular who's been in several times. He never approaches me, but a few of my managers have told me that he's been feeling them out, asking questions about me and my 'business partners.' He's not buying the usual spiel, either. Keeps saying he knows there's more to the story, all while trying to play himself off as just some nosy townie. Then, one of my guys overheard him talking on the phone in the back alley one day. He couldn't make out what he was saying but said it sounded like Russian."

Russian? There hasn't been a Russian presence in town in more than 20 years. Damien's dad made sure of that when the last group tried to move in on his shipping contracts.

I thank Vic for the intel and tell him to let me know if he hears anything else. We chat for a while longer, but then it's time for me to go if I want to hit the last two stops on my list today. As he's walking me back to the front of the restaurant, he suddenly stops. In a low voice, he tells me that the man he mentioned is sitting at the bar. I spot him easily and give Vic a subtle nod.

I continue on my way out and clock the man's eyes tracking me as I leave, so I make sure to go through all the usual motions. But once

I hit the sidewalk, I pivot around to the side alley instead of heading towards my car. It's a good thing I parked in a nearby lot and not right out front. Might as well take advantage of the opportunity to learn a bit more about our new friend since he was so kind as to show up at a convenient time.

I use the fire escape to scale the building and take up a perch on the roof. If nothing else, I want a bird's eye view of where he heads after this, but maybe I'll get lucky, and he'll step out for another call while I'm here. My Russian is rusty and was never fantastic to begin with, but I'm confident that I'd be able to make out enough to get by until I can have the rest decoded professionally.

Lady Luck is on my side today. After about an hour, the man steps out of the back exit and leans against the wall to light a cigarette. Pulling out his phone, he looks both ways before making a call. *He's got to be a rookie. That was the sloppiest solitude check I've ever seen.*

My suspicion is confirmed as I listen in on his conversation. From what I can tell, he's been sent specifically to gather information on Marchetti partnerships and businesses in town. It sounds like this is one of his first big jobs, and he says something about the person on the other end of the line learning to take him seriously once he proves himself with the intel he's certain he'll gather. *Eh, don't count on it, comrade.*

I've already decided that he and I need to have a private chat of our own, but I can't grab him here. It's too far to my car and too busy a time of day to be hauling an unconscious man around without drawing attention. When he finally strides off toward his next destination, I make my way back to street level and follow him, waiting for the right opportunity.

Thankfully, he makes that easy on me, too. After stopping in at the corner store to buy more cigarettes, he heads toward a nondescript blue sedan parked down a deserted side street. Right as he unlocks the car and moves for the handle, I close the distance between us and slam his head into the door frame. He crumples immediately, and I make quick work of restraining him in the backseat and swiping his keys. Sliding into the driver's seat, I throw the car in gear and head toward the docks.

* * *

It's a mesmerizing symphony. The melodic sounds of guttural screams and whimpers of pain are accompanied by the echo of my footfalls and the scrape of tools on metal as I make my next selection. There's something so cathartic about methodically extracting every drop of pain from an enemy. It's almost as though every pleading cry from his mouth fills a well of mana within me, replacing something that was lost and rejuvenating my demon with strength and vitality for the upcoming battles. I feel unstoppable, holding the fate of not just this one man but his entire organization in the palm of my hand. I am in control. And there's nothing that he nor anyone else can do about it.

And at the same time, this is how I know. The mere existence of moments like these is irrefutable proof that I'm a monster masking as a human and not the other way around, no matter what Elizabeth says. Hell, not even Damien truly understood the depths of my depravity nor the sheer amount of pleasure I feel from enacting this very specific form of justice. I am fucked up beyond all human recognition. There's not a soul alive who could ever truly understand. And that's exactly the way it should be.

Setting my ruminations aside, I return to the task at hand. I have to hand it to the Russian soldier seated before me. Granted, I started slow, but he's withstood several hours of increasingly painful persuasion without giving up anything of value. He's clearly determined to prove himself. Perhaps pain isn't the answer with this one. Perhaps fear would be a more suitable motivation. But fear of what is the main question. If not pain or death, then perhaps his greatest fear is something less physical. I examine him curiously as I speak.

"You know, you've done so well this far. I think you've earned a bit of a break. Besides, I've always been curious about how the bratva do things. Why don't you and I just have a normal chat, nothing confidential?"

Grabbing a second metal chair from the back wall, I place it down in front of the soldier before dropping into it. I adopt a relaxed posture, legs spread wide and one arm slung over the back. He doesn't believe me. I can see that plainly from the tension of his shoulders and the way he's looking at me through the side of his eyes as if preparing to flinch away from a blow. But that's okay. I grab a bottle of water from the table and break the seal, the snap echoing through the room.

"I'll tell you what. For every question you answer, I'll give you a sip of water. How does that sound?"

He does nothing but continue to fix me with a steady look, and I take his lack of refusal as agreement.

"Excellent. Let's see, what to ask first? Oh! I know! Are the neck tattoos mandatory, or is that just something most soldiers opt to do as a show of solidarity?"

He doesn't respond right away, so I shake the bottle tauntingly and see his tongue dart across his lips in temptation. After a few seconds, his thirst wins out over his pride, and he answers. We continue in that fashion for several more rounds, each question relatively innocuous but still interesting insight to have. You never know what might come in useful one day. But now that he's put his guard down a bit, it's time to get back to business.

"Okay, okay. Last question. How badly do the families of traitors suffer? Do they really torture *everyone*, even the kids?"

Jackpot. The way his pupils immediately dilate confirms my suspicions, and I know it'll be all downhill from here. I lean forward in my chair now, elbows on my knees as I bring my face close to his. I can't help but smile at my impending victory, plus it adds nicely to the theatre of the thing. There's nothing quite so terrifying as a villain who smiles as he commits atrocities against mankind.

"I see," I purr. "It would be a terrible shame, then, if photos of you buddying up to Marchetti soldiers were to make it back to your brothers in arms. Wouldn't it?"

He pulls at his restraints in a final, futile attempt to find some other way out of this situation. I'm content to watch and wait, my gaze fixed squarely on his face so that I don't miss the moment he finally accepts defeat. It doesn't take long. Soon, he stops squirming and spits in my direction, though he's weak, so it doesn't quite reach my face.

"I'm glad to see you've finally realized that you only have one option here. Tell me everything you know about your bosses and why they're nosing around my city, and I'll kill you quickly and discreetly. You'll never be linked to the Marchetti family in any way. Refuse or provide information that I later discover to be false, and well...my head of intelligence also happens to be extremely talented at Photoshop. It would be your loved ones who would pay the price for that."

It's over in a matter of minutes after that. He spills everything he knows, which honestly isn't much given his level in the organization, but it's still enough for me to have a better idea of who and what I'm up against. I make good on my promise and put a bullet through his brain before sending the recording off to Mono and calling in a clean-up crew and a driver to take me back to my car. Now that that's settled, a shower and a stiff drink are calling for me at home, and I don't intend to make either one wait for long.

Chapter 10

Elizabeth

Several Days Later

"Yes, Francine, I swear I will be back in time for the client meeting this afternoon. No, there's no need to move it. Yes. Alright. I'll see you then."

I hang up the phone and place both it and my face on the table with a groan.

"Mono, you're a genius, right?" I mumble as coherently as possible from my prone position. "How long do you think it would take you to come up with a cloning device?"

"Ha! I appreciate your faith in me, but I specialize in machines, not humans," he quips. "Why don't you just tell your boss over there to stop slacking off and take some things off your plate?"

I expect Vince to protest, but when I twist my head to glimpse his way, I see a contemplative look on his face instead. *Aw, hell.* I don't want him to think I can't handle things on my own.

"I see that look, Vincenzo. You can go ahead and wipe it off right now. I promise I'm not truly overwhelmed, and I have everything fully under control. It just makes me feel better to whine about it sometimes."

He raises his hands in supplication, an affronted look on his face.

"Okay, okay, I get it. Geez, isn't a guy allowed to care about the well-being of his employees? Who's the client you're meeting anyway? Is it the same one from the lobby the other day when I dropped you off?"

Client from the lobby? Huh? Thinking back to the day he's referencing, I don't recall meeting any clients in the lobby. *Unless...*

"You mean the guy I was talking to at the elevators?"

He nods.

"Oh, that's not a client. He's just someone I ran into back when I worked for Cerberus. I'm not entirely sure what he does, but he used to have meetings at the Cerberus building, and just by coincidence, he happened to have a meeting with another company in the MI building that day."

"Oh. You two just seemed to know each other pretty well, so I assumed he must be a client."

"Eh, I think that's just how Lance is. He's just got one of those extra-friendly personalities. Well, actually, I think he's trying to hit on me, but unfortunately for him, that avenue is closed. I keep up a polite rapport, anyway, though. Who knows when we might need him for a business purpose, right?"

Vince nods thoughtfully, but I'm distracted by the chime of my phone. When I look back up, I catch him and Mono exchanging meaningful looks. *Lord only knows what that's about.* Sometimes I swear those two have figured out telepathy and are just refusing to share with the rest of the population.

Vince gets up and says his farewells. He's off for a meeting with Luca and Adrian Nuñez, leaving Mono and me to keep digging through intel on the Russian group that's been skulking around.

"Hey, tell del Rio that he still owes me those tickets," I call as he leaves. "Patience has never been my strong suit. Plus, it's rude to keep a lady waiting!"

Vince just chuckles and waves in affirmation as he strides down the hall. Luca del Rio has warmed up to me the fastest of the three generals, maybe because he's the youngest and the least set in his ways, or maybe he's just the smartest of the three. It likely also helps that I've had a few opportunities to show off not only my keen observational skills but also my trustworthiness as of late.

A couple of weeks ago, I noticed several small discrepancies in the shipping manifests from one of our transport partners and took the information to Luca directly. It turns out that the partner was "misplacing" bits of cargo during transport and paying off one of Luca's lower-level guys to look the other way since the amounts were so small. I never mentioned anything to Vince, so Luca got to be the hero for uncovering the betrayal and dealing out swift retribution.

That alone was probably enough to get on his good side, but getting to show off my signature party trick the other night at dinner with him and Vince certainly didn't hurt either. I don't know why these men are always so surprised at my ability to spot infidelity. The couples in question are always so stereotypically obvious. But, I suppose I'm grateful for their predictability this time since it further proved my value to Vince's closest general. Which is good, since Vince has put me in charge of all of the finer details and communication surrounding his strategy for dealing with the Russians. The last thing I need is the Marchetti generals refusing to adhere to orders simply because I was the messenger.

Speaking of the Russians, Mono and I have been spending every spare moment together the past few days, piecing together everything we can find on where they're likely operating and who they're interacting with. I've barely had time to breathe between keeping things running at MI, researching this, and doing my best to be home for Sam at normal hours. It usually means I just end up back on my laptop after Sam goes to sleep, and I've been almost entirely neglecting my workouts this week. But I decided earlier today that needed to change.

"Suit up, code monkey," I tell Mono, grabbing my duffel bag from the floor. "We can talk through what this latest info means while we run a few laps around the block. I can't afford to miss any more workouts."

"Surely you don't expect me to join you," he deadpans. "I can talk to you just fine with these fancy new devices they've invented called earbuds. See, you put it in your ear and..."

"Ha, ha," I snark back. "Remember what Vincenzo said. When he's not here, you have to act like I'm him, which technically means I'm in charge."

"Oh, well, in that case, what I'd tell him is that he can go fu-*umph*."

Cut off by the ball of socks I chucked at his face, he shoots me a sarcastic smirk, tongue playing with the inside of his lip ring.

I didn't want to have to play the damsel, but he's left me no choice.

"Oh, come on. Pleeeeaase?" I whine. "Don't make me go alone. I don't know this neighborhood well. What if something happens?"

He sighs and drops his head. *Got 'em.*

"Alright, I'll go with you. Just give me a minute to change."

He throws my socks back at me and trudges down the back hallway, muttering something under his breath while I dance out my celebration in the kitchen. *These mafia men and their absurd insistence on gentlemanly manners make it so easy.* Not that I'm complaining. These are the kinds of men most women only long for, and I'm surrounded by them. There are far worse places to be. Doing one final celebratory spin, I skip over to the guest bath and get changed myself.

In reality, it only takes us about 10 minutes to analyze the latest intel. We run in silence for a while, but it feels strained. I want to get to know Mono better. I'm just not sure where to start. Small talk has never been my strong suit, and it seems like it's not his either, which makes sense considering the highly isolating career he chose. In the end, I decide to forget even attempting chit-chat and just ask the thing I've been most curious about.

"So, feel free not to answer this if it's too personal, but I've noticed how close you and Vince are. Were you that close with Damien as well?"

His breathing has been steady throughout our run, but he blows out a heavy sigh at my question and drops his gaze to the ground, his shaggy black hair bouncing over his eyes as his feet hit the pavement. *Ah, crap. Why did I have to be so nosy?* I'm frantically trying to think of something else to say to change the subject when he speaks.

"It was...different with Damien. Vince and I feel more like brothers, you know? Like we were always on an even playing field, challenging one another while working side by side through everything. But Damien was harder for me to relate to, and it took longer for us to bond. Honestly, he felt more like a father figure than a brother, even though we were almost the same age. I looked up to him and felt this intrinsic desire to impress him. That probably sounds stupid..."

"No!" I rush out too quickly, thanks to my panicked state. "Honestly, I know exactly what you mean. Hell, I sometimes felt that way myself. It made me wonder if my daddy issues were deeper seated than I'd realized."

Thankfully the joke lands, earning me a scoff and skeptical side-eye.

"Truly, though, I get what you mean. Damien was just so pulled together and unflappable all the time. It made you want to strive for his level, to prove yourself as worthy of his affection."

Mono nods in agreement, and I decide to press my luck since we're on the topic.

"So you said it took longer for you to bond, but I'm assuming that after almost 10 years of working together, you did anyway. Are you... doing okay? Grief is tricky enough when you're surrounded by people, and I know you're on your own out here by choice, but if you need someone to talk through anything with, you can always call me."

"Mmm, you're right. These past few years, Damien and I had grown pretty close. Spend enough all-nighters waiting for Vince to get back from some perilous mission or another, and you're bound to spend the time talking about everything under the sun to keep from worrying. He knew pretty much everything about me. And while he didn't openly share as much as I did, there are certain things you just learn after spending enough time with a person. Like what a time bomb you were going to be, for example."

I whip my head to the side, expecting to see a teasing grin on his face but finding a stoic, contemplative expression instead.

"Me?!"

"Absolutely. I knew after the first night you met, when he followed you out of the restaurant, that you'd get under his skin in short order. I just wasn't sure yet whether it would be in a positive or a negative way. I started keeping tabs on you then, which is why it took less than 12 hours for me to put together a comprehensive report on you when Vince finally asked."

"Oh? And what did your little psychoanalysis predict?"

"Oh, don't get me wrong. Analysis is Vince's strong suit. I just find the intel. I was reminded of my lack of instinct in that area the last time we bet on possibilities, and I ended up with a tattoo of his name as punishment."

"Wait. *What*?! Oh, now I have to know! What was the bet about? And where is the tattoo? Can I see it?!"

He flips up the sleeve of his shirt and flashes his shoulder to display a heart with Vince's name embedded in a ribbon. I can't help it. I start cackling so hard that I have to stop running entirely, bracing my hands on my knees and eventually just dropping to the grass in glee. That is so Vincenzo I can hardly stand it. *The absolute menace.* Mono gives me a minute to get it out of my system, rolling his eyes but resisting the urge I'm sure he has to just leave me behind.

"Okay, okay, I'm sorry," I finally breathe out. "I'm done. But I do still want to know what the bet was about."

Mono offers a hand to help me up, and I brush grass clippings off my leggings. With a cock of my head towards the path we were on, we drop back into a steady jog.

"Okay, I'll tell you what it was about, but you have to promise not to hit me."

I'm instantly suspicious, but curiosity has always been my most dominant emotion, so I agree with a raise of my palm.

"Well, we made a bet on whether you'd end up with Damien. Vince was convinced you would, but I had other ideas. We know how that ended up."

"Well, obviously. But wait, what do you mean you had 'other ideas'?"

He hesitates, and I'm immediately twice as invested in whatever he's about to say. After about half a block, he finally finds the words, or the courage, to spit it out.

"I just thought, you know, based on what I saw, that you were more likely to end up with...Vince than Damien..."

"*What*?! How on God's green earth did you come to that conclusion?!"

"I don't know! That's just the vibe I got from watching y'all interact. You weren't intimidated by his charm or his ice, and he seemed to open up to you more than I'd ever seen him do with a woman. I just assumed. I told you analysis is not my strong suit! Anyway, we're almost back to the house. Race you for the last leg?"

I'm too shell-shocked trying to process what he's just said to do more than blindly agree without really hearing him. When he sprints off, I have no choice but to tuck away his incredibly off-base assumptions and kick myself into high gear. I can muddle over the insanity of what he's just said after I smoke his ass.

Chapter 11

Vincenzo

One Week Later

The sound of the electronic lock activating is music to my ears. *Fucking **finally***. I've been waiting in this small apartment for hours, having expected him home well before midnight. As it stands, I'll be lucky to get any sleep at all before my first meeting in the morning. But, oh well. We do what we must to protect our family.

Lance flicks on the small light in the entryway and takes his time placing his bag in the closet. I wonder briefly if he's drunk, but he seems steady on his feet as he finally steps back and loosens his tie. I don't announce my presence, partly curious to see how long it will take before he notices me.

Too long. Blowing out a breath, he moves toward the kitchen, not bothering to activate any more lights along the way. Unholstering his sidearm, he places it atop the fridge before pouring himself a glass of water. I wait until he drains it and steps toward the sink before I speak.

"For a man who's so clearly desperate to meet me, you sure took your sweet time getting here tonight."

He spins instinctively towards my voice while also retracing his steps toward the fridge, but I'm faster. I'm out of my chair and across the small living room in three strides, blocking his path. The only light available comes from the small entryway fixture and the moon outside the window, but it's enough for me to enjoy the positively murderous expression on his face. No need for introductions tonight. He knows *exactly* who I am.

"I don't know what you're talking about. What interest would I have in meeting a *stronzo*[13] like you?"

"That's exactly what I was hoping to find out. You see, I've looked into you, *Nikolai*, and you seem to be an intelligent guy. So intelligent that I can't imagine you expected to be able to get close to Elizabeth Greystone *without* drawing my attention. You must have done so as a way to purposely draw me out. So, here I am."

I spread my arms wide and shoot him a syrupy grin, even as my eyes track every twitch of his muscles. I can't tell yet if he's going to try to run or fight. Not that it matters in the end. If he thinks he has any chance of leaving this apartment alive tonight, he's not quite as intelligent as I thought.

He doesn't bother with a reply, instead darting a hand toward the counter to grab a chef's knife, brandishing it in my direction. I feel a true smile cross my face, adrenaline rushing through my veins now that the real fun is about to begin. He rushes me, feinting toward my left side with the blade, but I catch the shift of his feet and manage to block his true jab to my right. He headbutts me and spins away, bouncing on his feet. *Fuck, that actually hurt. This Neanderthal has a stone skull or something.* I force away the flashes in my vision and slip a small knife from my pocket. Before he even notices the movement, it's flying through the air to lodge in his right forearm.

As the kitchen knife clatters to the floor and he instinctively moves to grasp at the blade in his arm, I rush him, my fist connecting with his jaw. I get in two more hits before he ducks and rams into my stomach, forcing my back against the wall. I stomp on the arch of his foot and

---

[13] asshole

bring my elbow down on the back of his neck to break his hold. He staggers back, and I don't notice that he's dislodged the blade from his arm until it's swinging straight at my face. I throw up an arm to stop his momentum and turn my head to the side just in time to avoid a deep cut, but he still manages to graze my left cheek with a thin slice.

He's a much better fighter than I expected. I haven't had to try this hard in a long time, and it's fucking *amazing*. A gleeful laugh spills from my mouth as my veins sing. *Now, **this** is what it's all about. But even so, no sense in drawing things out. Some sleep would be nice, after all.*

I grab his swinging wrist and wrench the knife from his grasp, exclaiming a quick "just what I needed" before driving it home into the side of his neck. A guttural cry escapes his mouth, and blood pours from the wound. He desperately tries to stem the flow with his hand, distracted enough that I'm able to palm a second blade and drive it directly into his abdomen, just for good measure.

He drops to his knees, his face already paling from the pain and loss of blood. He tries to speak, but it comes out as nothing more than a wet gargle.

"Oh, don't strain yourself, Nikolino[14]. Nothing you say at this point matters anyway."

I crouch down beside him, staring directly into his eyes as I watch the life fade from them, even as he conveys as much hatred as he can muster. After a few more seconds, he slumps fully to the floor, still refusing to break his gaze. We stay locked like that until the end, making silent promises to meet each other in Hell. I want to tell him not to hold his breath. I don't plan on joining him anytime soon. When the last shred of life finally leaves his eyes, and his breathing stops, I dip my fingers in the blood at his neck and draw my calling card on his cheek. A quick search turns up his cell phone, and I pocket it before pushing back up

---

[14] diminutive nickname for Nikolai

to my full height.

It's 3 a.m. now. If I head straight home and take the quickest possible shower, I might still be able to catch an hour or two of rest before I need to get up again. Striding out the front door, I beeline for the stairwell and do just that.

* * *

By noon, Mono has cracked into Nikolai's phone and gotten the final bits of intel we need to deal with his cohorts. I'm just waiting for Liz to arrive so I can give her the news and work out when we want to pull the trigger. Plus, I need to tell her about his duplicity. She's been in meetings off-site all day, and that wasn't exactly news I wanted to impart over the phone. I'm sure she'll be shaken by the thought that she was targeted once again, but hopefully, my swift handling of the situation will reassure her to some degree.

I recognize her familiar double rap, and she strolls through the door moments later, already rambling a mile a minute about the insane lines at the cafe where she picked up our lunch. She walks over to set the food on the table but drops the bag to the floor before she gets there, eyes wide and mouth gaping. Snapping my gaze around the room, I can't find whatever spooked her, but I draw my hand towards my sidearm just in case.

"Oh my god! What is this?!"

She rushes me, hands coming up to cup my face as she turns my head from side to side. Her thumb grazes a bit too close to the slit on my cheek, making me wince. She drops her hands immediately, covering her mouth instead.

"Oh, shit! I'm sorry. I didn't mean to hurt you. But what the hell happened?!"

I guide her toward the couch, gently pressing her shoulder so she'll sit and stop fussing.

"I'm alright, Copperhead. And I promise I'll tell you everything. But for now, just take a seat, and let's have lunch while we talk, yeah?"

Realization dawns in her eyes and she moves to pick up the abandoned takeout bag, but I keep my hand on her shoulder, holding her in place. Stepping over to grab the meal myself, I bring it to the table and divvy out the slightly battered contents before taking the seat beside her. Only once I've personally unwrapped her sandwich and forced it into her hands do her eyes leave my face. She takes the smallest bite I've ever seen, then looks back at me expectantly.

"Okay, I'm eating. Now tell me what happened."

I let out a heavy sigh and rub the bridge of my nose before remembering the black eye I'm sporting makes that a bad idea. *Fuck, that smarts.* And so will what I'm about to tell her, but there's no real soft way to say this. *Probably best to just rip the proverbial bandage off.*

"What I'm about to tell you sucks no matter how I say it, so I'll just give it to you straight. Lance wasn't some executive you happened to run into by coincidence. He was an intelligence agent for the Russians. His real name was Nikolai Stoletsky. I paid him a visit at home last night, and he turned out to be a better fighter than I anticipated, hence all of this. But I'm fine. I promise he got the worse end of the deal."

I pause to let her process the information. She blinks several times in quick succession, disbelief and anger slowly creeping into her expression until she suddenly shoots off the couch, her forgotten sandwich falling to the table.

"You've got to be fucking kidding me!" she seethes, pacing away for several steps before turning back, hands flailing as she speaks. "Is it that obvious to everyone that I'm the weakest link? Do I have some sign on my forehead that only Marchetti enemies can see? Pick this one. She's easy to fool and a direct ticket to the boss!"

I let her pace and rant, using the time to take a few bites of my lunch.

I was expecting fear to be her primary reaction, but seeing her fired up like this makes me feel silly for worrying. She has every right to be pissed, so I'm happy to let her get it all out. But then her steps slow until she stops completely. Her back is to me so I can't see her face, and she stays like that for several moments. When she turns around, her brows are drawn and her expression has morphed into one of regret mixed with the fear that I was expecting.

"Vince, I don't think I should do this anymore."

Fuck. I was afraid she'd say that. Not that I can blame her for wanting to protect herself. This situation just highlights what we both already knew. Working for me puts her directly in the line of fire, and I'm not so much of a monster that I'd guilt her into staying there against her will.

"Okay," I say with a long breath. "I completely understand. I'd never pressure you to keep doing something that makes you feel unsafe. I can respect that you'd rather not keep putting yourself at risk, especially since this isn't the first time something like this has happened. You have Sam to think about as well."

But where I expect to see reluctant agreement, I'm met with a look of annoyed disbelief instead.

"No, I don't think you *do* understand," she says, marching back towards me. "I'm not saying that I should stop doing this for *my* sake. I think I should stop doing it for *yours.*"

Okay, now I'm the one in disbelief. *How, on any mortal plane, could her leaving* **help** *me? She's the only reason I have a spare moment to breathe these days.* I shoot her a questioning look, but she averts her gaze, looking sideways toward the windows.

"Vincenzo, look at yourself! You put yourself in danger, yet again, because of me. I naively let my guard down with a stranger, and *you* paid the price. This is freaking Maria all over again, except this time, you were closer to the situation and able to step in before things went too far! But what if you hadn't seen me talking to Lance that day? What if I never said anything, and we didn't know about his allegiance until it was too late? What if..."

She stops and drops her head on a shuddering breath, hands clenching at her sides. When she raises her eyes to mine again, they're glassy and rimmed in red.

"I could never live with myself if I lost you too because of something like this. I'd rather cut ties now if it means that you'd be safer for not having to come to my rescue."

I'm up in an instant, folding her firmly into my arms as the first tear falls. I simply hold her as she cries, softly but steadily, for several minutes. I don't say anything, mainly because I don't know *what* to say. I just run one hand down the back of her head while the other keeps a firm hold on her shuddering ribs.

Out of everything about this situation, the thing she's most worried about is *me*? I don't know what to do with that. My chest tightens, and my heart starts racing just as hard as it was last night. It feels like I'm in full fight or flight mode, but I'm not even sure what my body thinks I'm meant to be fighting for or running from. Feminine displays of emotion? Surely, I'm not that stereotypical.

Eventually, her sniffling stops, but she keeps her head down and retains a death grip on my lapels. Assuming she's afraid of looking like a mess, I pass her my handkerchief to wipe her face.

"I'm pretty sure that's the first time I've ever gotten to whip that bad boy out. I feel so dashing."

She laughs drily and moves her head back to look me in the eyes. It's a bit unnerving. She doesn't say anything; she just searches my eyes with her own as if she expects to find the right answer in them. Needing to get myself back on firm footing and far away from the wild set of emotions the situation has surfaced, I transition back into business mode, dropping my arms to put a bit more space between us.

"Hear me now. You are not the weak link. If not you, the Russians would have just tried to worm their way in through someone else. Removing yourself from the equation won't change that. Things like this," I say as I gesture toward my face, "are just part of the package when you're dealing with monsters. It's been this way for decades, and I doubt it will change anytime soon."

She seems to accept that truth, her eyes resigned to the reality I've painted. But I don't want her to think I'm pressuring her to stay if she still wants to leave. I just don't want her to feel any responsibility or guilt for what happens to me, now or in the future.

"And I mean it when I say that I will support you no matter what you decide. I was born into this life. I don't know anything else, and frankly, I'm not sure I want to. But you have a real choice. You can quit and go back to being a perfectly normal citizen who just so happens to have a guardian demon watching her back. I'd never resent you for making that decision."

In the end, she asks me to give her a couple of days to think it over. I agree easily and tell her in no uncertain terms that she is not to do any work for MI or the family over the weekend. I don't want her burying herself in work to avoid the situation. When she gives me her final answer on Monday morning, I need to know that she has sufficiently thought it through and made the choice that's best for her.

That being said, one of the luxuries of being the boss is the ability to do what you want, no matter the advice you've given to others. For my part, I firmly box up the confusing rush of emotions I felt at seeing her so upset on my behalf, as well as the strange twinge in my chest as I watched her walk out of my office, and stash them far away in the back of my mind. Who has time to feel feelings when there's an empire to run? Answering a call from Luca, I drop into my desk chair and spend the rest of the afternoon deep in work mode.

Chapter 12

It only took about six hours for me to decide that I had been short-sighted earlier, and the best way to protect Vincenzo was to remain at his side, albeit far more suspicious and alert than I had been previously. And since I've got a naturally combative personality that can't stand being told what to do, I ignored his orders to avoid doing any work over the weekend. Most of my time was spent combing through any final details that might give us an extra advantage over the Russians.

Which is why, as I stand in front of Roberto, Emilio, and Luca in Vince's office, I'm fully confident in the information I've prepared. The Marchetti generals may not like me, but they'll have no reason to question the accuracy of my intel. Or so I think.

"Look, that all sounds very nice, Ms. Greystone," Roberto drawls, seemingly unimpressed with the detailed strategy I've just laid out. "But do you really expect me to trust that you've uncovered every possible weapon in the Russian's arsenal? I mean, do you even have any prior experience with intel at this level? We're not talking profits and losses here. This is actual life or death."

Vince's reaction is immediate and visceral, living up to his rattlesnake moniker with the speed of his bite.

"She speaks for *me*! If any of you have a problem with that, we can discuss it personally."

While I appreciate his unwavering support, I don't need it today. I've known since the day Vince introduced me that Roberto would eventually need a special demonstration of what I'm capable of, so I'm well prepared to handle this on my own. I wave Vince off and step closer to where Roberto is seated.

"Ah, I see you still don't trust me," I tell Roberto, offering a sickeningly sweet smile that I hope comes off as demeaning as I intend it. "That's fine. I expected that. Which is why I've been spending time at Lucille's over on 5th Street. It's a cute little place, excellent for really focusing on a problem. And the espresso was absolutely perfect."

I see the flash in Roberto's eyes at my mention of the cafe and know I've caught him by surprise.

"I enjoyed it so much that I almost forgot why I was there and invited some of the Marchetti wives out to join me for a coffee date. Oh, but don't worry. I realized soon enough how awkward that might get."

Roberto's face is solid red by now, and he's breathing audibly, nostrils flaring as he white knuckles the arms of the chair. I'm sure he'd like nothing more than to jump out of that chair and strangle me into silence, but he's at least smart enough to realize that would only result in his death, not mine.

"I can see by your expression that you've shifted from disbelief to disgust, so I'll assume that my ability to gather detailed and valuable intel on our enemies is no longer in question. Though, if you still want to talk that through, perhaps the two of us could meet one-on-one at Lucille's. I am dying for an excuse to return and try one of those cinnamon tarts I saw in the pastry case."

The other men in the room are still as gravestones, eyes darting between Roberto and me with curiosity written plainly on their faces. The only sound is the soft whir of Vince's laptop and Roberto's enraged breathing. He looks to be in actual physical pain as he forces out a strangled response.

"No. That won't be necessary."

I shoot another syrupy smile in his direction and trill my pleasure at his acquiescence. Continuing with the briefing, I wrap up with notes on the rendezvous locations before stepping back to allow Vincenzo to give the final orders. He keeps it brief, reiterating the assignments I've already covered and telling the men to ready their soldiers to move out in 48 hours. He dismisses them, and the three file out of the room swiftly. As soon as the door snicks shut, Vince rounds on me, eyes sparkling with mischievous glee.

"What the glorious fuck was that, Copperhead? Who the hell is Lucille?"

I give him all the details, pacing across the room to help expel some of my excited energy. When I tell Vince that Lucille is Roberto's 26-year-old love child with whom he somehow maintains a relationship without his wife knowing she even exists, he almost slips right off his perch on the edge of his desk.

"Elizabeth, I think I may be in love with you."

My gaze shoots to his face, and I stumble on my next step, almost crashing face-first into the wall. His impish smirk confirms that he was joking, but it still takes my pulse a moment to return to a normal rhythm after a scare like that. *And that would be scary because how messy would it be if your charming, intelligent, fit, ambitious boss slash best friend suddenly professed romantic feelings for you? Terrifying right? Obviously.* Whatever spiral inner Elizabeth is going down is interrupted when Vince continues.

"Roberto's been keeping that a secret for almost three decades, and you just demolished that man's sense of stealth after having only been with the organization for a few weeks. I mean, talk about going in for the kill. The venom in that bite was fucking lethal."

I preen under his praise. I know I'm smiling like an idiot, but I freaking did it! I shut down a seasoned mafia general with nothing more than cunning and a sharp tongue. Sure, Mono helped with identifying his habits, where he spends his money, where he likes to go, and whatnot. But I was the one who did the leg work. I staked out place after place and talked to countless strangers before uncovering the connection between Lucille and Roberto. But it was well worth it because, boy, is it a connection.

"I am truly impressed. I think you've earned yourself a new nickname. From now on, I'm calling you Venom."

Venom. I like the sound of that. I wriggle my eyebrows and chomp my teeth at Vince in approval, earning a deep laugh in return.

"Alright, Venom," he drawls, checking his watch. "Put the fangs away for now. We need to roll, or Francine will have my head for being late to the shareholders meeting."

Chapter 13

Vincenzo

Two Days Later

I'm on a rooftop again, this time under cover of darkness, the bodies of two Russian guards lying lifeless beside me. I wipe a bloody hand on the pants leg of the closest one. A gun would have been cleaner, but even a silencer makes noise in a wide-open space like this, and I couldn't risk the second guard outing my presence sooner than planned. That would ruin the dramatic entrance I've cooked up. I even dressed for the occasion in a three-piece suit, albeit in solid black, just in case. At any rate, it's impossible to avoid at least a bit of a mess when knives are involved, but luckily, this one cleans off relatively easily.

Mono's voice is clear as he feeds me status reports. Elizabeth is listening in, but she's on a muted line. Listening to the central feed will be good experience in case she ever needs to fill Mono's role, but I didn't want to risk her voice on the line being a distraction to the team, Roberto especially. He may have submitted to her authority for now, but it's not willingly, and the last thing I need is for him to be more focused on his distaste for her presence than the mission at hand.

"Breach confirmed. I repeat, breach confirmed. We're inside all three safe houses. Stand by for fall reports."

Excellent. That's my cue. I confirm receipt and that I'm initiating phase two as I slink toward the rooftop entrance, pulling out the keys I snagged from one of the guards. The door squeaks, but only slightly, and a brief pause seems to indicate no one noticed. *I'll bet not. They're probably a bit busy by now with the mayday calls coming in from their safe houses.*

Prowling silently down the steps, I make my way toward the back room of the restaurant where the Russian boss and his generals like to spend their nights. The closer I get, the more I can make out of the commotion inside. They're in full panic mode, and it sounds like two of the three voices are recommending the group scatter and lay low until they can assess the damage. *Too late for that, segaiolos[15].*

I pause before turning the last corner. There should be two more guards stationed outside the door, assuming they haven't been sent to aid their falling comrades. The distance between them is too tight for knife work, so I carefully slip a pistol and silencer from inside my coat and assemble the weapon. Back to the wall, I pull my earbud out and focus all my attention on listening to the movement further down the hall. The soft clack of a rifle being shifted around sounds to the left side, and the scuff of a boot echoes off the right. Okay. Two guards, it is. Replacing my earpiece, I breathe in and out slowly one last time to center myself before whipping around the corner.

I get both shots off before either guard can sound the alarm, and the commotion inside the room hides the muffled thud of their bodies hitting the wall before slumping down to the floor. Once again, I swipe the guard's keys, but I take a moment to stow my silencer and straighten my appearance before I unlock the door. There won't be any need for stealth after this point. It's a circus spectacular from here on out, and I'm the mother fucking ringmaster. A sinister grin crawls across my face as I reach for the door handle. *It's time to go round up the clowns.*

Swinging the door wide, I stroll into the room with my pistol trained

---

[15] Wankers/Douchebags

on the boss, Maxim Sokolov. His father, Mischa Sokolov, and I have made a special agreement. I called him just minutes before our operation began tonight and offered to spare his son's life if he ensures that Maxim and what remains of his organization never set foot in my territory again. He also agreed to personally deliver a shipment of Russian-made weapons to my operatives in Spain as penance for the trouble his son has caused. But Maxim doesn't know that, and neither do his lapdogs. Both of them leap to their feet, weapons pointed at my head, while the women who were previously in their laps shriek and run to crouch in the far corner of the room.

"Ah ah ah, boys," I tut. "If you think my reflexes aren't fast enough to pull this trigger before your shots hit, you should take a peek outside to see what I did to your guards."

Neither man moves, and I raise a taunting eyebrow at Maxim as he grits his jaw and stares at me with hatred flaming in his eyes.

"Mr. Caputo," he spits. "To what do we owe the pleasure?"

"Ah, Maxim. I thought it only polite that I stop by personally to see what you thought of my housewarming gifts. My generals tell me they made quite the splash with your soldiers throughout town."

He yells something in Russian that's outside of my limited vocabulary, but I'm sure he's cursing me and every member of my family or something close to it. Then he starts to laugh.

"You think that just because you took out a few safe houses that you've won? You haven't done your homework. Our team here was merely the first wave of scouts. The bratva's forces are much larger and stronger than your adorable little local gang could imagine. And you've all but guaranteed they'll be arriving on your doorstep within days. Your only hope of survival now is to drop your weapon and try to buy your way out of annihilation. Though it will have to be a rather compelling offer..."

His generals chuckle alongside him, though it's clear they're still uneasy. I am, after all, still pointing a gun at their boss' head.

"I think you're the one who hasn't done his homework," I taunt back. "Do you know nothing of what they call me? What I'm capable of?"

He doesn't answer, but he doesn't need to. I can see it in his eyes, in the way his pupils quiver, fighting the urge to dart around looking for an escape. He's not nearly as confident in the current situation as he'd like me to believe.

"I can see that you're familiar. So you should know that I never do anything without extensive research. I know *exactly* how powerful the bratva's forces are and how ruthless their leader can be. That's why I called Mischa directly before we began this little interlude. He's a reasonable man, your father. And clearly a family man as well. He was objective enough to recognize that indulging you in your misguided bid to encroach on Marchetti territory was a mistake, and he was willing to accept tonight's losses in manpower and resources in exchange for just one thing. Your pathetic life."

As soon as I finish speaking, the Marchetti soldiers who crept into the building behind me clear the doorway and take out both Russian generals with simultaneous shots. Only Maxim remains, seething but silent. *It must sting to have Daddy clean up your messes like an errant toddler.*

"My men here will escort you to the airport. Your father has already booked you a flight back to Russia. Per the terms of our agreement, you are never to set foot within a hundred miles of this city again, nor will you interfere in Marchetti operations anywhere else in the world."

I exchange a loaded look with the soldier to my right. At his affirmative nod, I turn to see myself out, infusing as much arrogant don swagger in my walk as I can muster. *Eat your heart out, kozel*[16].

---

[16] asshole (Russian)

* * *

"No, you did not!"

Elizabeth bursts into laughter, head thrown back and wine glass tipping precariously as she progresses to full-on cackling. When she finally sits back up, wine miraculously preserved, she has tears of glee in her eyes.

Following a brisk debrief at Mono's after everything was said and done, I offered her a ride home and ended up agreeing to a celebratory nightcap before heading home myself. That was several drinks ago, though, at least for Liz. At this point, she's moved fully past nightcap into potential blackout territory.

I've never seen her drink this much, and certainly not in such a short time span. Her face is flushed, her speech has been steadily becoming more erratic, and it's clear she's having trouble staying balanced even while seated on the leather sofa. She looks happy, though, and there's very little on Earth that would compel me to kill her good mood. Besides, she's earned a night, and let's be honest, she'll need the day off, as well, to let loose and unwind.

"God, I wish I could've seen his shhhtupid shhmirky face when you told him about dear old daddy."

She mimes a crying baby with her fists, and if I needed any further confirmation that she's toasted, I don't anymore. As she downs the rest of her wine in a single swallow, I start to wonder if I should tactfully cut her off just to keep her from feeling like complete death in the morning. That thought is solidified when she tries to put her glass down and misses the table completely, causing it to shatter on the dark wood floor. A hiccuped "oopsie" is her only response before she bends down and tries grabbing at one of the larger pieces with her bare hand.

I'm up like a shot, my hand closing around her wrist before she can hurt herself. *Alright, Miss Independent here clearly needs looking after.* I get her seated upright, then use my free hand to turn her face upwards so that she'll be focused on me instead of the wine glass.

"Hey there, Venom. I'll get that. But first, why don't I help you to bed? You've had a long day. I'm sure you're tired."

She bats away the hand at her chin with a slurred scoff, head bobbing like a newborn.

"You shoul' putchurself to bed. You were the one out assasstimating emenies and whatev. I just sat in Mono's lair and had snacks. Not tired at all."

Riiiight. Even as she says it, her head leans into my hand, dropping all of its weight against my palm in a sort of vertical pillow situation. *Okay, no more talking. It's time for more decisive measures.*

I bend down and scoop her off the couch in a singular, swift motion. Her arms seem to move on instinct, wrapping around my neck as her head comes to rest on my shoulder. Her steady breaths fan across my neck, and a jolt runs through me, sizzling down my spine and through my stomach in equal measure. *Jesus, Vince, pull it together.* I tighten my grip, pulling her closer to make sure she's solid in my hold before I start walking toward her bedroom.

She seems to be already asleep as I lay her down on the bed and start tucking the blankets over her. Her soft breathing is punctuated by occasional short humming sounds, and I can't help but smile at how unexpectedly adorable that is. For someone so feisty and vicious while she's awake, she sure does fit the sleeping angel stereotype.

I'm about to head toward the bathroom in search of painkillers to leave for her when her hand grips mine tightly. I turn back to find her teal eyes open and fixed on my face, though still glazed enough that I know she hasn't magically sobered up in the last five minutes.

"I'm like, really drunk, huh?"

I bark out a sharp laugh at the unexpected question.

"Yeah, I'd say that's a fair assessment. I think it's actually the first time I've ever seen you drunk."

She nods solemnly.

"Well, *duh*. I'm a smart woman, dammit! And smart women don't let their guard down around dangerous men. Or any men for that matter..."

I raise an eyebrow and gesture at my general physique with a questioning look.

"I'm not sure if I should be insulted or concerned."

She waves a dismissive hand at me, her entire arm swaying as if her limbs weigh a metric ton.

"Oh, you know what I mean. Marcus was a manipulative bastard. Couldn't give him a chance to be a bigger dick. And Damien was just... well, you know."

I'm not sure I *do* know, so I stay silent and wait for her to elaborate. She does, laughing softly to herself.

"I mean, could you imagine? Me shitfaced while Damien just sat there, all broody and intimidating? Talk about mortifying."

"Okay..." I drawl. "So you weren't comfortable enough to get drunk around them, but you're somehow fine with doing it around me? I think you might be drunker than you realize, Venom, because that doesn't make any sense."

Her reply is mumbled, so I lean closer to be able to make it out.

"It makes total sense, you numbskull."

She flicks me on the forehead as she says it, and I huff out a laugh as I rub the spot.

"You let me just be...me. Safe. S'really frickin nice."

Her hand squeezes mine tighter as if to punctuate her point. Meanwhile, I'm pretty sure I've stopped breathing, or my brain has stopped processing, or maybe both. I don't... How could she...? Why would I...?

I have the unmistakable urge to throttle something at the thought of her feeling so insecure for so many years, but at the same time, I have no idea what to make of what she said after that. *I make her feel safe?*

Me? The man who orchestrated mass murder and even personally saw to a few of them just a few hours ago? And wait, is she saying that even when she was with Damien, she didn't feel secure enough to let her guard down and be herself? That doesn't make any sense. She fully trusted him. *Didn't she?*

My brain kicks into overdrive, running through memories and snippets of conversations. Now that I think about it, there were more than a few examples of trust being an ongoing problem between Damien and Liz, but I never thought it ran so deep as to keep her from feeling like she could be vulnerable around him. *Shit.* That's sure as hell not the fairy tale romance I had them playing out in my head.

Bringing myself back to the present, I'm even more lost at what to do with this new information. Her eyes are still open, though drooping, and she's just looking at me silently, but she hasn't dropped my hand. Quite the opposite, in fact. Her thumb is running across the back of my hand, and her fingers keep curling in and out against my palm. The hair on my arms rises as the tactile sensations make my skin pebble, and I just barely stop myself from crawling onto the mattress and wrapping myself around her in a human cocoon.

Nope. Not doing that. Fuck, seriously, no more whiskey for you, Caputo. Maybe the events of today made you more susceptible or something, but you've clearly hit your limit. I decide she's probably not thinking straight, either. After all, she had far more than I did.

"Now I *know* you're talking nonsense, Venom," I tease. "How could I make you feel safe? You do remember what I do for a living, right? Hell, what I did earlier tonight, even? With this very hand you're holding, I might add."

She scoffs and rolls to the side, taking the offending hand with her.

"Whatever, Rattles. You may scare the rest of the world, but you can't scare me away. You and I both know that I've never been safer than I am right now."

Once again, I have no idea how to respond, so I just don't. This works out because, in a matter of seconds, her breathing deepens, and her grip on my hand loosens as she falls back asleep. I slowly slide my hand free and risk tucking her hair behind her ear to keep it out of her mouth before resuming my quest for painkillers and water to leave on her nightstand. Once I'm sure her alarm is set and she has everything she'll need to nurse her hangover in the morning, I slip from the room and out of the apartment. I make sure to text her from the elevator to take the day off. She's more than earned it, and I'm sure she won't complain about being able to head right back to bed after getting Sam off to school in a few hours.

Chapter 14

Elizabeth

The Following Week

"I've got that meeting with the marketing team at 4:30, and then I'll be leaving straight after for that dinner with Richard Barswick. We're very close to an agreement on the contract renewal, so I'll do my best to close the deal tonight."

Vince looks up from his tablet, and I suppress a triumphant grin at the red slit still decorating his bottom lip. I finally, *finally* got around his defenses to land a hit during training last night. It wasn't as powerful as I'd have liked since he caught on quick enough to dance back a step, but I still managed a solid blow that left his lower lip swollen and bleeding. While it's already mostly healed, you can still see the cut from his top fangs up close, and it's a nice reminder of how far I've come in the past few weeks.

"Would you like me to join you at dinner? You know, apply a little extra pressure?"

While I appreciate the offer, I'm determined to close this deal myself. Honestly, I think Barswick is just stalling as a power play. He hasn't even raised any solid objections. He just keeps saying that he needs to think about it some more. I can't tell if it's because I'm new to the organization or a woman. Maybe it's both. But I've already resolved not to take any more of his wishy-washy bullshit tonight. He's either in, or he's out, but either way, I'm not leaving this dinner without a solid answer.

"Don't you have dinner with Adrian Nuñez tonight to talk through the Madrid deal?" I remind Vince, tactfully sidestepping an outright refusal of his help.

Swiping quickly on his tablet, he confirms with a nod.

"It seems I do. Guess you're on your own then, Venom. Give him hell, but also, try not to scare the poor guy too badly, hmm?"

He's teasing, but he's hit awfully close to the mark on my game plan for the night. I shoot him a playfully wicked smile in return and start to gather my things to head to my next appointment.

* * *

Wishy-washy he may be around contract negotiations, but it's clear Barswick has no such compunction when it comes to good food. The restaurant is one I haven't tried before, and the food is amazing. It's Japanese-themed, with dark wooden tables in the main dining area, as well as a series of private rooms where you sit on the floor in a more traditional style. Barswick booked one of those rooms, and after hearing the dull roar of the dining room I'd say it was a wise choice.

The meal has been incredible. I'm not big on sushi, but the soups, seared meats, and side dishes I've tried have all been fantastic. I've already made a note to bring Vince next time. He's got to try their yakitori. There's something addictive in that marinade, I swear.

Barswick has skived off of any business talk up until now, more concerned with "building rapport" and indulging in several glasses of the insanely expensive sake he ordered alongside the meal. I let it slide while I was enjoying my own meal. But now that my hunger is sated, it's time to get down to brass tacks.

When he returns from a trip to the restroom, he drops gracelessly into the seat closest to the door instead of his original one across the table. Perhaps that sake was a bit stronger than I realized. Now that he's seated beside me, I notice the flush crawling up his neck and hope that indicates he's imbibed enough to be more forthcoming and impulsive than usual without having crossed the line into utterly useless. I'm tired of dealing with him. I need to get this signed tonight.

"So, Richard, I'm eager to hear your final thoughts on the contract. Your team had no further revisions to share, and you have to admit that we've been more than fair with the tier-based fee schedule. Do we have a deal?"

"Straight to the point, eh, Ms. Greystone? I do like that about you. You're very direct."

He smiles as he says this, but it seems off somehow - more oily than agreeable. My guard goes up immediately, and I watch him closely as he continues.

"Perhaps I should be direct as well. The contract is solid. I have no concerns about the deal itself. But, as you know, Barswick Materials is in high demand these days. Several Marchetti competitors are clamoring to make similar deals, so I'd like a little something *extra* to sweeten the deal."

Called it. I had a hunch that his stalling was less about the Marchetti International deal and more about wanting to cut a deal with the Marchetti family. It seems I was right. But officially, I don't work for the Marchetti family. Vince's inner circle are the only ones who know about my true role, so I'm forced to play dumb.

"Ah, well, perhaps we should set up some time for you to speak with Mr. Caputo directly. I deal only with the Marchetti International business, but I'm sure he'd be more than happy to discuss his other business ventures with you in person if you're interested in...additional partnership opportunities."

Barswick lets out a deep chuckle and shakes his head. His hand raises, and he runs a finger down my cheek as he responds.

"You misunderstand, Ms. Greystone. It's not Mr. Caputo's 'other business ventures' I'm interested in. It's you."

It takes every ounce of training that Vince has put me through to maintain my poker face in that moment. My skin crawls at the graze of his beefy hand on my cheek, and I recoil instinctively. I'm disgusted, but I need to think this through carefully. I'm not naive. I knew something like this was inevitable at some point, and I have no intention of losing months of hard work on this deal over it. But I also don't want to leave any room for misunderstanding. I am *not* on offer, and if he has any business sense at all he'll apologize and pretend this never happened.

The question is, is he the type whose ego needs protecting so his pride doesn't prevent him from continuing the deal, or the type who needs to be told no with a firm hand to respect the answer? He's praised my direct approach on several occasions, so a stern yet polite refusal is probably my best bet. I subtly inch away as I deliver my rejection, eager to put more space between us.

"Unfortunately, Mr. Barswick, my social company is not and will never be on the table. And while I can appreciate that you have several other potential partnerships to consider, I'll need to know your final answer on this particular deal tonight. Marchetti International has also grown significantly in recent years, and we need to protect our interests as well. If our current offer is not compelling enough, we will respect that decision and look for an alternative supplier."

I keep a reserved expression on my face as I await his response, hoping I'm coming off as confident and not antagonistic. But he doesn't take my meaning. Moving surprisingly quickly, considering his inebriated state, he slides closer to me and wraps his arms around my back, pressing me tightly against his doughy chest.

"Come now, Ms. Greystone. There's no need to be so prudish. I'm sure you have much better things to do with your time than start an entirely new negotiation. Wouldn't it be much more expedient to offer up a single night of your time? I promise you'll enjoy it just as much as I will."

I'm squirming with all my strength, but his hold is tight, and I'm not able to free my arms. Adrenaline has set in, and my heart is already racing. *Stay calm, Elizabeth. Vince has been training you for exactly such a moment as this. Just figure out where you have the most leverage.*

With my arms trapped and our positions on the floor restricting my leg movements, my choices are limited. Just as Barswick leans his face toward mine, disgusting lips puckered for a kiss, I rear my head back and slam it into the bridge of his nose as hard as I can.

He roars in pain and releases me on instinct to grip his face. Scrambling to my feet, I kick him in the groin for good measure and feel a sweet sense of retribution when his shouts turn to high-pitched shrieks. Snatching my bag from the hook on the wall, I take a final look at him squirming pathetically on the floor.

"Consider our offer revoked, Mr. Barswick. You'd be wise to lose the contact information of everyone at Marchetti International. We won't be doing business together again."

I slide open the door and step out, not bothering to close it behind me. Let passersby enjoy his suffering as much as I did. I walk briskly from the restaurant, focused only on putting as much distance as I can between us in case he grows a pair and fights through the pain sooner than expected. I get into my car and make it half a mile down the road before the trembling sets in, the immediate danger having passed. I'm pulling the car over to the shoulder to collect myself when my phone rings.

Shit. It's Vince. Is he done with Adrian already? Did Barswick call him? Or has something gone wrong with the Saltero discussion? I blow out a deep breath and connect the call, trying to infuse as much normalcy in my voice as possible.

"Hey, b..boss, what's up?"

Fuck. So much for that. But maybe he didn't notice.

"Venom? What's wrong?" he snaps.

Nope. He noticed.

"Huh? What do you mean? Everything's fine. I'm just heading home. There's more work to do on the supplier agreement, but I can fill you in on all that tomorrow. But what about you? Are you done with Adrian already? Did everything go okay?"

I'm trying to sound nonchalant, but my voice comes out too high-pitched, and I know even before he speaks that there's no way he's buying my act.

"Elizabeth," he growls. "Don't fucking lie to me. What. Happened?"

What's the point in even trying to hide it? I'll have to tell him eventually, so I might as well get it out of the way. I quickly run through the night's events, making sure to emphasize that I am perfectly fine and left that bastard regretting his choices. But it doesn't matter. Vince is too quiet on the other end of the line.

"Vincenzo, listen to me. I know what you're thinking, and you *cannot* mafia don this one. This is legitimate business, and we need to handle it as such. I've already told the bastard to forget we exist, and we'll find another supplier in no time. If you want to dole out punishment, do it in the form of blacklisting him from our other partners or orchestrating a hostile takeover of his stock or something. No murder. Not this time. We keep these two worlds separate for a reason. Okay?"

It's a tense few seconds as I wait for his response. But that tension doesn't fade even after he answers.

"Text me when you get home so I know you're safe. I'll be in late tomorrow, but I'll see you at our 12 o'clock in my office."

The call disconnects and I immediately dial him back, but he doesn't answer. I don't bother leaving a message. Whatever he's planning, I won't be able to stop him. All I can do is get some sleep and be prepared to help deal with any fallout in the morning.

Chapter 15

Vincenzo

The Next Morning

I park my bike in the underground garage and stow my helmet in the storage compartment, closing it roughly. It's been almost 12 hours since I spoke to Elizabeth, and my blood hasn't cooled in the slightest. I want nothing more than to beat the living hell out of Richard Barswick and toss his lifeless body in the bayou for the gators. But Elizabeth's right. We have a strict no-crossover rule regarding Marchetti International and the family business. It keeps our assets and employees safe. It's *important*. But fuck if there's not a very large part of me that wants to say "to Hell with it all" right now. Because this asshole deserves far worse than what I'm about to put him through.

I don't bother masking my fury as I march through the lobby of Barswick Materials. Even if I won't be ending any lives today, I still want every person in the building to believe that I'm capable of doing that and so much more if their boss doesn't clean up his act. The elevator doors open, and the moment I step inside, the other passengers suddenly have urgent reasons to be elsewhere, leaving me alone for the ride to the 34th floor.

I storm right past Barswick's protesting assistant to pull the cover off of the control panel at his office door. A few carefully placed slashes of my pocketknife disable the electronic lock, granting me access.

"Christine, I thought I told you I was not to be distur-"

Barswick freezes when he realizes who has entered his office. I close the door firmly behind me, latching the manual deadbolt to ensure we won't be interrupted before I'm through. I'm at the front of his desk in two strides, and I slam both hands down on the glass top, startling him into ceasing his pathetic stammering. I lean toward him until my face is mere inches from his.

"Listen closely, you worthless piece of filth. You made a very large, very stupid mistake last night, and you will be reaping the cursed harvest of that decision for years to come. From this moment forward, you will have no contact with anyone at Marchetti International aside from Gabriel Martoza and me. You will never speak about or appear in front of Elizabeth Greystone or any of my female employees again. If I so much as hear that you *described* someone who resembles her to another person, I will be back to issue a much stronger form of retribution."

I pause to let my words sink in. Barswick's eyes are wide, and he's pressed as far back as he can be in his desk chair, but it seems his ego is overpowering his survival instincts. He starts to protest, telling me that I have no right to storm into his office like this, but I cut him off with a shout.

"I'm not finished yet!"

He shuts up immediately, all bluster and no backing in the face of a snarling predator, just as I expected. I pull a small stack of papers from the inner pocket of my suit coat and slam them on his desk.

"You will also sign this newly revised version of the supply agreement with Marchetti International, granting us an exclusive partnership for the next five years under an all-new pricing structure."

He starts blustering again as he skims the updated terms.

"You're completely out of your mind! I can't agree to this. It would ruin the entire company!"

I lean back in menacingly, an honest-to-God growl escaping my lips before I can reign it in. But it works. Barswick's eyes widen anew, and a line of sweat begins to form on his hairline.

"Perhaps you should have considered that before disrespecting the much more favorable offer that Ms. Greystone presented you with last night," I snarl. "As it stands, you'll sign this agreement, or I'll make sure that you're blacklisted from working with any of the major players in the country. Your products serve a niche industry, after all. Surely, you know we're all well acquainted."

I rise back to full height, giving the impression of relenting before I drop my final bombshell.

"Not to mention, I'm sure the IRS would love to know the true purpose behind Peachtree Unlimited. Fucking weird name for a paper company[17], by the way."

And just like that, it's done. Barswick signs the contract with a shaking hand, and I stow the document in my coat before striding for the door. I breeze through the onlookers and security guards crowding the hallway.

"Don't bother, gentlemen. I'll see myself out."

They follow me anyway, but I don't care. All I care about right now is getting to the office to see Elizabeth in person and verify that she's truly alright. She'd better be, or Barswick will be seeing me again unthinkably soon.

* * *

After seeing for myself that she's not sporting so much as a bruise from that bastard, I fill Liz in on how I've handled the Barswick situation.

---

[17] company that exists on paper only with no actual business operations, often used for laundering money or evading taxes

She listens quietly, but I can see the reservations in her eyes. I reassure her that there will be no repercussions, and after a while, she seems to wash her hands of it, moving the conversation on to Spain and some preliminary strategies she's been working on with Mono.

Our meeting is cut short when my phone rings. It's Vic, and he's just put eyes on Maxim Sokolov ducking into a shop inside the flea market over on Airline Drive while he was out doing some shopping with his wife. *What the fuck is he doing back in town? My orders were very specific.*

I thank Vic for the intel and tell Liz that Luca needs to see me about a shipment. She doesn't question it, used to me ducking out at all hours when duty calls. I'm not entirely sure why I'm lying to her. I just have a gut feeling that I need to keep this quiet for now, at least until I decide what I'm going to do about the rogue Russian heir. Wanting to put my own eyes on him before I give Mischa a call, I jump on my bike and head towards the market.

* * *

I've got to hand it to him. This fucker has some serious balls. Well, either that or he's completely delusional. Maxim has been creeping around the market in what he probably believes to be a stealthy manner, visiting a handful of suppliers who deal in weapons, information, and even manpower out of their backrooms. It's clear he's trying to rebuild his forces in town and that he's not getting any support from the bratva, or he wouldn't have any need of local mercenaries.

Once he leaves, blissfully unaware of the tracker I planted on his car, I double back into the market. One by one I stop into the same shops he visited. I'm already well acquainted with most of the owners, and the ones I'm not are still well acquainted with me. It doesn't take much to get the full details of what Maxim is up to. One would have to be truly oblivious to think it was better to hold loyalty with a lone newcomer instead of the reigning king of the Houston area, and these are smart men and women. It's exactly why they've managed to fly under the legal radar for so long and why the Marchetti family has always treated them with respect as we've ruled over the city.

My original suspicion was correct. He's attempting to buy weapons and soldiers to wield them. Given how hard he was negotiating, I think it's safe to assume he's financing all of this from his personal accounts, further indicating that Mischa is either unaware of or refusing to support this suicide mission his son has embarked upon.

I have approximately zero desire to spend any more time or man-power dealing with this coglione[18]. My men are all busy dealing with things that actually matter, both for normal business or in preparation for the Madrid operation. As I mull over my options, only one really makes any sense at all. I need to take care of Maxim myself, quietly and permanently. Maybe I should have done it this way in the first place, but at least I gained some goodwill with Mischa for my attempt at sparing his son. He won't have any space to retaliate this way, considering Maxim is blatantly disregarding the agreement we made.

My first call is to Luca. I tell him that I'm going dark for a day or so and that he's in charge while I'm gone. My next calls are to Mono and Liz, reiterating those orders. I specifically tell Mono not to look for me. As far as anyone else is concerned, I'm meeting with a potential new partner offshore, and only in the case of a life-threatening emergency to him or Liz should he contact me. I don't want Mischa catching wind of my plans before I'm done. Maxim is mine now, and even dear old daddy won't be able to save him.

---

[18] idiot

Chapter 16

Elizabeth

36 Hours Later

"Liz, are you listening to me? Liz! Elizabeth! Elizabeth fucking Greystone!"

I snap back to reality and very nearly leave it again via a blow to the head. My reaction upsets the precarious balance of the wooden chair I'm reclining in, but thankfully, Mono's near enough to steady me before that happens. He slowly returns all four chair legs to the floor before fixing me with a disapproving glare, raised eyebrow and all.

"Sorry..." I mumble sheepishly. "I'm just worried about him, and my mind is running away with me. I'm focused now. I promise."

He sighs deeply, dropping his head back against his desk chair.

"Look, I hate it just as much as you do, but we both know that Vince is more than capable of taking care of himself. He's going to show up in a day or so completely fine and telling some stupid fish story about how he took out an entire armada with just his pocketknife. We just need to have faith and keep the Marchetti machine running smoothly in the meantime."

"Ugh. I know. You're right," I grumble begrudgingly. "Wait a second. Did you just call me 'Elizabeth fucking Greystone'?"

"Yeah, well, I couldn't remember your middle name, and that was definitely a three-name moment. I'd been talking for almost five

123

minutes before I realized you hadn't heard a word I'd said."

Eh, fair enough. I apologize one last time for zoning out and dive back into the report Mono and I have been pulling together on Adrian Nuñez and all of his top players. If we're going to do business with them in Spain, or even pretend to, we can't afford any surprises or loose lips. Once we finish with that, I read through the Marchetti International briefings that I hadn't gotten to yesterday and send off a few emails. It's Saturday, so things are quiet on that front. By 2 p.m. I'm caught up and itching for something else to take my mind off of Vince's absence. Sam is at his dad's this weekend, so I don't even have normal mom duties to keep me occupied.

Deciding that I could always use a little extra training, I let myself into Vince's home gym for a workout. He did say I could use it anytime, and if it means I'll also be aware the very moment he returns from his top-secret mission, well, that's just a bonus.

By 9 p.m. I've trained, showered, cleaned the already mostly neat apartment from top to bottom, ordered dinner, and started a movie and there's still no sign of Vince. I'm debating asking Mono to take a quick look at his location, just to see if he's at least moving around when the electronic lock chimes.

I spring off the couch and sprint for the door, reaching the hallway just as Vince appears from the other side. His hair is disheveled, and there's blood covering his clothes and almost all of his exposed skin, but I don't care. I know it's not his. It's never his. I'm too relieved that he's okay to resist throwing my arms around his neck and holding on tight.

"Oof," he grunts. "Hey there, Venom. You act like I've been gone for months. Did you miss me that much?"

Wait. His words are normal, but his voice is not. Leaning back to inspect his face, my stomach drops. I was too excited that he was alive to notice his clenched jaw and the strained look in his eyes, but now they're all I can see. *Oh shit. No, no, no, no, no.*

"Where?" I ask, my voice tight as I release my hold.

My hands are moving of their own accord, running across his chest and arms in search of injury.

"How bad is it? Do you need a doctor? Why aren't you answering me? Vince, where are you hurt?!"

He hisses as I brush against his ribcage and grabs my wrist to halt my search.

"Listen, it's not that bad. I promise. Just...let me sit down first, and then you can inspect away, yeah?"

Oh, right. Sitting would probably be more comfortable. What am I doing, making an injured man stand in the hallway?

Ducking under the arm opposite his injury, I help him to the couch. I don't know that he really needs my help. He made it this far on his own, after all. But I need to help. I need to fix this. He *has* to be okay.

He settles onto the couch and I make him bring his feet up so he can recline back. As I kneel down and reach for the hem of his black t-shirt to lift it, I realize that the bottom is jagged and frayed. I see why as I raise it to his chest. A thin strip of black fabric is tied tightly around his stomach, knotted over a still-bleeding wound. The strip is already completely soaked through, and blood is slowly running in rivulets down his abs onto the leather couch. I can't tell how wide or deep it is, but I can guess by the amount of blood that it's not something I can handle with rubbing alcohol and a butterfly bandage. *Not that bad, my ass.*

With as firm a grip on my emotions as I can manage, I look back up at Vince. He's already staring at me, and his gaze flits between my glassy eyes and gritted teeth before he grimaces contritely.

"Who do I call?"

My voice is raspy, but at least I'm not openly crying.

"Dr. Thomas is already on his way. He should be here in the next 10 minutes."

I nod. Of course, he's already called someone. This probably isn't the first time he's needed a house call, after all. But that thought doesn't make me feel any better. If anything, it makes my chest even tighter to think that this sort of danger is so commonplace for Vince that he's not the slightest bit fazed by the situation.

"Don't worry," he croons. "I'm pretty sure they didn't hit anything vital. I'll be stitched up and back to normal in no time."

He tries to flash me a cheeky grin, but it falters at the end. I can't imagine how much pain he's in, and yet he's trying to hide it for my sake. I want to smack him for purposely putting himself in danger in the first place, but instead, I lay my head on his shoulder and throw my arm across his chest. He freezes in place for a few moments, as if he, too, was expecting me to hit him instead of hug him. Once he realizes I'm not budging, he brings his hand up to rest atop mine.

Neither of us says anything. I can't. I know if I tried to speak, it would release the floodgates of my emotions. And he's probably tired. He's had an intense 48 hours. The adrenaline from whatever fight resulted in his injury has to be wearing off by now. We stay like that until Dr. Thomas arrives, me clinging to his shoulder and him running a soothing thumb across the back of my hand.

I do my best to make myself useful while Dr. Thomas cleans and stitches up Vince's wound. Vince was partially right. While the knife didn't hit any major arteries or totally puncture an organ, it did most likely nick a kidney, or so the doctor thinks, based on the location and the amount of blood. Without actual operating tools, he can't be sure, but he does reassure me that most kidney wounds will heal themselves with time and rest alone. Leaving Vince strict instructions to take it easy for the next several days and to call if he notices any signs of hemorrhaging, Dr. Thomas finally leaves a little after 2 a.m.

Since Vince can't get the wound wet, I help him wash his hair over the side of the tub and use a washcloth to clean as much of the grime and blood off the rest of him as I can. He makes all the expected dirty jokes about sponge baths and hot nurses, but I can only manage a weak smirk. Even my penchant for humor in dark situations has limits, it seems.

After helping him dry off and slip on a pair of clean pajama pants, I get him settled in bed. Disappearing into his closet, I commandeer a t-shirt and a pair of drawstring shorts. There's no way I'm leaving him on his own tonight. What if he needs to get up to use the restroom or his wound re-opens, and someone needs to staunch the bleeding until Dr. Thomas gets back? *Nope. Out of the question.*

I avoid making eye contact as I step out of the closet and make my way to the other side of the bed, afraid he'll try to convince me to leave. He doesn't make so much as a peep even after I'm fully burrowed beneath the covers. *Maybe he's already asleep.* I turn around to check, moving slowly to avoid waking him.

Nope. A pair of amused honey-brown eyes meet mine, and he stretches out the arm closest to me, closing his palm in a beckoning gesture. I don't need to be told twice. I slide into the opening and rest my head on the pillow next to his, throwing an arm over his chest again. He closes his arm around my back and chuckles, shaking his head.

"While I appreciate your resolve, there's no need to sneak your way into staying the night. I'd be foolish to turn down any comfort or care you were willing to offer, Venom. Even if I still don't understand why you'd want to offer it to someone like me in the first place."

I do hit him this time, but only lightly on the shoulder. Though by the way he feigns injury, you'd think I socked him for real.

"Oh, hush. You're my best friend, you idiot, and someone has to make sure you don't bleed out in the middle of the night. And enough with the self-deprecating bullshit. I'm pretty certain I've proven that I'll defend you against anyone who dares to speak ill of you, and that includes yourself. You're just lucky I like you or I'd have hit you a lot harder for scaring me so bad. I told you that you're forbidden from dying on me, and that *includes* terrifying me with near-death experiences."

"I hardly think this classifies as a near-death experience," he argues, but I stop him with narrowed eyes.

"Okay, alright. You win," he concedes.

He settles further into the pillow and doesn't say anything more. I'm just drifting to sleep when he speaks again, voice soft.

"Don't you even want to know if I got him? It's not like you to not hound me for details."

I shake my head as much as I can without lifting it.

"I already know you got him. You wouldn't have come back until you had. And don't worry, I fully intend to hound you for all the details tomorrow after we've gotten some sleep. I'll probably yell at you more, too."

He chuckles again, squeezing me tighter.

"Fair enough. Goodnight, Venom."

"Goodnight, Rattles."

Chapter 17

Vincenzo

The Next Day

It takes all of my well-honed persuasion skills and a fair amount of puppy dog eyes, but I eventually convince Elizabeth that "taking it easy" does not mean that I have to be confined to bed the entire day and that a quick trip to a nearby cafe for brunch will not, in fact, cause me to spontaneously keel over and die.

My motives for wanting to go out are two-fold. Showing my face in public will quell any potential rumors of my being weakened or dead in case anyone saw anything they shouldn't have yesterday. But also, all of Elizabeth's fussing over me is about to put me in the loony bin. It's not that I don't appreciate her concern. I do. God, I swear I am more grateful than she'll probably ever understand. It's just that my intimacy-starved body keeps interpreting every touch as a very different kind of care. It's both terrifying and excruciating, trying to hide my physical response from her while also being able to do absolutely nothing about it.

I manage to walk into the restaurant with a pretty natural gait, though I struggle to hide my relief at being able to sit down when we finally reach the table. We've just ordered our drinks when Elizabeth's phone starts blaring TLC's "No Scrubs" at full volume. *Well, that's new.* I cock a quizzical eyebrow in her direction as she scrambles to silence the

129

ringer, but she just mouths an apology as she connects the call.

Between the ringtone and her monotone greeting, it doesn't take a genius to figure out that it's her ex on the other end of the phone. I've done some digging, and based on what I've gathered, he's an unfaithful, self-absorbed, controlling asshole. Liz swears he's a decent parent to Sam, which is something I guess. But given everything else I've heard about him, I have to wonder if that's just willful delusion on her end.

After a few moments of deep breaths, bitter facial expressions, and clipped responses, Elizabeth hangs up the phone and shoves it face down on the table. She closes her eyes and takes in a few more breaths before fluttering them open and shooting me unmistakable "what the fuck" eyes.

"Well, that seemed...fun," I poke, earning myself an eye roll in return. "Does he need to be brought down a peg or two? Should I call Mono to plant an embarrassing virus on his phone? We can have it play loud moaning sounds periodically during work hours."

Her face brightens at the idea, and she laughs despite herself.

"Ugh, as tempting as that sounds, no. I'd rather hang on to the knowledge that I am *always* the bigger and better person between the two of us. Self-righteousness can be very soothing, you know."

"Whatever makes you happy, Venom. But the offer stands if you ever change your mind. What did Scumbag McGee want anyway?"

Elizabeth explains that Marcus has some "urgent issue" to take care of and needs to drop Sam off early today. She doesn't believe him, of course, but agreed to let him bring Sam by the restaurant for Sam's sake. The last thing he needs is to be stuck with Marcus when he's throwing a hissy fit over not getting his way.

"Actually, I'm sorry," she says, grimacing. "I didn't even check with you before agreeing to let them crash our lunch."

"Oh, shove it. Only a douchebag would pout over something like that. I have zero objections to Sam joining us. My only question is, what's our story?"

She looks at me quizzically.

"Our story?"

"Yeah. I mean, it's a bit weird to be out to lunch with your boss on a weekend. I'm sure if Sam is even remotely like you, he's going to have about a thousand questions, so we should probably agree on the answers."

"Oh, well..." she hesitates, looking down at her cutlery before continuing. "I was just going to introduce you as my...friend, who also happens to be my boss. I mean, it's true and requires a lot less explanation, so I just figured..."

I shift in my seat, trying to find a more comfortable position. The twinge in my chest is most likely the pain radiating from my wound. I mean, it's not like it's a big deal, being introduced to Sam as something more than his mom's boss. A totally normal situation.

"That's perfect," I assure her. "You're right. It's the truth. I just didn't want to assume. I know how much you want to keep Sam away from the darker side of things, and there is a not-insignificant chance that one of his friends at school will have parents who recognize my name..."

She finally looks back up, determination radiating in her eyes.

"I do want to protect him; that's still true. But I'm confident that once Sam gets to know you on the light side of things, he'll be able to brush off any rumors without a second thought. And to be honest, it's exhausting trying to keep the two sides of my life so separate. You're both important to me. Plus, it'll be good for him to have a male figure he can learn from besides his dad. The older he gets, the more I worry that he'll pick up all of Marcus' bad habits and beliefs purely by default."

What started as a firm declaration morphs into a meek suggestion by the time she's done speaking. Uncertainty creeps back onto her face and she worries her bottom lip between her teeth as she looks at me.

Surely, she doesn't believe I'd reject her desire for me to play a more significant role in Sam's life. I mean, I've literally killed for the woman. And, come to think of it, I've also intentionally *not* killed for her, which is frankly more telling if we're being honest.

I can't stand being the cause of her discomfort, so I reassure her as solidly as I can. I'm honored to be allowed into Sam's life, and I can only hope that I pass his inspection. I don't even want to consider what might happen if Sam openly objected to our friendship.

Thankfully, I don't have long to ruminate on what-ifs. Marcus and Sam appear through the entryway, glancing around for Liz. I call her attention to their arrival and she waves them over, standing to speak to Marcus as she takes Sam's backpack and motions him into the chair between us. I rise as well, doing my best to mask my slow movements as nonchalance, and button the lapels of my jacket.

"And who the hell is this?" Marcus says as he looks me up and down with a sneer.

I hate him already, but offer a handshake anyway. Partly to goad him and partly to make a good impression on Sam.

"Vincenzo Caputo. I'm a friend of Liz's. You must be Marcus."

He stares at my hand for a beat too long before deigning to return the gesture. That's fine. I'm going to enjoy playing this game.

"Yeah, I'm Marcus. Glad to hear Lizzie can't help but talk about me. Can't say the same for you, unfortunately."

Liz steps between us, ending the handshake and forcing Marcus to take a step back.

"Don't be a dick, Marcus. Didn't you have somewhere urgent to be?"

He shrugs, feigned innocence on his face, as he places a hand on Liz's shoulder. The urge to cut it off is swift and fierce.

"Ah, don't be so stiff, Lizzie. I'm sure Vince here can take a joke."

Liz smacks his hand away, and I snap my eyes up to Marcus', infusing pure frost into my sardonic grin.

"Of course. In fact, I'm glad to hear you have a sense of humor, Marcus. But, please, don't let us keep you."

I gesture towards the exit as my other hand gently guides Liz toward her chair. She takes the hint and sits, her eyes trained on me while Marcus' are trained on my hand at her elbow. Without her playing defense between us, I close the gap between Marcus and me, leaning down to highlight the height difference between us and lowering my voice so that Sam can't hear me from his seat across the table.

"And it's Vincenzo, or even better, Mr. Caputo. Only those close to me call me Vince, and I don't think we're destined for that particular kind of relationship."

I straighten without waiting for his response and shoot him a wink, turning to return to my chair. He doesn't have any witty retorts to offer. All I get is narrowed eyes and the click of his jaw. *Guess I won't be enjoying any verbal sparring matches from that quarter.* Though he's not entirely idiotic. When Liz shoots him a death glare and gestures to the exit, he opts to cut his losses and turns to leave.

Liz refocuses her attention on Sam, who's been watching the entire exchange with rapt attention and is currently staring at me the way a zoologist might examine a newly discovered species, openly curious but cautious. He drags his gaze away to answer Liz's questions about how his weekend was ("fine") and what he wants to eat ("french toast with berries and whipped cream") before settling on me again, questions practically pouring out of his eyes. *Well, here's your chance, Vince. Don't fuck it up.*

"It's nice to finally meet you, Sam. I've heard a lot about you from your mom. I'm Vince."

I stretch out my hand for a shake, but he doesn't meet it right away, either. *Greystone men are a tough breed to please.*

"I thought only people close to you get to call you Vince."

I'm stunned still for a full second, and Liz is even worse. She chokes

133

on her water, setting off a coughing fit that has both Sam and me concerned until she takes another drink to get it under control and waves us off. *Keen eyes **and** ears on this one, it would seem. Noted.*

"You're right. But given what your mom has already told me about you, and how important you are to her, I'd like for us to be friends. Consider the name a friendship offering of sorts. What do you say?"

After a short beat, he nods and meets my hand. I feel a swell of pride at the firm shake he delivers. Though I shouldn't be surprised. I'm willing to bet that Liz pays particular attention to teaching respect, both the giving and receiving of it. A well-delivered handshake is a crucial symbol of both.

By the end of the meal, Sam has warmed to me significantly. I've found his weak spot for silly jokes, and my inherent knowledge of young boys' humor gives me a decided advantage when thinking up ones he might like. Liz has given up trying to get us to behave, though I can tell she's happy to see us getting along so well. When the check arrives, Sam and I are so busy cackling conspiratorially at my latest punchline that Liz almost manages to grab the bill before I do.

"Ah, ah, ah," I scold her playfully as I swipe the register off the table. "A gentleman never lets a lady pay the bill, no matter how very capable of doing so she may be."

Sam backs me up with a determined agreement and a firm nod, and I shoot Liz a wink. Never let it be said that Vincenzo Caputo doesn't take his role model duties extremely seriously. A few more weeks, and I'll have any traces of Marcus' self-absorbed narcissism fully expunged. Maybe not even that long. Sam seems like a sharp kid who clearly takes after his mom. He's probably already seen through most of Marcus' bullshit without my help.

* * *

After dropping Sam and Liz off back at their building, I spend the rest of the day catching up on work. Going completely dark for two days has me feeling out of the loop, so I start with intel reports from Mono and slowly make my way through to MI proposals and approvals. On the plus side, it's clear that Liz, Luca, and Mono had things well in hand while I was out. This turned out to be a pretty good practice run for my extended absence when we head to Spain.

At some point, my eyes start to grow weary, and I realize it's already dark out. Deciding that I'm caught up enough to be able to finish the rest tomorrow, I stand up to stretch out my tense muscles. *Cazzo Madre di Dio*[19]! In my focused state, I forgot about my injury and moved too quickly. *This proof of mortality shit is for the fucking birds, I swear.* Moving more carefully, I exit the office and head toward the kitchen to throw together a simple dinner before I call it an early night.

I'm midway through a roast chicken sandwich when my phone sounds a telltale chime.

> Liz: If I have to hear one more punchline about farts, I'm replacing your shampoo with hair removal cream.

> Me: Ahahahaha! I take it Sam's been on a roll since this afternoon?

> Liz: He thinks he's a comedic genius. Bedtime took twice as long as normal because he'd prepared so much material and was simply not capable of saving any of it for tomorrow.

> Liz: But in reality, thank you for today. He had a blast, and he even made a special point to open the door for me when

---

[19] Fucking mother of God!

we ran out to grab dinner earlier. Your gentlemanly ways are rubbing off already.

Me: The pleasure was mine. Seriously. He's a fantastic kid, and you trusting me enough to introduce us means more than you know.

Liz: I swear one of these days, we're going to finally kick this nasty habit you have of undervaluing your worthiness.

Liz: Anyway, I'm turning in early. You should do the same. Whatever work you haven't already gotten through can wait until tomorrow.

Me: I'd already come to the same conclusion, but also, who's the boss of who here?

Liz: Oh, gee. I don't know what I was thinking. My apologies, SIR. I am but your humble servant.

God, she's so refreshing. I don't know how narcissists operate. How could you not love the rush of sparring with someone who's not afraid to give as good as they get?

Me: Goodnight, Venom.

Liz: Goodnight, Rattles.

I'm chuckling to myself as I set my phone back on the counter. But before I can take another bite of my sandwich, I catch a glimpse of my reflection in the far window and realize that I am well and truly fucked.

I look like a teenage girl whose crush just told her she "had a cool vibe." My grin is wide enough to compete with the freakin' Cheshire Cat, and my flushed face and bright eyes belong on an anime character, not a ruthless mafia don.

It's one thing to chalk my carnal reactions up to sexual withdrawals or the urge to murder anyone who mistreats her as friendly protectiveness, but when a simple text exchange has me acting like a blushing schoolgirl... It's not even worth trying to lie to myself anymore. *Fuuuuuuuck.* *Cazzo*[20]*!*

I have *feelings* for Elizabeth. And I have zero fucking clue what to do about it.

---

[20] Fuck, but with Italian seasoning

Chapter 18

Elizabeth

12 Days Later

Gah. Finally. I sink into the tub with a moan. Things have been insane over the last two weeks. We've been preparing for several new product launches along with expanding the Marchetti family presence into Spain, and my shoulders have apparently been cataloging each and every stressful task with a new knot. As the bath salts and near-scalding water start to ease the tension coiled throughout my body, my mind runs through a mental checklist of the most critical details, making sure I haven't forgotten anything.

Eventually, satisfied that I haven't inadvertently caused the downfall of the Marchetti empire, my mind shifts to wandering. I wonder what Sam and Marcus are up to tonight, and hope it's something more than Sam situated squarely in front of the TV while Marcus scrolls on his phone. Thinking about Marcus reminds me of our conversation at drop-off earlier this evening, which only serves to undo some of the relaxation that's settled into my bones.

Ugh, no. Do not give him the satisfaction of getting under your skin. I will myself back into a peaceful state of mind with a few deep breaths and the comforting thought of the stupid look on his face the other weekend when Vince put him in his place. One thing is for certain. Vince *definitely* got under Marcus' skin. I'm sure that's exactly why he couldn't help but throw out a few unoriginal barbs about my guard dog having sniffed out a tastier treat when I showed up to drop-off alone.

I didn't even bother to reply. Marcus could never understand Vince and I's relationship. Marcus only has two modes when it comes to women; completely, suffocatingly, possessive and controlling, and give-zero-fucks selfish abandon. Vince and I's relationship built on mutual trust, respect, and confidence in one another would be a concept he'd never be able to grasp. And that's without adding in the fact that it's purely platonic.

*Mmhmm. Platonic. That explains why you tried to dry hump the man's leg when he had you pinned against the wall, right? Or why you were practically drooling at the sight of him shirtless, even when he was being treated for a **stab wound**?*

Hey, whoa! Whose brain are you anyway? I think we can both agree that Vincenzo is objectively attractive, and considering that I haven't slept with anyone since Damien, it's only natural that my erstwhile hormones would target the man in closest proximity. It's biology, nothing else to it.

Opening my eyes, I sit up and shake my head gently. Arguing with yourself is surely one of the first signs of insanity, but it's probably just due to all the mental strain I've been through lately, right? *Right?* Whatever. That's my story, and I'm sticking to it.

Climbing out of the now-lukewarm tub, I ready myself for bed. A good night's sleep will surely have me back to normal in no time. It won't be hard to come by, either. I'm so exhausted that climbing into the cool sheets feels like heaven, and I drift off mere moments after turning off the lights.

* * *

A large gloved hand covers my mouth, and I'm dragged backward down the hall, my captor's other hand pinning my arms down at my sides.

It's dark, and I can't see much, but I can hear muffled thumps coming from behind us, almost like the sound of someone beating the dirt out of a rug.

I donkey kick back, connecting with my captor's shin. It doesn't have the desired effect. He curses and breaks his stride momentarily, but his grip doesn't loosen even the slightest bit. *Not completely inept, then. Dammit.*

We cross through the threshold at the end of the hall and I stumble on the transition. The man holding me barks out something in Spanish and throws me onto the hardwood floor. My newly freed hands shoot out to keep me from faceplanting, but it's a short-lived victory. I end up cheek to wood anyway when he presses a knee into my back and jerks my arms behind me, securing them with a heavy-duty zip tie.

The thumping is louder here, and the accompanying grunts make me realize it's not a carpet being beaten. It's a person. I can't tell who, though I assume it's one of Vince's men. His protective detail isn't as suffocating as Damien's, but I know there's still always someone watching. That thought leads to a sobering realization. *These guys must be more than just good if they got by Vince's man.* He doesn't assign me the new kids, and his seasoned soldiers are some of the most lethal I've ever seen.

Oh, shit! Are they about to torture me for information on Marchetti operations? I think I can hold out until I pass out, at least. Maybe? We never covered handling torture in Vince's training sessions. Those were more focused on not getting into this situation in the first place.

I'm pulled roughly off the floor by my bindings, my shoulders burning in protest. Once I'm steady on my feet, Thug One pulls me back against his chest and brings a blade to my neck. He says something else to Thug Two, who stops his pummeling long enough to reply. I can see my guard now, or at least his arms. He's tied to a column, trussed up as they wail on him. Every few moments, Thug Two stops and asks a question. But the guard never responds, and the beating resumes.

Do I really think I can withstand something like that? I mean, the guard is barely even grunting when he's hit. I'm about to embarrass the entire Marchetti empire. But I'll be damned if they get anything out of me. I may scream, or cry, or plead for mercy, but Elizabeth Greystone will never be broken. Besides, maybe the guard got a message out to Vince before they took him down. Surely, he'll burst in here at any moment and save us both. Yeah! It's Vince. He always saves me.

My newly formed resolve strengthens my spine, and hope steadies my steps as Thug One walks me past the pillar, knife still at my throat. Thug Two pauses again to ask another question, but this time, when he gets no response, he doesn't resume the beating. Instead, I'm turned around and Thug Two gestures towards me, taunting the guard with my presence. Except...

My knees buckle, but Thug One keeps a tight grip on my bindings to hold me upright. A stilted sob escapes my throat as my eyes rake over his broken body. His face is already swollen, and blood is pouring steadily from his nose and mouth. I can only imagine what the rest of him looks like under his clothes. Despite everything, he's still lucid, and when I finally meet Vince's eyes with my own, I see the same fear, anger, and anguish that I'm feeling reflected straight back at me.

There's also surprise in his gaze, as if he didn't expect to see me here. That theory is reinforced when he starts struggling against his bindings in a burst of renewed energy. He's practically feral, thrashing about and spewing curses and threats in a multitude of languages. Thug Two strikes him hard across the face, telling him in English now that he can ensure my safety by simply telling them what they need to know.

Vince looks at me again, struggle clear on his face. He can't save me, not at the expense of everyone else in the organization. But I can see him weighing the options anyway. I shake my head, signaling for him to keep silent, even as tears track down my cheeks.

Seeing this, Thug One presses the blade tighter against my throat, preventing any further movement. Thug Two, growing impatient, grabs his pistol and whips Vince across the head with it. Vince's eyes glaze over, and I scream at them to stop despite the sting from the blade slicing shallow ridges into my skin. He'll die if they keep striking him like that, and I can't watch him die. I *can't*. Maybe if I distract them, he'll have time to break his bindings.

I succeed in stealing Thug Two's attention, but the sinister smile spreading across his face is not the result I was expecting.

"Maybe we're going about this the wrong way," he says. "Maybe we'll have better luck getting *her* to talk when it's *your* life on the line."

He raises his gun again, pressing it against Vince's temple. *No. No, no, no, no, no!*

"So, Principessa[21], tell us everything you know about the Marchetti family, and we'll let you both live. If you don't, you'll get to watch as we send the infamous Ice Demon down to Hell, where he belongs. Hope he can stand the heat."

I can't. He's lying. Neither Vince nor I will leave here alive, regardless of what I tell him. I lock eyes with Vince, looking for telepathic guidance on what to do. The resignation in his face confirms my thoughts. My tears flow faster, but I blink them away and raise my chin to glare at Thug Two as I prepare to speak.

"I'm not telling you anything, asshole. I will prepare a nice, friendly welcome for when you join us in Hell, though. I'm sure it won't take too long. The entire family was trained by the Ice Demon himself, after all."

Thug Two roars and presses the gun tighter against Vince's head. He repeats his threat, saying he's giving me one last chance to save Vince's life. I ignore him, focusing on the pride that I see in Vince's

---

[21] Princess

eyes. He smiles slightly, and I return one of my own. The gun sounds, and everything goes dark.

* * *

"Vince!"

I shoot up in bed, heart racing and chest heaving as I cry out. Everything is still dark, and I don't hear any sound. *Where am I? Am I being held captive somewhere? Is Vince really...gone?* But no, a captive wouldn't be covered in soft blankets in a king-size bed. After a few blinks, my eyes adjust, and I realize I'm in my bedroom.

Running my fingers along my throat, I don't feel any cuts. My wrists feel fine as well. *Was it all just a dream?* But my cheeks are damp, and there's an ache in my throat that makes me think my screams were all too real.

I grab my phone to check the security cameras, struggling to open the right app with my shaking fingers. Once it finally loads, I breathe a sigh of relief. All is still and quiet. Even Sam is deep in a peaceful sleep in his room. But my nervous system doesn't seem willing to trust the data. Tears are still running down my face, and my whole body starts to shiver as the final scene from my nightmare replays on a loop in my head. *What if that dream was my intuition telling me something was wrong?*

I know it's the middle of the night, but I *need* to confirm that Vince is truly okay. My finger hovers over his speed dial photo for a few seconds while I try to talk myself down, but eventually, I give in to my neuroses and activate the call.

"Are you alright?"

His voice is gravelly but full of intensity, even though I likely woke him from a deep sleep. A relieved breath rushes from my mouth, mixing with my reassurances.

"I'm fine. I'm sorry to call so late. I just... I needed to be sure that you were okay."

"What? Liz, you're not making sense. What do you mean you needed to be sure that *I* was okay?"

"It's stupid, really. I just. It was just a dream. I'm sorry I woke you."

I hear rustling and assume he's sitting up in bed.

"Nuh-uh, you're not brushing this off," he says, his voice clearer now. "Tell me about the dream."

I already feel incredibly stupid for calling him, but his tone is one I know all too well. I'm not getting out of this without an explanation. *Here goes nothing.*

"Alright. Well... I had this dream that I was abducted, but then they took me to a room where you were being beaten, and you were all bloody and swollen, but you wouldn't give them any information, so they thought taking me would get you to talk but then they realized by the way I reacted that it would probably be easier to get *me* to talk if *you* were in danger, and so they threatened you with a gun, but I couldn't say anything because I know you wouldn't want me to give up the entire organization just to save you, and you were looking at me with these big proud eyes and I knew I was doing the right thing, but then they pulled the trigger and I heard the shot ring out but everything went dark and I woke up in bed terrified and I just had to call and make sure that it was all just a horrific dream."

I heave in a deep breath, my lungs starved for oxygen after my rapid-fire monologue. Vince is silent on the other line for so long that I pull the phone away to check that the call hasn't dropped. Replacing the phone at my ear, I hear a scraping sound but still no Vince.

"Vince? Can you hear me?"

There's more rustling, and then his voice sounds through the line.

"Yeah, sorry, Copperhead. Had trouble connecting to my in-helmet Bluetooth for a bit, but I'm here. I heard everything."

"Oh. I didn't realize you were still out. I thought I'd woken you. At least I don't feel so bad anymore."

"Well, I mean, I was asleep at first. But you still shouldn't feel bad. I'm glad you called."

Wait. What?

"I'm confused. So you were asleep, but now you're out on your bike?"

"Well, yeah," he says as if it's the most obvious thing in the world. "It's the fastest way to get to your place. I'm almost there. I'm pulling into the parking garage now."

While he's apparently breaking the laws of physics to get over here in record time, I'm doing an excellent confused retriever impression, head twisting this way and that as I process his words.

"Wait, you're here?! I wasn't trying to call you out of bed. I just needed to prove to my anxiety that you were alive so I could sleep. I didn't mean to disrupt your entire night."

"Venom, be honest. Were you seriously going to just turn over and go right back to sleep after we talked, or would you have been watching the security cameras like a hawk and listening for every sound to make sure no one was actually coming to turn your nightmare into a reality?"

A ding signals that he's reached the garage elevator.

"I'll take your silence as an admission of my accuracy. Anyway, I might lose you in the elevator, so see you in about 15 seconds."

He hangs up, and I'm left gaping at my phone. *What is even happening right now?!* I scramble out of the blankets and make a beeline for the front hallway, my sock-clad feet sliding around the corner right as the elevator doors open. Vince steps out, helmet in one hand while the other pushes his unruly curls off his forehead. I'm still at a loss for words, and it only gets worse as I take in the grey sweatpants, black t-shirt, and black leather jacket he's wearing. *Oh my god.*

He strides toward me, dropping his helmet haphazardly on the side table before pulling me into him. The tension in my body instantly

145

releases. I hadn't even realized I was still so on edge, but the most dangerous man in the Southeastern US lending me his strength does more than the most experienced masseur ever could. I wrap my arms around his waist and press my cheek against his shoulder, drinking in every drop of his soothing presence.

Vince says nothing, just stands strong, occasionally punctuating his hold with an extra squeeze. After a few minutes, I pull my head back and look up at his smirking face.

"Better?" he asks.

"Much," I confirm with a nod.

"Good. Do you want to talk about it?"

I pause, considering his question. But I can already feel my heart rate increasing just thinking about recounting the entire thing, so I shake my head vehemently.

"Alright, then, let's get you back to bed, huh? I'll sleep in the guest room, and I've added a second guard in the lobby, so you can rest assured that no one is getting in here tonight."

"That sounds amazing," I say, adding a much softer, "Thank you."

"No 'thank you' necessary. I'd happily do that and a thousand times more if you needed it, Copperhead."

He gestures with one arm for me to precede him down the main hall, and I pad toward the bedroom. When I don't feel him behind me, I turn to check and find him still rooted in place at the entryway. He's gazing my way, but with a faraway look in his eyes, deep in his own head.

"Earth to Vince," I call. "Did you forget something?"

He snaps back to awareness, eyes focusing as he clears his throat.

"Sorry, just, uh, running through a mental checklist. All's well. Let's get some sleep."

Hmmm. Weird. He's not usually the type to hesitate in his words. I narrow my eyes in his direction, trying to assess whether or not he's telling the truth. He just shoots me one of his signature smirks and closes the distance between us. Something still feels off, but I decide to let it go. I trust Vince with my life. If he says everything is fine, then it's fine.

Vince follows me to my room but hangs in the doorway. I perch on the edge of the bed, not fully settling in just yet.

"Think you could check the closet for monsters before you go?" I joke, earning a bark of laughter.

"Not to worry, Copperhead. I had this place fully warded against monsters before you moved in, excluding yours truly, of course."

"I suppose that's fine then," I say. "Your very presence should scare any others off anyway."

"Damn straight," he quips. "Now, get comfy. I'll be just next door if you need me."

I nod my head, burrow under the comforter, and give him a thumbs up when I'm settled. He flips off the light switch with a snap.

"Goodnight, Rattles. And thanks again."

"Goodnight, Copperhead. Sleep tight."

He shuts my door with a soft click, and I'm alone again. I close my eyes and try to drift back to sleep. The only problem is that my senses are still on high alert. I hear every tick of my watch and creak of the building. The sounds are the same ones that happen all day, every day, but tonight, my brain insists on interpreting them as potential danger. Though, to be fair, how can I really be sure that was a typical building sway creak and not a nimble intruder floorboard creak? *Get it together, Liz. Vince is right next door, and he can absolutely tell the difference between the two sounds. You're perfectly safe.*

Repeating the mantra does little to help, but I'm determined to overpower my paranoia with logic and sheer stubbornness. I close my eyes and focus on my breathing as the seconds tick by. But then another creak sounds, and I can't take it anymore.

I'll just do a quick lap around the loft to put my mind at ease. Throwing off the blanket, I get out of bed and look around for a semi-decent

147

weapon. It's slim pickings for sure, but my eyes land on my nightstand drawer, and an insane thought crosses my mind. *No. Absolutely not. What are you going to do, pleasure them to death?!* But it's solid and heavier than anything else in easy reach. Sure, it's embarrassing as all get out, but it's better than *nothing*. Besides, how satisfying would it be to make some thug explain that he got a black eye from this crazy chick's dildo? Decision made, I open the drawer and grab my trusty friend before I can change my mind. I only need it for a long-distance attack anyway. Vince has spent months teaching me close-quarters combat, and I'm confident I can hold my own long enough for him to join the fray if need be.

I ease open the door, supporting the weight of the hinges to make sure they don't make even the tiniest squeak. Stepping as lightly as I can, weapon arm locked and loaded above my head, I look down the hallway toward Sam's room and back the other way toward the main living area. I set a course for the living room first. As the only entry point, it's a reasonable bet that if it's secure, then everything else is too.

My foot barely connects with the plush wool of the living room rug before two large hands restrain me from behind, one grabbing the hand with the dildo while the other covers my mouth. My scream is muffled, but it's unnecessary anyway once I hear Vince's smooth timbre in my ear.

"Elizabeth," he drawls, amusement clear in his tone. "What on God's green earth are you doing?"

Spinning me around to face him, one hand still gripping my wrist, he raises a brow and waits for my answer.

"I was just doing a perimeter check. I kept hearing creaking and while I *know* it was probably just building sway, I couldn't sleep until I did at least one lap around the place to be sure."

"Mmhmm," he says disbelievingly. "And you thought a *sex toy* was the most appropriate offensive weapon against any would-be intruders?"

I plaster on a guilty smile, hoping he'll take pity on me and leave it alone, but he only reinforces his expression and looks pointedly at the "weapon" in my hand. *Ugh, fine.*

"It was the best I had!" I whine. "I don't keep any actual weapons in the bedroom, though I suppose I should probably start."

My voice trails off, the realization that I should have thought of that a long time ago making my cheeks flame in embarrassment. Vince watches me carefully, his intelligent brown eyes calculating something as he takes in my appearance. I'm sure I look ridiculous, and I'm fully expecting a raunchy joke in retort, so I'm surprised when his voice is laced with concern rather than amusement as he speaks.

"How can I make you feel more safe?"

"What? No, I'm fine. I just needed to prove to my overactive imagination that all was well. Really."

"Elizabeth," he deadpans, shooting me a flat look. "You're prowling the house in the middle of the night, wielding a sex toy as a weapon, and you haven't stopped shivering since I got here. You don't feel safe enough, even with me sleeping in the other room, and I'll be damned if I leave you to suffer when I am perfectly capable of doing something about it. *So tell me.* What would make you feel secure?"

As much as I hate to admit that he's right, an idea pops into my head immediately. But it's too much to ask. I'm a grown woman, for Christ's sake, not a preschooler. And yet...

"Would you be willing to, maybe, stay in my room with me?"

My eyes are glued to an incredibly interesting spot on the floor while I await his response, and I resist the urge to press the backs of my hands to my burning cheeks. I jolt in surprise at the touch of Vince's finger under my chin as he raises my eyes to meet his. His gaze is searching, but a smile slowly spreads across his face as he confirms my request.

"You would feel better if I slept in your room tonight?"

I nod, not trusting my vocal cords to form normal sounds in my mortified state. His smile is in full beam now.

"I don't know. Are you sure there's enough space for me with El Capitán Grande²² over there?"

His chin gestures toward the dildo still gripped in my hand, and I just *barely* resist the urge to smack him with it. *I suppose I did set myself up for that one.* He must register his near escape because his tone turns placating.

"Okay, I'm sorry. I couldn't resist. I promise to behave for the rest of the night and would be honored to protect Lady Greystone in her bed-chamber."

"Okay, now you're just making it weird," I say, pulling a face at his regency reference.

"Alright, alright, being serious now. I swear. I have no problem at all sharing a room. I mean, it's not like we haven't done it before, right? So, let's go. Precious rest time is a'wastin'!"

We walk in silence back to my room, and it continues as I switch the pillows and turn down the far side of the bed before sliding under the blankets. Normally, I prefer to sleep on the right side of the bed, but since that's closer to the door, I opt to give Vince that side tonight. If he's going to protect me, might as well give him the side closest to potential danger, right?

The silence lingers for a few minutes after we've both settled in until we simultaneously blurt out towards the ceiling.

"This is weird, right?"

"This feels awkward, doesn't it?"

We look at each other and dissolve into laughter at the coincidence. As our laughter wanes, I start to worry that perhaps we meant different

---

²² Captain Big

things, but my concerns disappear as Vince opens the arm closest to me and gestures me over. I slide quickly into position before he changes his mind and am momentarily reminded of the night he came home injured after dealing with the rogue Russian heir. I shiver at the memory of one of the most terrifying nights of my life. Vince squeezes me tighter in response, though he doesn't ask what's triggered the reaction. Perhaps he's reliving the same memory, too.

Finally feeling safe again, my body starts to feel heavy, and I drift off within a matter of moments to a dreamless sleep.

Chapter 19

Vincenzo

The Next Day

Despite it being Saturday, I wake up early to make sure I'm gone before Sam gets up. Finding myself with extra time on my hands and not wanting to go home yet, I decide that I'm overdue for a chat with my brother. On the drive to the cemetery, I'm assaulted by flashbacks of last night. I get the singular pleasure of reliving everything from my protective concern when Elizabeth first called to the mortifying panic I felt when she almost caught me zoning out on her fucking amazing, scantily clad body in the hallway to the warring senses of peace and shame as she fell asleep curled into my side. It's almost enough to make me run my bike straight off the overpass. *What the fuck am I going to do?*

Pressing harder on the throttle, I cover the last few miles in record time and am soon kneeling in front of Damien's grave. I don't have an offering. In my mental haze, I forgot to stop and get something. But that's not why I can't bring myself to raise my head from its bowed position in front of his headstone.

"Brother, I...." I start but falter.

Nothing I say will be good enough. There are no excuses, no acceptable reasons for betraying the only person who's ever truly felt like family to me. In the end, I decide to just lay it all out honestly and pray that he can forgive my weakness.

I talk for hours, telling him absolutely everything that's happened since I last visited, almost two months ago. When I get into the details of Liz's training, I forget myself and start to chuckle as I recount how excited she got when she thought she finally had me during disarming practice. But my smile drops as I remember what happened next. Rethinking her reaction, I wonder for a split second if that was purely a fear kink or if the fact that it was me who had her pressed against the wall had anything to do with it. *Son of a bitch! What are you doing? You're supposed to be apologizing, not daydreaming about your traitorous feelings being reciprocated.*

Snapping back to my original intention, I tell Damien more about our recent successes with Marchetti International and how close we are to finally heading to Spain to take care of Raphael once and for all.

"I may be a shitty friend, but I hope I'm at least making you proud to see the Marchetti name still flourishing. Though I can't take anywhere near all the credit. You should see Elizabeth in action, Damien. She's a damn savant. She even had Roberto by the balls after only a few weeks in the organization. She's a thing of real beauty, I swear."

And we're back to Liz again. No matter how I try, there's no hiding that she's entwined with every thought and damn near every significant memory I have of the last few months. I feel like, at this point, the only way to stay true to Damien is to cut all ties with her. But it's not just me she's entwined with. Removing her from the organization would send shock waves through both the family and MI. It would take several people in each group to fill her shoes and likely delay our progress for months. Not to mention the fact that I'm not sure I could even do it. I'm weak when it comes to her. Which is an even bigger reason to break things off now before anyone else uncovers that weakness and uses it against us all.

Embracing that weakness, even if just for a moment, my posture crumples, my head landing atop Damien's gravestone as my hands clutch the grass beneath.

"What am I supposed to *do* here, fratello[23]? I've never felt like this. For anyone. I'm out of my depth and a traitorous bastard for even asking you for advice about this. But I have no one else. You were the only person who ever truly saw me, the only person who understood me. But now, Elizabeth... Damien, she sees me too. I don't know how, but she sees every fucked up part of me. And instead of pushing her away, it only makes her hold on tighter."

I pause out of pure necessity. I'm gasping for air, trying with everything I am to keep my emotions under control, even though I can feel the pressure building behind my eyes.

"I don't know if what she feels for me is purely platonic or something more. But that also doesn't matter if I need to let her go. Send me a sign, brother, *anything*, to tell me that I need to let her go and I'll do it. I may not be strong enough to do it for any other reason, but I know I could do it if you tell me to. I swear to you. Just tell me what to do here. Please..."

It's a testament to how fucked up I am that I don't notice Mono's arrival until he's almost directly behind me. I snap my head to look at him, pressing my lips into a thin line in an attempt to hold back the evidence of my desperation. As he kneels next to me and throws an arm across my shoulders, I realize I needn't have bothered. It's clear by the look on his face that he heard plenty already.

"Listen, you're free to tell me to shut up and butt out, but before you do that, you should know that just like you swore to Damien on his grave that you'd look after Liz, I promised him that I'd look after you. So, at least hear me out first, yeah?"

I nod once, surprised at his confession and not confident enough in my voice at the moment to do anything more. Mono blows out a long

---

[23] brother

breath, then looks me dead in the eyes.

"Damien loved you, Vince. You were his brother, but you were also his best friend. And the only thing he ever wanted for you was for you to realize that you were *worth* that love. That you *deserved* it. And I understand man code and all that bullshit, but the Damien Marchetti that I knew would *never* have wanted you or Elizabeth to live in loneliness for the rest of time simply because he was taken from you both too soon."

He stops, a contemplative look on his face before he mutters something that sounds a lot like "fuck it" and continues.

"I know this next bit may sound sacrilegious, considering we're kneeling on the man's grave, but I never thought that Damien and Elizabeth were a perfect match. Don't misunderstand. I know they loved one another. But I'm not sure that love would have really stood the test of time, not in a romantic way, at least. And you know why? Because of you. Because you and Elizabeth were such a natural fit, where she and Damien had to try so fucking hard that they were basically forcing it. Because you ebbed when she flowed, and she pulled when you pushed. I spend every day of my life watching all of you. And I could see it clear as day. I can still see it, Vince. There's something beautiful there. And Damien would want you to be brave enough to grab onto it. You think you're weak because of your feelings, but believe me when I tell you that the real weakness would be in continuing to deny them out of fear of rejection or some misguided sense of loyalty. Let it in. Let *her* in. That's what I think Damien would say, what I think he sent me here to say in his place."

My entire body is shaking by the time he's done, whether with fear, sorrow, anticipation, or maybe some twisted combination of all three, I don't know. What I do know is that everything Mono said feels *right*. But the question of whether or not I'm brave enough to act on it and risk Elizabeth's rejection is still up in the air. I'm a strong man. I can withstand physical and psychological torture just as well as I can inflict it. But if I bare my soul and it turns out that her feelings were purely platonic? Or even worse, if she sees my feelings as too much of a burden and she leaves altogether? I don't know if I'm strong enough to withstand that.

Even so, my cathartic confessions, combined with Mono's piercing counsel, have lifted a crushing burden from my shoulders. I can decide whether or not to act on my feelings later. For now, it's enough to realize that Mono is right and that Damien would never begrudge me those feelings. As long as all is right between my brother and me, I can tackle anything else that comes my way.

As I rise slowly to my feet, I reach out a hand to Mono and pull him in for a hug.

"Thank you, man. Seriously. And since you're out of the bat cave, what do you say to breakfast at Lucille's on me?"

He barks out a laugh, the mischievous gleam in his eye matching my sentiments exactly as he gestures for me to lead the way. I tip my head toward the clouds as I walk and send up a silent prayer of thanks to my fallen brother. *Whatever happens, fratello, I'll always protect her and your legacy. La famiglia è tutto.*[24]

---

[24] Family is everything.

Chapter 20

Elizabeth

A Few Days Later

"So, Captain Dingbat is okay with keeping Sam for the month while we're in Spain? He's not going to try to call you back to the States with some ridiculous personal emergency that precludes him from parenting his child?"

"Oh, come on," I scoff. "That was *one* time. Not that I wasn't equally annoyed by it, but I can assure you that even Marcus is not clueless enough to think something like that would fly under these particular circumstances."

The incredulity on Vince's face doesn't budge despite the flat look I give him, but I can't muster the energy to worry about it. Even if Marcus did try to pull another dickhead move like that, his mom is around as a backup option, and she's wonderful with Sam. I often wonder if Marcus might not have been switched at birth because he's the total opposite of that saint of a woman.

I swirl my wine, more as an absent mannerism than for any flavor benefit. I doubt it would do much anyway, considering I've been nursing the same glass for the last 30 minutes. It's a weekday, and between Sam's extracurriculars, everything going on at Marchetti International, and the final planning for Vince and I's clandestine operation in Spain, I can't afford to be poorly rested, let alone hungover.

Vince is sprawled across the leather armchair next to me, one hand supporting his chin while the other fiddles with the clasp of his pocketknife. His drink also remains mostly untouched on the coffee table. Though he seems to have dropped the Marcus bashing, it's clear there's still something on his mind. Reaching over, I press my fingers into the furrowed skin of his brow. He rears back and shoots me a wary look, rubbing his forehead dramatically.

"Oh, quit whining. I barely tapped you. But if you keep worrying so hard, you'll get wrinkles and ruin the whole aging gracefully routine you've got going on."

"You take that back! Caputo skin does not *wrinkle*. And I also do not *worry*. I assess. It's kind of critical to the whole enacting-vengeance-on-a-narcissistic-psychopath-without-being-killed thing we're doing here."

It's a wonder I can still breathe with Vince's puffed-up chest taking up every spare inch of space in the room. Even still, he does make a decent point. Not that I'll ever tell him that.

"Pardon me, *oh invincible one.* Please, do enlighten me as to what you were *assessing* before I so rudely interrupted."

I punctuate my reply with a cheeky smirk, but much of my bravado vanishes at the look on Vince's face. As he traces his bottom lip with his middle finger, his tongue runs between his back teeth, predatory eyes locked on me. His jaw flexes, and he tilts his head just the tiniest amount as he considers me. His *assessment* has shifted fully in my direction, and I can't tell if he's trying to decide whether to read me in on his thoughts or how to best punish me for my bratty remark.

Oh. Just the thought of the latter option does things to my nervous system that I will *not* be assessing, now or in the future. I lock that shit down quickly, doing my best to keep a syrupy smile on my face to protect my embarrassing train of thought from his notice.

Thankfully, he seems distracted enough by his own thoughts. His face shifts from predatory to resigned, and he leans forward with his elbows on his legs, dropping his head as if he already knows he's going to regret what he's about to say. When he looks back up at me, it's with a placating expression that only serves to send my hackles up in anticipation.

"I was assessing our recent training sessions, and while you've made amazing progress, I'm having second thoughts about sending you in alone. I, more than anyone, know what Raphael is like, what he's capable of. Maybe we should postpone the trip and give ourselves more time to prepare. Or perhaps reconsider bringing a third into this. I'm sure we can find someone suitable who's flown under the radar enough not to be recognized."

Yep, hackle activation was justified. *I know this man is not sitting here underestimating me to my face. Unacceptable.*

"Yeah, that's not happening," I tell him flatly. "I have been working my ass off to be ready for this because *you and I* owe this to Damien. No one else would be as committed. This isn't just some random job, Vincenzo. This is personal."

He opens his mouth to reply, but I cut him off. I don't want to hear any excuses or concerns for my safety. I'm perfectly capable of managing my own well-being.

"If you need proof that I can handle Raphael and his scumbag ways, why don't you test me? It's been a while since we've sparred, and I don't think you realize quite how far I've come."

I stand, raising a brow in his direction, one hand on my hip in full "try me" mode. After a few tense moments of stare-down, he meets my challenge. Rising from his seat to crowd into my personal space, he tucks his hands in his pockets and peers down at me through hardened eyes, a sinister grin on his face.

"Alright, Venom. Let's see what you've got."

That's the only warning I get before he presses forward determinedly, making me stumble backward as I try to navigate out of the seating area and into a more open space.

"Oh, come on, princess," he hisses. "Who says we can't mix business with pleasure, huh? You want to take the best deal back to your boss, don't you?"

His hand is on my ass, groping hard enough to hurt, while the other is tight around my waist. I try to spin away as soon as we clear the coffee table, but between his grip and the speed of his advance, I'm unsuccessful. He tsks, capturing my wrists and raising them above my head as he presses us both back into the wall of windows overlooking the city.

"Now, now. There's no need to pretend. I've seen the way you look at me, cariña[25]."

His voice is a low, predatory growl.

"I'm sure you've thought about what it would be like. Feeling my hand around your throat, my tongue running across your breasts, and my cock buried deep in your cunt while you moan my name."

He leans in close, his lips brushing against my jaw as his breaths flutter across my neck. My entire body is trembling, and I swear I can feel actual electricity arcing across the places his lips graze against my skin. *Fucking hell.* I know I'm supposed to be afraid, or at least I would be in any real situation. And perhaps a part of me is. But not because of what he's threatening to do to me. No. Right now I'm only afraid of how much I want him to follow through on those threats, disastrous as that would be to both our personal and business relationships.

Fucking focus, Elizabeth. If you can't pull yourself together, maybe Vince is right. Maybe you do need more time to prepare.

But I can't let that happen. We've been planning this for *months*. And every day that Raphael walks free is one more day that we've let

---

[25] doll

Damien down. He was so close to taking out Raphael himself, and I am the reason he'll never get that chance. I owe it to him to do this and do it now.

Traitorous libido somewhat under control, I decide to reuse a tactic that's served me well in the past. Tilting my head back, I bare my neck to Vince's ministrations, letting out a whimper as his teeth nip at the skin of my neck. I can't see his face to know if he's buying my act, so I assume he is until he shows me otherwise. Pressing my hips against his, I suddenly wonder if I'm not the only one struggling to draw a line between acting and reality. He's hard against me, and my whimper turns to an involuntary moan as he presses back, hitting that perfect spot between my legs.

He slides my hands down to transfer my wrists behind my back, gripping both in a single hand so that the other is free to settle around my throat. Applying just the right amount of pressure, he pulls my gaze down to meet his eyes. I lower my lids, shooting him my best lusty siren eyes as I release a weighted breath. His gaze is dark, darker than I've ever seen it, with his pupils blown so wide that I can barely see a hint of his signature honey brown around the edges. He's searching my eyes with his own, deliberation clear on his face.

Not wanting to give him time to see through my ruse, I lean forward to break our eye contact. Angling my head, I bring my lips to his ear and blow a soft breath across his lobe. His answering shiver sends a rush of feminine satisfaction through me, even as I deliver my veiled warning.

"God, I've wanted to do this so many times," I whisper just before I position my mouth over his earlobe and bite. Hard.

He rears back on instinct, and his grip on my throat loosens enough that I'm able to smash my head into his nose, causing him to stumble away just enough. Freeing a single hand from his grasp, I reach out and grab a candlestick off the nearby end table, pointing it at him like the gun I'd be carrying in any real situation.

He stares at me for a beat in shock, but a smile quickly overtakes his expression. Removing his hand from his ear, he claps proudly and laughs as he celebrates my victory.

"That was brilliant, Venom. Seriously. I thought you'd lost the plot. I mean, fuck, you looked, well, you looked like you were begging to be fucked if I'm being honest."

His expression falters, and he starts talking faster, seemingly only just then realizing what he's said.

"Not that we would have. I mean, I was just waiting to see how long you took to snap out of it, you know. Needed to know how much work we had to do to get you ready for Madrid, and whatnot. But shit, it never even occurred to me that you were pretending. Probably because I was so wrapped up in my own acting. I mean, you know I wasn't...it was just for the test. I had to make it seem real, too, you know?"

He trails off, one hand coming up to scratch at his neck as he looks anywhere but at me. I've never seen Vince visibly uncomfortable before. He's always so controlled and unfazed, even when shit is completely hitting the fan.

Jesus, is he really that put off by the mere idea of sex with me?

I'll have to dwell on that blow to my ego later. As he scratches at his neck, his fingers graze his ear and I catch the flinch that he tries to hide. Setting down my mock pistol, I move to his side and rise on my tiptoes to get a look at the damage I caused. Blood is trickling steadily down his neck, though thankfully, it's a slow stream. It's going to need cleaning and some sort of ointment to avoid scarring, though.

Shit, I guess I bit harder than I meant to. Not that I've ever had to think about the right amount of bite force to apply on an earlobe before. But still.

I turn his face back towards me so I can get a good look at his nose, too. It's not bleeding too badly either and seems to still be the same shape as it was before, so I'm relatively confident that it's not broken.

162

Wrapped up in nurse mode, I don't realize how close I've gotten. But a slight shift of my gaze locks our eyes together, and I become acutely aware of both the proximity of our mouths as well as my fingertips still resting on his cheek. He doesn't look away, and neither do I. The only thing I can manage for several seconds is an audible swallow.

Snap out of it, Elizabeth. You're probably freaking the poor man out!

"Come on," I tell him, clearing my throat and ending our awkward staring contest as I look toward the hallway. "Let's go to the bathroom so I can see better in the light. We need to get that cleaned up."

Vince gestures for me to go first, following silently. I bustle around the master bathroom, grabbing the supplies I need and trying to avoid any more awkward eye contact. Once I can no longer avoid it, I turn to face him and find him watching me with a contemplative look.

I stride purposefully toward him, setting my gathered supplies on the counter next to us. After dabbing a cotton swab in ointment I reach for his ear before realizing that our height difference makes this more complicated than it needs to be.

"Could you, um, sit on the, uh, the makeup thingy, please?"

He chuckles, arching a brow at me.

"The makeup thingy? I'm afraid you'll have to be more specific, doll. I'm not very well-versed in what women get up to in their private chambers."

His golden eyes are positively twinkling now. Heat rises to my cheeks, embarrassment rearing her ugly head. It's not like me to stumble over my words, and I don't like the feeling, harmless mistake or not. I'm not sure why I'm so out of sorts tonight. Must be just residual adrenaline from my earlier rush of victory.

"Oh, don't be dense. You know what I meant! The low counter with the bench thingy. The, the vanity! Yes, please sit on the vanity counter and stop being such a smartass, you weedy giant."

He does as I ask, chuckling the entire time. I narrow my eyes in warning but don't say anything else. Instead, I pick up an alcohol wipe and press it firmly against his ear, causing him to flinch back.

"Yow, hey! You did that on purpose!"

Vince cups his ear and pouts, but I'm not buying it.

"Oh, shove it," I snark. "You can sit through stitches without so much as a whimper, but one measly alcohol wipe has you crying for Mommy? Please."

"It's about the intention behind it," he whines dramatically. "You wanted that to hurt. I could feel it. You're a cruel, wicked woman who delights in my suffering."

Oh, give me a break. The kicked puppy face he's shooting my way should make me laugh, and it almost does, but something about the look in his eyes just makes me feel guilty instead. *Ugh, fine.*

"Alright, alright, I'm sorry. I promise I'll be gentle from now on. Okay?"

He makes a show of considering before giving me a single, resolute nod. I step back between his legs and pick up the ointment, making an equal show of gently applying it to the teeth marks on his ear.

Once I've bandaged his ear and cleaned the blood from around his nose as best I can, I lean back to examine my handiwork.

"Do you want an ice pack? Might help with the swelling."

He stands up from his perch on the counter and turns to look at himself in the mirror, running his fingers gingerly over his purpling nose.

"Nah, it'll be fine. Besides, it's late. I need to get home and get some sleep."

I check my watch and realize that he's right. It's almost 2 in the morning.

What the heck? Where did the time go?

"Why don't you stay here? Like you said, it's already late. Plus, I don't think your face will appreciate being squashed into your riding helmet right now."

He stops mid-stride to look at me, pulling a surprised face.

"Huh, I hadn't thought of that. Though, I mean, I could ride without it just this once."

"Oh, nuh-uh. Absolutely not," I say, marching up to him and poking him in the chest. "We've talked about this. You're not allowed to die on me. And with my luck, this would be the one night some drunk asshole sideswipes you into a ditch. Nope. Not happening."

I cross my arms and give him my best mom look. It works. He backs down, agreeing to stay the night. As we exit the bathroom, he looks toward the bed for a long second before pivoting and heading toward the door.

"Alright, well, I'm off to bed, then," he chimes, way more cheerily than is necessary. "Sleep tight, Venom."

With barely a look in my direction, he's gone, the door clicking softly shut behind him. Part of me wants to call him back, to insist that he stay with me just like the last couple of times he's stayed over.

But that would be weird. There were valid reasons for us sharing a bed the last two times. This time? This time would mean something entirely different. Even so, I can't shake the feeling of wrongness as I slip into bed alone after changing into my night clothes. The feeling doesn't wane, but thankfully it's no match for my fatigue. After a few long minutes of determined steady breathing and numerical sheep visualizations, I manage to drift off to sleep.

Chapter 21

The Next Morning

I'm already wide awake when my phone chimes, the security system alerting me to Vince's twilight departure. Though my blanket cocoon is incredibly comfortable in the physical sense, my mind is trapped in something more akin to a thorn patch of intrusive thoughts, most of them focused on how much my performance last night has likely fucked up my relationship with Vince. I fling the covers off my head, hoping the fresh air will shock some sense into my pathetic brain.

What the fuck? We are not pouting. Nor are we analyzing every minute detail of our interactions. There is nothing to worry about. What in the high school hormones is happening here?!

Logical, independent, grown-adult Elizabeth knows that Vince only snuck out at the ass crack of dawn without a goodbye because he's a gentleman and he respects my boundaries with Sam. I have no desire to explain to my son why a man spent the night at our house, no matter how innocent the true reasons.

But irrational, insecure, regressed-to-high-school Elizabeth is convinced he did it because he mistook my acting last night for actual interest. He's probably so uninterested in me in that sense that now he doesn't know how to face me.

Ugh!

166

I channel my frustration into kicking the rest of the blankets off with my legs, but I'm still not ready to get up just yet. Instead, I adopt my best disgruntled starfish impression as I give in to the urge to recount every awkward encounter in obsessive detail.

To be fair, he's the one who started it. He didn't have to put on a sleazeball act for my test. He could have made it a kidnapping or something else less...sexual. I mean, okay, Raphael *does* have a reputation, and even I have to admit that I seem to be exactly his type from the profile that Mono worked up on the guy. But still. He could've tested my skills with some other scenario, so he can't get upset when I played into the scene instead of fighting against it.

And another thing! He has no room to pretend like I'm the only one making things awkward when he was the one smuggling a freaking steel pipe in his pants while he had me pressed against the windows. Physical reactions are such a bitch for precisely that reason. They aren't ruled by logic or emotion. And he's an intelligent man, so I'm sure he knows that my reactions to him were in no way an indication of any real desire to evolve our friendship into something else.

Yeah. So, maybe I'm overthinking things. Logical Liz is right. I'm sure he just wanted to be gone before Sam woke up. Yep. That's what we're going with. No more thinking about this.

After close to five minutes of definitely *not* thinking about it, my phone chimes with a reminder. *Holy crap, that's right!* It's Sam's birthday today. Thank god for technology when the human mind fails us. With a renewed resolve to put all things Vince out of my mind so I can focus purely on my brand new eight-year-old's big day, I slide out of bed and pad toward the bathroom.

My resolve lasts approximately 47 minutes. Though, in my defense, it's only natural to think of someone when you walk into your kitchen to find that they brewed a fresh pot of coffee for you before they left, even though they don't drink the stuff themselves. I am still just a girl underneath all the emotional trauma and stubborn bravado.

I smile as I pour a cup, adding milk and honey until it's the perfect shade of dark beige. *I guess things aren't as fucked as I feared.* Before long, Sam joins me in the kitchen, the smell of bacon and pancakes having roused him from sleep right on time.

"Happy birthday, my big, wonderful boy!" I croon as I wrap him in a tight hug.

"Moooooom," he whines as he pats my arm limply.

"Oh, nuh-uh! You may be eight, but you are still my baby. None of your friends are around to see you, so quit acting like you're too cool for your mom and give me your best squeeze with those big kid muscles."

He cracks a grin, and I know I've got him. After feigning crushed ribs from the force of his hug, I ruffle his hair and point him towards the kitchen island, where I load him up with all of his favorite breakfast foods.

"So, kiddo," I ask between bites of my breakfast, "what do you want to do today? Still thinking we should hit the boardwalk?"

"Yeah! Definitely the boardwalk, but you have to promise to let me ride the roller coaster and play all the games at least once!"

"Alright, alright," I laugh. "It's a deal. Did you decide which friend you want to bring?"

"Well, actually," he starts but hesitates.

I stay quiet, having learned long ago that it's better to just wait him out than to try to guess what he's thinking. Finally, he looks up at me uncertainly.

"Do you think Vince would come with us?"

It's a good thing my coffee cup is already on the counter; otherwise, I would probably have dropped it.

"Umm, Vince? You mean Mom's friend, Vince, that you met the other day at lunch?"

"Yeah!" he perks up. "It's just, well, I was gonna invite Robert, but he had to go out of town with his dad, and I don't really like any of the other kids in class all *that* much. But Vince was super cool and funny, so I was wondering if you think he would wanna come. You know, if it's not too lame, hanging out with a kid."

*Oh, well, now he **has** to come.*

"Hey, there is nothing lame about hanging out with you, young sir. That I can guarantee. I'm not sure what Vince has planned for today, but I'll call him up and ask, okay?"

Sam nods and tucks back into his pancakes. I head back to retrieve my phone from my room and pace for a moment, still fighting lingering reservations about where we stand after last night.

Suck it up, Buttercup. This is for Sam.

As always, Sam is just the push I need to get over my own issues. I'd commit multiple crimes for that kid, so risking a bit of personal embarrassment is child's play in comparison. I press the call button and hold my breath until Vince picks up.

"Morning, Copperhead. Did you find the present I left for you?"

Oh, thank the heavens.

"I did. Thank you for the coffee. It tasted extra delicious this morning."

"Well, duh," he teases. "Anyway, what's up? Surely you're not working already?"

"No, nothing like that. It's Sam's birthday today and our tradition is that I always let him pick something fun to do along with a friend. He wants to go to the boardwalk to ride the rides and play the games and that sort of thing."

I'm rambling, but Vince humors me.

"Cool, sounds like fun. Want me to book you guys something nice for dinner, my treat? I didn't realize that his birthday was so soon. I feel bad that I didn't get the little man a gift."

"Well, actually...he asked if you would be willing to come with us this

169

year as his friend."

It's silent for a while. I'm pulling the phone back to check that we're still connected when Vince finally responds.

"Are you serious?"

"Yeah, I mean... He just thought... I mean, don't feel obligated. I told him that I wasn't sure if you already had plans, so I could just tell him that you're busy. It's no big d-"

"No, no, no, Copperhead, you misunderstand me. I meant are you serious that Sam picked *me* to spend the day with instead of any of his friends at school?"

"Umm, well, yeah. He said you're super cool and funny, and he wanted you to come. So, what do you think?"

"I'll be right there. Just give me 30 minutes to go home and change. Actually, make it 25."

Vince hangs up after a quick goodbye, and I stride out to give Sam the good news. He gives an excited whoop and runs into his room to get ready. I'm not sure how to interpret Vince's reaction to the invitation, but that doesn't stop me from trying to do so anyway as I clear the dishes and put away the leftovers. By the time the elevator chimes to signal Vince's arrival, I've accepted once more that I may never fully understand the enigma that is Vincenzo Caputo.

Sam runs to greet him, literally squealing around the corner of the front hallway in his new sneakers. The two fist bump, and Vince shoots me a wink before pulling out his phone.

"I got you a little something, but I didn't have a chance to print them out before I came over, so please forgive the presentation. Three tickets to go see Rick Haverty in a couple of months. You can take your mom and a friend. What do you think?"

"Oh, my god, I love it! Mom, we get to go see Rick Haverty! This is awesome!"

"That's amazing, bud," I say, only a little lost. "He's that comedian you like, right?"

After being educated that Rick Haverty is not just some "comedian he likes," but instead the funniest human to ever walk the planet, I express my apologies for the slight and suggest that we start heading out if we want to beat some of the crowd. Vince insists on driving, so we make our way to his black BMW and settle in for the ride.

* * *

We get home late, well past Sam's usual bedtime, but you wouldn't know it to look at him. As I put away my things in the hall closet, he and Vince are deep in an animated conversation about whether the manager of the restaurant we ate at for lunch was the man in the blue button-down or the woman in the red blouse. Apparently, Vince has been coaching Sam on situational awareness throughout the day, along with some other tricks that I'm sure I'll have to smack him for later, and this question is his final test.

"Ehem, gentlemen? Perhaps it would be simplest to look up the restaurant's website and see if they have a staff page?"

They both blink at me for a moment, as if they'd forgotten I was even there, before exclaiming their thanks and diving back into their discussion. Vince pulls out his phone, and Sam hops on his tiptoes to peer at the screen while he searches. A few taps and several shouts of "No, not that one!" later, Sam lets out a victory whoop.

"Ha! I knew it! Eat that suckah!"

My head snaps in his direction, ready to remind him about the concept of manners, when Vince waves me off to handle it himself.

"Alright, I'm not afraid to admit defeat. You were right. *But!* Remember our talk about presence? How would a real boss have said that?"

Sam thinks for a moment, squinting in concentration before his eyes light in recognition. He clears his throat and stands up straighter, looking Vince square in the eye.

"Huh, it seems I'm right once again. Imagine that."

He punctuates the statement with a smirk, and I have to press my lips together to keep from sputtering in impressed shock at the confident little sasshole who has just replaced my son. Vince just grins proudly and pats him on the shoulder.

"That's what I'm talking about! Nicely done, big guy. Now, I remember your mom said it would be time for bed as soon as you got home, so why don't you go brush your teeth while I chat with her about some work stuff?"

Sam nods once and jets off down the hallway, the two stuffed toys he won at the carnival flailing in his grip. Vince strides over to me, a conspiratorial smile on his face.

"You knew the whole time that the woman was the manager, didn't you?"

"Oh, absolutely. I just wanted to see if he'd stick to his guns or let the fear of being wrong make him question himself."

I shake my head, unsurprised but reminded that life ends up in places you never expected sometimes.

"Mmhmm, and what other handy mob-boss-in-training skills were you teaching my son today? Advanced interrogation techniques? The merits of blades versus firearms in reconnaissance situations?"

He laughs, and I smile despite myself.

"No, that's all still a bit too advanced I fear. We focused mainly on moving silently and some light lockpicking. You know, the easy stuff."

I narrow my eyes at him, trying to determine if he's still joking when it hits me.

"You rat! So that's how you both snuck up on me holding stuffed animals when you'd said you were just going to the bathroom?! I thought you'd detoured by a carnival game on the way back."

"Ha! Guilty. There was a storage closet right next to the bathrooms. But I did leave a $50 bill on top of the stack, so there was no stealing involved."

My head lands in my hand as I contemplate why I find that more amusing than concerning. *Oh my god. What have I gotten Sam into? Maybe it wasn't such a good idea to let the two of them meet.*

Vince must be able to gauge my thoughts because he's quick to reassure me.

"Wait, it's not like that, I promise. I'm not trying to train Sam up or anything. I just think there are certain skills that all young men can benefit from. Being aware of your surroundings, reading the room, being able to remain inconspicuous. These are all exceptionally useful in the blindingly bright legal realm. I know you don't want Sam involved in the family business. I'd never infringe on those wishes. I swear it."

I take in his solemn expression and the serious tone of his voice and decide to believe him. He's not wrong. Those are incredibly valuable skills in the regular business world. And Vince isn't Damien. He'd never step around my wishes thinking that he knows better.

*Woah. Where did that comparison come from? Apparently, I've been harboring more resentment for Damien's interference in my career than I've been willing to admit. Anyway, putting all **that** back in its box for the moment...*

Sam returns to the living room to say goodnight, clad in his favorite PJs. I walk toward him, ready to go tuck him in, when he steps around me to Vince and wraps his little arms around Vince's waist. The surprise is clear on Vince's face, but he recovers quickly, giving him a gentle squeeze and pat on the back in return. Sam pulls back with a smile and a cheery "Goodnight, Vince!" before grabbing my hand to head to his room. I glance back as we walk down the hall to see Vince staring after us with unfocused eyes, lost in his thoughts.

Sam turns out to be full of surprises tonight. As I'm tucking the blankets around him, he asks matter-of-factly if Vince is going to start staying with us the way Catie stays with his dad.

"Umm, what?" I stumble, thrown off balance by the question. "Why do you ask, buddy?"

"Cause I really like him. He's cool. He listens to me and teaches me things, and seems really smart. Plus, you're really happy when he's around, and I want you to be happy."

Oh, sweet Jesus. Now I'm gonna cry.

"You're right, baby. He is cool. And he's a great friend to Mom. But I'm already happy, bud, because I've got you. You know that, right?"

"I know, Mom. It's just a different kind of happy, I think. Like Dad and Catie. Except, no kissing! I *hate it* when they're kissing. Yuck."

I can't help but chuckle a little, more grateful than I can express that he's still so innocent.

"Alright, mister. Well, anyway, it's time to sleep now. I love you, and I'll see you in the morning."

At his whispered goodnight, I turn off the light, shutting the door softly behind me. When I walk back into the living room, Vince has made himself at home on the couch, remote in one hand, as he looks for something to watch. He smiles and waves me over, patting the seat next to him. I move to his side, more out of habit than anything, still stuck in my head. Vince's arm is slung across the back of the couch, a perfectly normal position, but Sam's question has me thinking about what it would be like if he dropped it down onto my shoulders while I snuggled into his side.

But then we're back to where we started this morning. Are my physical reactions to him purely the result of biology? Am I only considering this because of the power of suggestion? Or have I been dancing around this idea for months, brushing it off under any plausible excuse for fear of ruining our friendship and seeming disloyal to Damien's memory?

Damien. What would Damien even think about this? I mean, I'm sure he wouldn't want me to be alone forever. But his best friend? And mere months after his death? It's too soon. Isn't it?

Then again, should I put my life on hold? Neither one of us is getting any younger and we're facing danger every day. Will I regret it more if I do nothing and end up losing my chance altogether? Or would it be worse to start something only to have Vince ripped away from me the way Damien was? Though, to be honest, I'm not sure I could handle Vince being taken from me even now, so does it matter? I'd be shattered either way.

And doesn't that say enough right there? Can I honestly say that I feel nothing more than platonic friendship for him and, in the same breath, admit that my entire world would crumble if he were killed?

Yeah, no. It's official. Even I can't delude myself any longer. I'm falling in love with yet another mafia don, and I have no earthly idea what to do about it. Thankfully, Vince either doesn't notice the bombs going off in my head, or he's purposely giving me space to work through them. Either way, I'm appreciative as I settle in and do my best to focus on the movie he's chosen as if my entire reality hasn't just flipped on its axis.

Chapter 22

Vincenzo

A Few Days Later

I step off the elevator and stride down the front hallway of Liz's apartment. I'm a bit earlier than I thought I'd be when I texted to confirm our movie night, but the stoplights were on my side tonight. Not seeing any sign of Liz in the main living area, I set the snacks I've brought on the dining table and head for the back hallway. The light is still on in her office, and the door is closed. She must be in a solid groove to still be working this late. She's lucky to have such a thoughtful partner who insists on making sure she takes time to have some fun every once in a while.

But before I stage an intervention, I need to check for one of my knives in her room. I'm certain I had it on me when I came over after her nightmare, and I haven't seen it in a while. I'm hoping it's still on the bedside table. I liked that knife.

As I walk into the master bedroom, I barely have time to register that there's a light coming from the en suite bathroom when the door slides open and Liz struts out, fresh from the shower and singing softly to herself with a towel on her head.

Correction. With *only* a towel on her head.

Dio cane[26].

I'm not strong enough for this. I can handle a lot of things - intimidation, starvation, torture. But finally knowing for a fact how delectable every inch of her body is and not being able to *do* anything about it? When all I've been able to think about for the past few weeks is how badly I want to run my hands over her skin and watch it pebble under my touch? When I've fantasized about my head between those perfect thighs as she shudders beneath me? *Fuck. No, I can't do this.*

Apparently, I can't do anything else either, though, because I just stand there, frozen like an absolute idiot. I have hope, for just the smallest second, that perhaps she'll be so wrapped up in her thoughts that she won't notice me, and I can sneak away once she's in her dressing room. But, no. I should have known better than to expect any help from the universe. Karma really is a bitch.

Liz catches sight of me in her peripheral vision and flinches, a gasp cutting off her song mid-word. I see the moment she recognizes me, and her stance relaxes, though her gaze is still wary as we enter the world's most painful staring contest.

Wait. Did I wreck my bike on the way over here? Because I'm starting to think I've already died and I'm standing in Hell, awaiting judgment while Persephone herself assesses my value. That's the only logical explanation for why all of my hard-won control has crumbled to the point where I'm incapable of turning my head, or closing my eyes, or offering up an explanation as to why I'm even in Elizabeth's bedroom in the first place. *Tell her about the knife! Tell her you thought she was in her office. Tell her fucking anything!*

But I can't. I can only stare in school-boy wonder, cataloging every single detail while I have the chance. She hasn't moved to hide herself. In fact, once she realizes it's me, she turns fully in my direction,

---

[26] Fucking God./Holy shit.

granting me an even better view, one hand on her hip as she stares me down with raised brows, awaiting an explanation, or a reaction, or *something.*

Her eyes drift downward from my face, and I realize too late that the grey joggers I wore over for movie night are doing me absolutely no favors. My dick is hard enough to puncture steel, and she's got a front-row seat to the show.

Wait. Hold the fucking phone. Did she just? Oh, holy shit, now I know I'm dreaming.

Her tongue darts out to wet her lips, and I watch as her pupils dilate in real time, heat entering her gaze as she takes in my reaction to her and runs her gaze slowly back up to my face. When she meets my eyes with her own, the challenge is clear within them.

"Let me guess, biology?"

Her words snap the invisible hold on my feet, and my decision is made. I swing a hand out to slam the door closed behind me and stalk toward her with purpose as I reply.

"No. I'm done pretending. Last chance to run, Venom."

She doesn't.

I'm on her in half a breath, shameless in my desperation. She tastes like sin, salvation, and everything I'm not allowed to want. My grip on her hip is firm, pulling her to me while my other hand cradles the back of her head, and I press her against the bedroom wall. I'm feral with the need to be closer to her. We're connected from lip to toe, every possible body part pressed into one another, but it's not enough. I know I'm kissing her too hard, devouring her, consuming her, as I struggle to stay in control of myself. But she meets my pace, her own need for me clear in the way she drags my bottom lip between her teeth, the way she grips the back of my shirt and digs her fingers into the side of my hip.

Fuck yes. She's not being gentle in the slightest, as if she's already read my owner's manual in preparation for just such an occasion. *Or maybe...*

I unwind the towel from her head and let it drop, her damp hair falling around her face. It's wavier than it is when it's dry and a bit messy, giving her a freshly fucked look even though we've barely gotten started. I slip a hand beneath her hair and run my fingers up through the strands before curling them and pulling gently, just to test the waters. She moans low in her throat and kisses me harder. *Oh, Venom. It's like you were **made** for me.*

My hand slides from her hip down to her ass, and I squeeze. *God, she's perfect.* My dick jumps in agreement at the feel of her. She grinds her hips into me in response, and I can't wait any longer. Sliding my hand further down her thigh, I pull her knee up to hook around my back, positioning her cunt in just the right spot. A slight bend of my knees is all it takes for my cock to be pressed directly against her clit, and we moan in unison this time, the feeling fucking exquisite, even with the layers of fabric still between us.

Her head is thrown back, as much as our position on the wall will allow at least, and I take the opportunity to direct my attention to the curve of her neck. I grind into her on a slow but steady rhythm and trail open-mouthed kisses down her jaw onto her pulse point. I can feel her blood rushing beneath my tongue, her heart beating almost as fast as my own. I wish for a moment that my canines were just a bit sharper. Something tells me she would be incredibly turned on by a bit of vampire play.

*Shit. **I'm** incredibly turned on by just the **thought** of vampire play.* I may have to make a few calls and set something up for the future. Though... Do we have a future? Is this real for her? Is this more than just built-up sexual need and hormones? God, I hope so. I'm not sure I could handle it if she told me that this meant nothing more than sex.

I'm pulled from my spiraling thoughts by her fingertips ghosting along my waistband. She hooks her index fingers into the sides, but I'm not done with her here yet, and there is absolutely no need to rush. I'm going to cherish this time, just in case I never get the chance again.

With renewed fervor, I nip and suck at her throat, reveling in the shiver that winds down her body. She tilts her head further to the side, giving me even better access, and I murmur my appreciation.

"That's it, Venom. Give yourself over to me."

Everything dials up a notch at that. Her grip tightens, her breath quickens, and she lets out the loudest moan yet. *Oh. So you like to be talked through it, huh, Venom? Or do you like giving up control? Either way, baby, I can fucking do that.*

But not here, not against this wall. Recapturing her lips, I release her leg and pull her into me as I step slowly back, angling us toward the bed. She follows instinctively, like a familiar dance partner. Pressing forward again, I stop just as her legs brush against the comforter.

"Sit on the bed. Legs open."

My voice is rough but firm, and she responds immediately. Watching this vibrant, intelligent, stubborn woman obey my commands without hesitation, with nothing but trust and desire in her eyes, is almost enough to do me in. God, the things I'm willing to do to make sure she looks at me like that forever.

I reach one hand over my head and strip my black t-shirt off in a single, fluid motion. Her eyes track every movement, and she's brazen in her perusal of my bare chest. I can't stop the self-satisfied smirk that takes over my face. *She wants me. Bad.*

Well, never let it be said that I'd deprive her of anything she wants. I step out of my shoes and socks quickly before moving my hands to my waistband and sliding my joggers over my hips. I'm standing before her in nothing but my black boxer briefs, and I can practically taste the anticipation in the air as her eyes remain fixated on the bulge beneath them. I reach out, grabbing the hair on the back of her head and pulling slowly, forcing her to look up at me.

I drop my voice to a low rumble to ask her, "Do you want my cock out, Venom?"

She swallows hard before confirming, her voice breathy.

"Have you dreamt about my cock, Venom? About wrapping those pretty lips around it? About how it would feel to have me thrusting deep inside you?"

Another ragged confirmation. She's squirming on the bed now, seeking relief for her throbbing cunt. It's not enough, I know. Only I can give her that. But I can't pass up the opportunity before me while she's being so honest and open.

"Mmm, what a filthy mind you have. But what about your hands? Did you touch yourself while you imagined those things? Did you come on those perfect fingers while you thought of me?"

Her frustration peaks, and she finally manages more than a one-word answer.

"Vincenzo," she growls. "I swear to God if you don't stop teasing me..."

My smirk has turned into a wolfish grin now. I can feel it. But I am still just a man, and fuck if it doesn't feel incredible to hear her say my name like that.

"I'll take that as a yes, then. That makes two of us, Venom. Did you know? Could you tell that I've been obsessing over touching you, just like this, for weeks now? That I've jacked off to the thought of you in every position imaginable while I fuck you? Was it embarrassingly obvious?"

Her eyes widen at my admission, and I believe her when she says no, though I am surprised that someone as sharp as her could have missed the signs I'm sure I was involuntarily broadcasting.

"Well, I suppose it's reassuring to know that my poker face is still sharp as ever. It's always been one of my most useful skills."

I slide my fingers from her hair around to grip her chin gently. I don't need to hold her gaze in place. Her eyes are locked on mine of her own accord. But I can't bring myself to break contact entirely.

"Would you like to see what other skills I possess, Venom? I've got several that I think you'll particularly enjoy."

"Less talking and more showing," she pants. "*Please*, Vince."

"God, I love it when you moan my name. Like you're desperate for me. Such a *good girl*."

I smirk as she shudders, just as I expected.

"Lie back and put your heels on the edge of the bed."

I kneel to the floor as she complies, ghosting kisses across her inner thighs, but realize that I can't see her face from this angle.

"Raise up on your arms, elbows bent, and look at me."

That's much better. She watches me intently, positioned between her legs. I blow a light breath across her swollen clit, and her head falls back. I nip at her thigh, bringing her gaze back to mine.

"Keep your eyes on me. If you look away, I stop. Understood?"

She nods, but that's not good enough.

"I need to hear you say it, Venom. Am I understood?"

"Yes, Sir," she breathes, her answers once again stilted and rushed, her thighs tightening around my head.

Fuck she's absolutely perfect. I infuse as much praise into my gaze as I can because my mouth can't wait any longer. It's only focused on one thing right now. I lean into her and run a pointed tongue across her cunt before capturing her swollen clit between my lips.

She cries out, and her hips dart off the bed, but I place a hand on her stomach to hold her in place. I'm in control of this experience. The pace, the angle, the pressure. Those are all mine to decide. I want full credit for bringing her pleasure like this.

And pleasure her I do. It's child's play to discover exactly what she likes and what her weaknesses are. She's so beautifully responsive that

I'd have to be blind *and* deaf not to catch the signs. And her eyes. Fuck, I'm in danger of coming right alongside her from the way that she's looking at me alone. She hasn't taken her eyes off mine the entire time, though I can see her fighting against the urge to close them and give in to the sensations I'm causing.

But I want this imprinted in her brain. I want my face to become synonymous with the feelings she's experiencing right now. There will be no fantasy scenarios or memories of other men while I'm giving her pleasure. There is only me and her.

Soon, I can feel her desperation cresting as she nears release, and I double down on my efforts. They pay off almost immediately, and she screams as the first orgasm rips through her. Her head finally shoots back, and one hand comes up to grip my hair in an attempt to pull me off of her. I slow my pace and gentle my pressure but don't relent, licking and sucking her through it until the last aftershock has left her body.

Once it has, I give her a mere moment to revel in the boneless feeling before I'm finally shucking the last of my clothing and crawling over her on the bed. Sliding a hand beneath her back, I gently lift her further up the bed, making sure her legs have plenty of room. Her face is angled toward me with a dreamy smile. I enjoy it for a moment before kissing her hard and settling atop her, angled to one side so that I can finally explore what I've admired from afar for so long. One hand runs up and down the side of her body as the other braces me above her.

These kisses are different than before, still just as intense, but more reverent. Now that the initial fear that she'd change her mind has worn off, I'm ready to take my time, to savor. She's kissing me back just as deeply, as though she wants to drink me in as much as I do her. Her hand runs along my side, trailing inward across my back in lazy strokes when she suddenly stiffens. Her fingertips trace and retrace a cluster of scars on my back, and I realize she's never seen them. Every time I've been shirtless, she's only seen my front. She probably didn't even know they were there.

But I don't want to talk about my scars. I don't want to think about how long I've had them or the bastard who put them there. All I want is to drown in her and forget that the rest of the world even exists. Unfortunately, I know her better than that. As expected, she pushes me gently away and looks into my eyes, her gaze hard.

"Who?"

She's all venom and hellfire right now; her vicious side activated on my behalf even before she knows the story behind the scars. But I won't lie to her. I never have, and I don't intend to start now, especially not when her trust is more important than ever. I let out a deep sigh and drop my head, resigned to having to do at least this much before we can continue with my earlier plans.

"Raphael," I say, no emotion in my voice. I learned a long time ago that it's easier to go numb when thinking of him than to feel sorry for myself. I see her mouth open, but I already know what she's going to ask.

"When I was a child, over many separate incidents, but I really don't want to talk about him right now. I promise to tell you everything, but later. He has no place here."

She nods, and her expression softens. Her fingers spread out, covering as much of my back as she can manage, and pulls me down for a kiss. When she pulls back, it's with a determined look. One I know all too well.

"He'll pay for that as well. I'll make sure of it."

It's my turn to nod. I don't know what to say. Her fury on my behalf feels...well, it feels incredible, but I don't want her to feel furious right now. So I file away my appreciation for her protectiveness and focus on redirecting her thoughts to the more pressing matters at hand. Namely, sliding my cock into her cunt in what's likely to be the most memorable moment of my life thus far.

Both my hands and my mouth make their way to her breasts, pulling and licking and sucking as I memorize every inch of them. Her hands are everywhere, in my hair, on my skin. She can't seem to stay still, writhing and caressing in response to my touch. My hand trails down between her legs, and she opens them immediately. I run a finger through her folds and find her still soaking wet. She presses into my hand, practically begging for me, and I oblige. My middle finger slides inside of her so easily, and I push into the hilt, dragging it back slowly as I curl the tip just slightly along her inside wall.

"Oh my god, Vince. NOW."

Her legs open even wider, knees falling to the side as she grants me complete access to continue. I know she wants more, but I'm in no hurry to give in to her demands. I continue teasing her with my finger, all the while keeping up my worship of her breasts. Her nipples are taut and overly sensitive now. Every graze of my tongue makes her squirm. Every breath of air across them earns a whimper.

"Vincenzo..." she whines, and it's the sexiest sound I've ever heard. "Please, I want. No, I need..."

"What do you need, love? Tell me."

"You," she breathes. "I need you. *All* of you. Right now."

As much as I love running the show in bed, I can't resist her when she's begging for me so openly. I'm certain there's not a man alive who could. But I'm not ready for this to be over so soon, so a position change is in order to ensure that I can last long enough to show her what I'm truly capable of.

Not bothering with instructions this time, I grab her sides and flip her onto her stomach, chuckling at her surprised yelp. She presses up on her hands and shoots me a glare, but there's no muscle behind it. She and I both know that one thing she is not is easily broken. My girl can handle a lot more than a playful toss, that's for damn sure.

Pulling her hips back and up, I line myself up behind her before I

185

pause. *Shit.*

"Venom," I grit out, barely able to stop myself from driving into her right then and there. "Please tell me you have condoms stashed somewhere in this room."

She looks back at me, considering for a moment.

"You don't need one," she says matter-of-factly. "Unless..."

"No! No, you're right. I have no reason to need one."

Her head tilts a bit, both of us processing the unspoken meaning behind our words. If she was any other woman, I'd be demanding proof - lab results, prescriptions, all of it. But this is Liz. She's not some random woman, and I'd trust her with my life.

She nods, and I let out a relieved breath before slamming my hips forward and driving into her. Our simultaneous moans say it better than words ever could. This. This is what Heaven feels like. Which is especially nice, considering it's likely the only Heaven I'll get the chance to experience.

I pull out slowly, savoring the feel of her fluttering around me, and press back into her just as slowly. I'm torturing us both, but it's exquisite. However, even I only have so much restraint. My pace picks up as I thrust until I'm pounding into her like a man possessed. But if I'm possessed, then we're heading to Hell together because she's matching my every move, pressing her ass back against me so hard I can feel the tip of my cock just barely grazing the edge of her cervix.

Fuck, she takes me so well. Reaching forward, I wrap a hand around her throat and pull her up to meet me, her back pressed against me as she shifts to a kneel, and I adjust my pace for this new angle. I leave my hand around her throat and squeeze just slightly with my thumb and middle finger, making sure to keep the edge of my palm off of her windpipe. This is purely about control right now. We can play with air restriction later if that's something she wants.

Turning her face to me, I capture her lips with mine, diving my tongue into her mouth in sync with the thrusts of my cock. My free hand slides down to her clit, setting a leisurely pace as I swirl around the swollen nub with just a hint of pressure. Her moan of satisfaction is muffled by my mouth, so I release her and bring her ear to my lips instead.

"I probably should have told you this before, but it's no secret that I'll play dirty when it's important," I purr. "You're mine now, Venom. Your brilliant mind, your glorious body, and most importantly, your very soul belong to me now. Mine to worship. Mine to protect. Mine to fuck into oblivion every night. *Mine.*"

The last part comes out as more of a growl with the force of my vehemence, but oh well. I'm not playing around, and it's best that she realizes that now. If she agrees to this, she's not just getting Vince, the playful businessman and mafioso. She's also getting my monster, the infamous Ice Demon, and I need to believe that she's prepared for that.

Turning her eyes back to mine, I study them carefully as I ask my next question. I need to know how she truly feels about what I've said and the claim I'm making.

"Any objections, Venom? Are you willing to give yourself over to me, demon and all?"

"My only objection is for lack of specificity," she says, her voice strained but determined.

Umm, okay. Not quite what I expected.

"I'm not sure if you meant your demon or mine, but it doesn't matter either way. You're welcome to mine anytime, and you forget that I'm already familiar with yours, and he doesn't scare me."

I'm still thrusting into her, our pace steady despite the weight of the conversation. She swirls her hips while her words sink in, and I hiss through my teeth, my grip on her throat tightening as my restraint wavers. She continues, a knowing smirk on her face.

"Also, you only outlined your half of the terms. I have my own claim

187

to stake. I'll be yours, Vincenzo Caputo, but you are *mine* in turn. Your mind, your body, and your soul are mine. Mine to challenge. Mine to satisfy. Mine to empower. *Mine.* And I will be just as vicious as your demon if that's what it takes to protect my claim."

Cazzo[27].

My last thread of control snaps at her words, and I practically roar my assent as I drive into her like a feral beast, increasing the pressure from my fingers. Her head drops back onto my shoulder, and she stops trying to match my movements. Her hand comes up to wrap around the back of my neck, and her fingers tangle in my hair. I can tell that she's getting close. Her breathing picks up speed, and she's whimpering needily with every thrust.

"That's it, Venom. Come for me. Come all over my dick. Mark me as yours."

That's all it takes to send her over the edge. She screams my name as she comes, and I barely stop myself from following her as she clenches and flutters around my cock. I wrap both arms around her chest as her body goes limp, peppering kisses along her jaw and praises in her ear.

"That was incredible."

Kiss.

"You're a goddess."

Kiss.

"You take me so well, Venom."

Kiss.

It takes her several minutes to come back to herself, and I hold her close to me the entire time. I'm still buried inside her, rigid cock twitching with every shift of her hips or deep breath she takes. But I can be patient. Besides, it's no hardship to hold her, to be her anchor while she drifts. It's more than I dared to hope for and far more than I

---

[27] Fuck

deserve.

Eventually, her heart rate steadies, and she turns her head to me, dragging a hand across my cheek to position my mouth for a long, lazy kiss. Slowly, she starts moving atop me once more, hips twisting and grinding as we savor one another. *This is the sweetest form of torture I've ever endured.* But I can't wait any longer. I break the kiss, nipping at her bottom lip when she whines in protest.

"Lie on your back, head on the pillows, and arms above your head."

She rises, and I growl at the loss of her, even though it's my own fault. She does as instructed, settling into position and fixing me with a come hither stare. I prowl towards her on all fours, nipping and laving my way up her legs to her stomach and finally reaching her face for another languid kiss. I settle the lower half of my weight over her, my hips nestled squarely between her legs. My hands trace her curves, her pebbled skin leaving visible evidence of their path.

"Now, keep those hands right where they are. Can you do that, or do you need some help?"

She shakes her head eagerly.

"I can do it."

"Excellent. I love the confidence, Venom. Let's see if it's warranted."

I know the challenge in my statement alone will be enough to have her hands glued to the top of the pillow for the rest of the night if necessary. She's always so determined to prove herself, even though she's already one of the most respected, and sometimes feared, people in any room she enters.

I grab hold of my cock and brush the head against her entrance, teasing her with slow strokes to make sure she's ready for me. She is. I slide easily into her and groan as I reach the hilt, deepening our kiss. While one arm braces most of my weight, the other is free to roam, eagerly finding a pert nipple and giving it a gentle pinch. Though restrained, Liz is still an active participant, writhing her hips and kissing me back with force as I pump into her steadily. It feels like she's trying to pull my entire body closer to her with just her lips, and I fucking love it.

I've never fucked a woman like this before. Sure, I'm not opposed to kissing during sex, but it's usually limited to foreplay. None of the women ever meant anything, so it didn't feel necessary to kiss them constantly, or hell, to even look them in the eyes while we fucked. If you'd asked me before tonight, I'd have said that doggy style and reverse cowgirl were my favorite positions. But now? With Liz?

This is addictive. I could do this for 12 hours a day and still complain that it wasn't enough time. It just feels like so much...more. *Fuck, I'm in so far over my head.* All I can do is pray to the God who long-ago disowned me that I don't fuck this up and hope that he still has some pity left to spare.

But never let it be said that I'm not doing my part. My pace increases steadily, spurred on by my own desperate need to fully claim her as my own, as well as her whimpered pleas. My free hand drops to the bed for support, and I break our kiss so that I can raise up for both better leverage and the distinct satisfaction of getting to watch as the pleasure I'm giving her is broadcast across her face. Her attention is rapt on me as well. I'm sure I'm broadcasting similar messages for her viewing pleasure.

I'm surprised I'm not seeing sparks, the way I'm pistoning in and out of her like a man possessed, my pelvis pressing hard against her clit with every thrust. Nonetheless, a fire is building. I feel the pull low in my stomach and know that I won't last much longer. Thankfully, Liz starts to pant louder, and her eyes drop shut periodically before snapping back open to lock with mine. I don't know if she's carried over my command from earlier or if she just doesn't want to miss a moment of what's happening, but it doesn't matter. She's perfection either way.

"Let go, Elizabeth. Come for me one last time, love. Then I'm going to fill you up and claim you as mine. You want that?"

"Holy shit, yes I want that. I want *exactly* that. Fuck. Vince!"

Her screams become unintelligible as I fuck her even faster, finding a secret reserve of strength that must have been hidden for just this moment. This orgasm is no less powerful than her first, and the pull of her inner walls along my cock sends me tumbling over the edge alongside her.

As we come down together, breathing hard, I notice my arms actually shaking. Whether from fatigue or adrenaline, I don't know, but the sight makes me laugh all the same.

"Holy fuck, woman. That was- I've never- Cazzo, you've destroyed me."

I collapse onto the bed on my side, being careful to land next to Liz instead of on top of her, and pull her into me. I may be spent, but I'm not ready to let her go just yet. She just smiles and stretches up to place a chaste kiss on my lips before snuggling her head into my shoulder. We stay like that for a long time, her tracing shapes on my chest with her fingers while I run mine up and down her spine.

I feel her starting to drift off and shift slightly so that I can get up for a second.

"Wait right here, love," I tell her with a kiss on her forehead.

Not bothering with clothes just yet, I head to the bathroom and return with a warm washcloth. I take my time running it along her legs and her cunt, cleaning her as best as I can, before returning to the bathroom to do the same for myself.

We'll both need a shower in the morning, but for now, this should do. I pad back over to the bed and pull at the blankets, freeing them from beneath her to lay them over the top of us both instead. Scooting into the middle of the bed, I pull her close to me again and press a final kiss to her temple.

"Sweet dreams, Venom."

Her answering murmur is too muffled to hear, but I smile anyway and settle in for the best night's sleep of my life.

Chapter 23

Elizabeth

The Next Morning

I wake up in a feverish sweat, my brain sluggishly rebooting to process the protests of my boiling body. *Ugh, what the heck? Has the AC gone out? Am I sick? I don't have time to be sick.*

But then the muscled arm across my waist flexes, and I'm shifted even further back against the human furnace behind me. *Vince.* I'm not suffering from faulty appliances. I've simply been claimed by a possessive, touch-starved, crime lord who generates enough body heat to warm the entire loft in the winter. Too bad it's only November and Houston still hasn't seemed to get the "winter chill" memo yet.

I try to gently slip out from under his arm, but even in sleep, Vince's reflexes are on high alert. His fingers grip my hip, and the hand that was under my pillow slides away as he rolls on top of me, pinning me firmly in place even as he braces his head on a bent arm and shoots me a lazy grin.

"Good morning, Venom. Where do you think you're off to so early?"

"Ideally? The freezer. I feel like I'm running at a thousand degrees sleeping next to you. Don't they call you the Ice Demon? Why do you feel like you're powered by pure hellfire?"

He chuckles, and his smile turns predatory, eyes raking over as much of my still-naked body as our position allows. Despite my discomfort, I catch my own eyes doing the same to him, lingering on his arms. I bite my lip, mostly to keep myself from drooling over the visible strength in his biceps. He may be lean, but he is most certainly not lacking in the muscles department. Though I suppose the way he so effortlessly manhandled me last night was already ample proof of that.

"Hmmm," he purrs, voice still gravelly from sleep. "I think you only have yourself to blame, Venom."

He leans closer, nose brushing up my jawline as he speaks, his tone low and measured.

"My temperature, like the rest of me, is typically very well regulated. But after last night, well...you've lit a flame that's never burned before, and now I need your help to release all this excess heat."

He reaches the top of my jaw and presses a slow kiss behind my ear, nuzzling my head to the side to give himself better access. His tongue darts out to tease the same spot, and electricity shoots down my spine, making my hips squirm. *Oh fuck.* He's barely touched me, and my body is already screaming for more of him.

He shifts his hips, and the head of his cock finds my entrance like a damn homing missile. He starts to move slowly, rubbing it up and down, teasing me but never pushing forward. It's not like I'm not ready. I've been wet for him since the moment he captured me beneath him, not that I'd admit that willingly. Gotta keep him humble and all.

I run my hands down his back, forcibly sidelining the rage I feel on his behalf at every stripe of raised skin. Raphael will pay for this, but not now. Right now, I have a much more *pressing* need. My hands reach his ass, and I wait until he's lined up perfectly before I pull suddenly. *Fuuuuuck.* His cock slides inside me, just a couple of inches, but it's enough to have me moaning loudly and winding my hips in hopes of drawing him deeper.

He huffs hot air against my neck and groans, the sound almost a whimper.

"Goddammit, Venom. You impatient little beast."

"Please, Vince," I beg shamelessly. "More. I need more of you."

"Oh, Venom," he purrs. "I'm not strong enough to refuse when you beg so sweetly. Especially not when it feels like this..."

He trails off as he slides deeper into me and starts to pump at a tortuously slow pace, his words turning to a low rumble while mine become an unintelligible chorus of "oh god," "yes," "fuck," and a slew of other encouraging moans. He's just started to pick up speed when I hear a soft "Mom? What's for breakfast?" and a light knock on the door.

Vince freezes in place above me, his wide-eyed shock echoing my thoughts exactly. I completely forgot that it's a school day. Hell, I completely forgot that Sam was even *home*.

"We're gonna pick up kolaches on the way, kiddo!" I call out desperately. "Mom overslept a bit, but I'll be out in a second!"

Sam yelps in excitement, and I breathe a sigh of relief as I hear him run toward the living room. Vince's brain finally reboots, and he rolls to the side, flopping back onto the bed dramatically.

"I feel like a kid who almost got caught sneaking treats in the middle of the night," he laughs. "Feel my heart. It's racing."

I smack him on the arm and roll out of bed, grabbing the nearest piece of clothing as a temporary nightgown while I go to get ready.

"And here I thought you said it was me who had that effect on you."

He clambers out of bed and makes it to my side in a few long strides. Wrapping me up from behind, he rests his head on mine and holds me tightly.

"Oh, Venom. You've turned me so fully inside out that I'm not sure I'll ever recover. Even now, seeing you wearing nothing but my t-shirt, my love marks peppering your skin, my scent mingling with yours on every inch of your body. God, it's enough to send me happily to Hell for the rest of eternity."

Jesus. He's always been a smooth talker, but damn, I'm not sure even a saint could resist the allure of his words. What's more, he says them with such ease, yet he sounds completely and utterly sincere. I never expected him to be so free and open with his feelings, especially given his overcautious nature and lack of intimate relationships in the past.

I turn around and kiss him slowly, infusing the words I'm not yet ready to say into his lips and hoping he's able to translate effectively. When I break away and step back, he releases me easily, a satisfied smirk on his face.

"Go get ready," he says. "I'll hide in here until you guys leave. I need to check in with the team anyway."

I nod and head toward the bathroom, doing my best to tame my haphazardly dried hair and calm my disappointed libido.

* * *

As I watch Sam debate the merits of blue versus red icing with the donut shop owner while he's placing his order, my mind finally crosses into the territory I've been avoiding ever since I realized I had feelings for Vince.

He and Damien may have been best friends, but the more I've gotten to know Vince, the more I've realized that they couldn't be much more different. I had real feelings for Damien. I know that to be true, and my feelings for Vince now don't negate that. But Damien was always so reserved. He never fully let me in, and I always felt like he was waiting for me to meet some invisible standard. It was just like I told Mono. Though I knew he cared for me, I felt like I had to prove myself worthy before he would truly respect me. Until then, I was just another asset to be managed.

Even when we had sex, he'd hold himself back. He was attentive and loving, but he was always so gentle, even when I encouraged him not to be. It's like no matter what I said or did, he couldn't believe that I was capable of holding my own, of possessing any true strength, figuratively or physically.

But *Vince*. I have never felt as sexy, strong, and valued as I did last night, or for the past several months of our working relationship, for that matter. Vince doesn't treat me as though I'm weak, something naive and breakable to protect. He sees me, all of me, and he treats me as something precious yet powerful, an equal who doesn't need to be coddled, who brings true value to him and his empire. When he was concerned for my safety, he trained me. When he saw me struggling emotionally, he challenged me. When we had sex, he wasn't afraid to be rough and domineering. He *fucked* me. And yet, it was the most intimate experience I've ever had. The entire thing has rocked me to my core.

Not for the first time, I think I may be in way over my head. But I don't care. This feels like it has the potential to be the best thing that's ever happened to me, and I will not sabotage this opportunity for myself.

Seeing that Sam has finally made his decision, landing on a blue-iced, guitar-shaped donut to go with his kolache, I step up to pay for our breakfast with an optimistic smile on my face.

* * *

I drop into my desk chair at Marchetti International and close my eyes for a moment. It's been a full morning of back-to-back meetings, which has been great for keeping my mind off of Vincenzo but not so great for calming my over-anxious mind. I always get a bit antsy when my to-do list grows at a faster rate than my accomplishments, but a few quiet moments and a fresh re-writing of said to-do list are usually enough to quell my nerves.

After I'm back on solid ground, I pull out the burner phone Vince gave

197

me to tackle the next item on my list. With our trip to Spain looming, it's time for me to take over all communications regarding the operation and negotiations with the Colombo family. I dial and wait, anticipation in my veins, as the call connects.

"Dígame[28]," a male voice answers.

"Andre, my name is Olivia Maizen. I am Mr. Destino's head of operations and will be speaking for Mr. Destino from here forward."

"Yes, of course. Mr. Destino told me to expect your call. What can I do for you, Ms. Maizen?"

After confirming that everything is ready for our arrival and that I'll be able to meet with Raphael's representative in person soon after, I hang up and lean back to run through the details in my head again. I'm fully confident in my ability to handle the negotiations with the Colombo team members, but I'm still not as confident in my ability to hide my emotions when I finally come face to face with Raphael himself. I'm hoping that thinking through all possible scenarios and imagining my cool-headed reaction to each of them will pay off when the real moment comes.

* * *

When I step out of the elevator into the front hallway that evening, I'm surprised to hear dual male voices shouting excitedly in the living room. I turn the corner to see Vince and Sam, controllers in hand, deep into a racing game. The sitter walks over from the kitchen, brushing her hands off on a towel.

"Welcome back, Ms. Greystone. Sam's finished all of his homework and he ate a small snack about an hour ago to hold him over until dinner. Mr. Caputo arrived about 30 minutes ago. He mentioned that you had a

---

[28] "Tell me" - common phone greeting in Spain

198

meeting later tonight, but since he was already in the area he stopped by early with dinner. It's keeping warm in the oven. Do you need anything else before I leave?"

I shake my head and thank her, my attention still fixated on the boys. Sam is whooping and dancing around, while Vince has his head thrown back on the sofa in apparent defeat. He catches my gaze and smiles, shooting me a wink. He rises and gets Sam to shut down the console with nary a whine, ushering him into the kitchen to wash his hands before dinner.

"You're going to have to tell me how you did that," I say as he sidles up to me, hands in his trouser pockets. "I swear, it's always a battle when screen time is over if I'm the one delivering the message."

Vince preens and steps closer to me, his chest brushing against my arm as he leans in.

"What can I say? My natural charisma knows no bounds."

"Right... So you bribed him?"

His smile turns sheepish, and his head drops for a second before he rocks back on his heels.

"I may have promised him a knife-throwing lesson when we're back from Spain."

I smack his arm, but there's no strength behind it. I trust Vince not to cross the line between potentially useful life skills and heir-to-the-criminal-empire training. I join Sam at the sink to wash up for dinner and soon we're all seated around the dining table while Sam gives us a detailed rundown of the drama unfolding between his tablemates at lunch.

Chapter 24

Vincenzo

Several Days Later

We land in Madrid around midday, having opted for the red-eye the night before since neither one of us wanted to waste 13 waking hours in the air. Andre sent through everything we'll need to get into the villa, but couldn't risk his cover to see us there directly, so I hire a car at the airport.

I'm traveling incognito, entering the country as Lucien Destino, thanks to Mono's vast digital network of "friends." Thankfully, keeping a low profile is easier than ever now that face masks are so commonplace, so I only have to don the facial prosthetics and mask I've brought along to pass through customs. Even after such a short wear, it still feels incredible to rip them off as soon as we're sequestered inside the tinted back seat of the town car.

"Ugh, I am not looking forward to having to wear those for an entire night," I whine.

Liz shoots me a sympathetic look but reminds me to think of the dramatic impact when I finally remove them in front of Raphael. It works. I'd withstand far more discomfort for that kind of satisfaction.

As we pull up to the villa, I'm even more impressed by the work Andre has done to select and set up our temporary base of operations. Well, I suppose not so temporary in the long run. Though our primary mission to avenge Damien by getting rid of Raphael should only take a couple of weeks, Adrian Nuñez and I have decided to make a solid run at distributing the Salteros' product through the Valencia docks. This villa, and the one in Valencia, will serve as barracks of sorts for the fledgling crew I'll be working to build once Raphael is out of the picture.

Elizabeth echoes my sentiments as she oohs and ahhs over everything, from the layout to the security system to the built-in amenities. After a quick call to Mono to check that he's able to access everything in the system, I wander through the halls until I find her lounging in the sunroom. Or maybe it's more of a greenhouse. Citrus trees and a variety of flowers fill the windowed space, creating a tranquil retreat to unwind. That's exactly what Liz is doing, laid out across the wicker sectional with one arm slung over her eyes to block out the afternoon sun.

I pluck an orange off the nearest tree and peel it as I make my way to her. She doesn't acknowledge me, but I can tell by the stillness in her posture that she knows I'm here. That's fine by me. I enjoy the feeling of reward I get when she ultimately surrenders to my bids for her attention. I take a seat next to her head and pull a piece of the ripe fruit away, setting the rest down on the coffee table.

I take a small bite to break through the skin, then run the dripping fruit softly across her lips. She opens her mouth slightly, just enough to let the juice run inside, and hums appreciatively.

"Mmm, that may be the most delicious thing I've ever tasted. Or maybe I'm just hungry."

She captures the rest of the fruit with her mouth, dragging her lips around my fingers purposely, and drops her arm, teal eyes shining up at me like precious gems. My heart stutters, still coming to terms with the fact that the goddess laid out beneath me actually wants me nearly as much as I want her. *God, I hope I never wake up from this dream.*

"Is that so?" I tease. "Well, now I need another taste. I'm not sure if that's possible."

I kiss her, taking my time to savor the taste of both the fruit and her natural sweetness. Her hand winds around the back of my neck, and her fingers begin to play in my hair. The longer we kiss, the hungrier we both become. I'm devouring her, and she's matching me move for move, the world's most perfect partner in the dance our lips and tongues have started. I lose myself in her mouth for several minutes, but eventually, my need for more of her builds to a high enough level that it demands release.

"Hmm," I hum thoughtfully as I pull away. "It is delicious, but I can think of one thing that tastes better."

Her gaze meets mine, and I let my eyes communicate my intent as I rise and move to the other end of the sofa, sitting near her feet and leaning over her to run my hands across her splayed form. As they slide back down, I hook my fingers beneath the waistband of her lounge pants and pull them down her legs along with her underwear.

She's watching my every move intently, though the only sound is the steadily increasing speed of her breathing. I reach over to grab the rest of the orange and break off a larger chunk of several pieces. Spreading her knees with a gentle hand, my other grabs the fruit and squeezes, juice running through my fingers and down onto her cunt.

Elizabeth gasps lightly and bites her lip, already anticipating my next moves. Never one to disappoint, but also determined to savor the delicacy I've prepared for myself, I slowly kiss and lick my way down her outer leg from knee to thigh until my lips are just barely hovering above the point where her leg meets her hip.

I look up at her through dark, hooded eyes, letting my breath blow across her sensitive flesh. She's so fucking beautiful, panting and desperate for me, her gaze begging me to feast on her like the ravenous beast that I am.

I take a long, slow lick through that sensitive juncture, relishing the feel of her trembling beneath me as much as I do the taste of citrus and sex. Wanting to hear her moan my name, I aim my next lick straight up her center, dipping my tongue just barely inside her as I travel toward her clit.

"*Fuck*, Vincenzo. Oh my god."

That's the sweetest fucking sound I've ever heard.

"That's right, baby. I'll be your god as long as I get to worship you as my goddess."

And worship I do. Shifting my position, I brace my elbows on the sofa and grip her ass with both hands, holding her perfect cunt in just the right spot as I lick, suck, and nip at her sensitive flesh until she's lost the ability to form actual words. Sliding two fingers into her, I curl them repeatedly against her and send her crashing over the edge, my mouth and tongue lapping up every last drop of pleasure.

"Now *that*," I say with certainty once her breathing calms, "is the best thing I've ever tasted."

She laughs and weakly throws a pillow at me. I chuckle alongside her, feeling rather pleased with myself. It's nice, just sitting in the afterglow of a woman well pleased and knowing that I had everything to do with it. But then I remember her earlier comment about being hungry and decide that it's only fair I feed her now that I've eaten so well.

As I stand up, I feel my phone vibrate and take it out of my pocket to see a series of text messages from Mono. I bark out a laugh as I read them, finding a sick sort of amusement in his discomfort.

> Mono: Hey asshole, next time you ask me to do a thorough review of the security system, maybe don't immediately go and fuck your woman in FULL VIEW OF SAID CAMERAS.

Mono: You're lucky I have fast reflexes or you'd have to choose between finding a new code monkey or living with the knowledge that I know what she looks like naked.

Mono: Also, congratulations you insufferable bastard. Just remember, I fucking called it. Don't fuck this up.

I just send back a sly-faced emoji and pocket my phone to head toward the kitchen. I have a goddess to feed, after all.

* * *

That night, we're lying together in bed, talking through the plan for tomorrow one final time. I know Liz has everything memorized and fully under control, but I'm still anxious. I'm not used to sitting on the sidelines, especially not while my woman walks directly into enemy territory without even a way to call for backup if something goes wrong.

I do my best to tamp down my fears and lock them away. Realistically, this isn't even a high-risk meeting. It's simply a formal introduction of Liz as my emissary and a way to open the door for further negotiations between our two organizations. It's a formality. And yet...

Thankfully, Liz doesn't seem to take my concern for doubt in her abilities. She indulges me with a thorough review of not only her ideal scenario but several alternative courses and methods of diversion if things begin to go off track. She's thought of everything, and I'm reminded again of just how brilliant she truly is. It's a shame we'd never met until now. Just imagine where the Marchetti empire could be if she'd been with us from the beginning.

Though, actually, that re-opens the possibility that she may have once again chosen Damien from the beginning, and I'd never have gotten the chance to feel...whatever this is that I feel for her and from her. Love? Acceptance? Completion? Some wild combination of all three? Ugh, I'm a selfish fucking bastard for the thoughts running through my head now. Let's not even entertain the debate of whether I'd rather have Damien back or keep Liz as she is now. Because honestly, the answer is likely to make me even more of a monster than I already am.

She kisses me then, bringing me back to reality, her eyes searching mine knowingly. I see an idea spark, and then she drops a promise that quickly shifts my thoughts from concern to anticipation for tomorrow's meeting.

"Tomorrow night, when I get back from showing the Colombo family just who they're dealing with, I'm going to kneel in front of you and suck your cock while you tell me what a good job I've done."

My jaw drops open, and I stare at her with wide eyes.

"Holy fuck, Venom. You are... I can't... How am I supposed to sleep now that I have that image in my head?"

She just smirks and presses another kiss to my cheek. I'm furiously debating options in my head and wondering if she's serious about going to sleep right now or if I could get away with fucking her into the mattress when her fingertips graze over my aching cock, making it jump.

"Well, I suppose quality sleep is important for peak performance. How about you come over here and finish what you started in the greenhouse?"

"Oh, thank fuck," I groan.

I flip her beneath me in an instant and spend the next hour worshipping her so thoroughly that we both fall into a dreamless sleep mere moments after the last aftershock rocks through our bodies.

Chapter 25

Elizabeth

The Following Evening

I drive myself to the meeting in one of Vince's cars. I'm dressed in the traditional armor of high-powered business meetings: dark slacks, a royal blue long-sleeved blouse, a matching waistcoat, and a pair of insanely expensive heels Vince gifted me. I'm carrying a simple bag with only two copies of the distribution agreement, a few business cards with my fake name and burner number, and some touch-up cosmetics for show.

The pistol I selected from Vince's armory will have to stay in the car along with my phone. No weapons or electronic devices was one of the stipulations of the meeting tonight. It's a bit one-sided, considering the Colombo family controls the restaurant we're meeting at, and it's likely chock-full of armed soldiers. But I'm not phased. I feel powerful, ferocious, and ready to prove I can hold my own in this dark, twisted underworld that Vince calls home.

I walk into the main entrance with my head held high and greet the hostess warmly.

"Olivia Maizen. Mr. Casuelo is expecting me."

The girl's eyes widen slightly. Maybe she's not used to seeing female representatives dealing with the Colombo men. Whatever the reason, she quickly recovers and gestures for me to follow her. We first pass by a security guard who inspects my bag and scans me with a metal wand. At his nod of approval, the hostess leads me to a private room in the back and knocks twice before opening the door.

"Ms. Maizen to see you, sir."

She motions me into the room and dips her head as she closes the door, leaving me alone with Christian Casuelo, one of Raphael's generals and the man Andre has been pretending to work for over the past several months. I make a quick assessment of the man before me. I've studied his photos before, thanks to Mono's intel, but he seems different in person. Maybe it's the aura he's giving off. It's a bit more annoyed bear and less cunning wolf than I expected. He's leaned back in his chair, one hand slung over the armrest and the other drumming on the tabletop. He doesn't stand right away, focused on looking me up and down first. He also doesn't bother to hide his sneer as he reaches my chest, and I resist the urge to roll my eyes. *This guy's going to be a fucking delight to work with, I can already tell.*

Done with his visual catalog, he finally stands and offers me his hand.

"Christian Casuelo. It's nice to finally meet you, Ms. Maizen. I've been intrigued by you and Mr. Destino ever since Andre brought you to my attention."

I shake his hand firmly but am careful not to show off too much. I want him to keep whatever prejudices he has about women being the weaker sex for now.

"Please, call me Olivia. I'm just as eager as you are. The Colombo family has been on Mr. Destino's radar for quite some time. You're very well-respected in the area, so it only made sense that you would be our first choice when looking to expand our distribution."

He sneers again, clearly buying my flattery and gently submissive demeanor. *God, why are they so fucking predictable? Aren't these men supposed to be abnormally cunning? Or are Vince and Damien just the exceptions to the rule?*

"Have a seat, Olivia," he gestures to the chair across from him. "And you can call me Christian. We may as well drop the formalities if we're about to be business partners, right?"

"My thoughts exactly."

I smile and sit in the indicated chair, sliding the proposals and a business card from my bag before placing it on the floor near my feet. I push the business card across the table to Christian with a demure smile.

"This is my direct contact information, just in case Andre hasn't shared it with you yet. We consider you a very important client. I'll be available any time to discuss the particulars of the deal."

He pockets the card and shoots me another leering grin. I suppress a shudder and keep my smile plastered on my face, sending over a copy of the proposal next.

As we dive into discussions of the proposed agreement, it's clear that Andre has been the one driving this until now. Christian seems to be reading over the proposal for the first time, reacting off the cuff to the numbers and timelines that his own team suggested. I agree to most of his requests, making a show of hesitating on several before agreeing to keep up the ruse and holding a firm line on the frequency of shipments. Even though I know that none of this actually matters, I can't have him thinking that I'm a complete pushover.

Eventually, he closes the folder and looks at me expectantly. I brace myself for whatever's coming next, certain I'll need my poker face more than ever.

"It's been a pleasure, Olivia. I'm sure this will be a long and *fruitful* partnership. Perhaps our next meeting can be of a more social nature. Estarías preciosa con mi collar alrededor del cuello[29]."

I'm not sure how to translate the second part of his comment, but

---

[29] You'll find out in Chapter 26 ;)

I can guess enough to know it'll probably make me want to knock his teeth out. I stand, hiding my assumptions behind a polite smile before thanking him for his time and promising to be back in touch after I've discussed the remaining points with Mr. Destino. At his agreement, I give a final nod of farewell and turn to leave.

I repeat the phrase in my head as I walk back to the car, aiming to commit it to memory so that I can look it up once I'm back home. With a quick text to Vince that I'm on my way, I put the car in drive and head back to the villa.

Chapter 26

Elizabeth

Later That Night

"Describe the room," Mono says. "Did you see any cameras?"

I think back and shake my head. I'm at the villa with Vince, and we've dialed in Mono for my official mission debrief.

"No, no cameras. It was just a normal-looking, private dining room. There was an oval table with seating for six. Oh, and a red velvet curtain along the wall facing the door."

Mono perks up at that, tapping his cheek in thought.

"Hmm, shitty design choice or concealment for a window or surveillance system?"

"Judging by the way the rest of the place was decorated, I'd vote for shitty design choice, but maybe that's the whole point," I tell him. "Though it doesn't even matter unless the next meeting is at the same location, and I'm pretty sure it won't be."

"How can you be so sure?" Vince asks, leaning forward and resting his elbows on his knees.

"If all goes well, I can handle the rest of the minutia with Casuelo over the phone. My next in-person meeting should be with Raphael himself, and he's never taken a meeting at that location before. He seems to prefer La Dolce in Valencia instead. We've only got limited time, so that's where we should focus our attention."

Mono shoots me a thumbs up over the video screen, and I catch a glint of pride in Vince's gaze. He nods and looks over to the webcam. "Alright, monkey boy, you heard the boss lady. Find out everything we'll need to know about La Dolce in the next 48 hours. I don't expect it'll take much longer than that to nail down the final details and set a meeting, assuming the actual meeting tonight went as expected?"

He directs the final question to me, and I nod.

"More or less. Casuelo wasn't quite what I expected, but the only major detail left to nail down is the price. I purposely didn't agree to anything tonight for the show of it, but since we aren't going through with this, we can pretend to concede in a day or so."

"On it, boss, er, *bosses*," Mono quips with a smirk.

I preen and take my promotion in stride. My ego likes a good stroking every now and again just as much as anyone's. Vince just chuckles and redirects us back to the briefing.

"What did you mean, Venom, that Casuelo wasn't quite what you expected?"

"I just thought he'd be more...shrewd?" I tell him. "I mean, having met your generals, I guess I was expecting someone like them. They're all so refined, their reactions controlled, and they know every inch of their business, down to the last comma."

"And Casuelo wasn't quite up to snuff?" Vince asks with a smirk, clearly pleased by my assessment of his generals being superior to Raphael's.

"No, not even close. For one, it seemed like he hadn't even read the proposal until tonight when I set it in front of him. I'm guessing Andre handled everything, and Casuelo just couldn't be bothered."

Vince and Mono scoff in unison, and I suppress a smirk. They really do act like brothers sometimes. It's endearing.

"Was that it?" Mono asks, picking up the line of questioning from Vince.

"Yeah, that's the gist of it. I mean, he was still a total creep, but that wasn't wholly unexpected."

"Are we talking sexual predator creep or just disrespectful asshole creep?"

Mono asks the question, but I see Vince go still from the corner of my eye as he waits for my answer. I scrunch my nose and try to think of how best to describe him so that they have an accurate picture without setting off Vince's protective side.

"Mmm, I'd say three parts of the second and one part of the first. He was obvious with his leering when I arrived, but he didn't try to touch me or anything like that. He did very easily buy into the idea that I was there to pander to him as a mere messenger instead of a true decision-maker. He kept calling me sweetheart and saying how hard it must have been for me to put all this together with this fake ass smile like he thought I was a total bimbo."

I snarl at the memory, before remembering the last thing he said to me.

"Oh! As I was standing up to leave, he told me that he hoped our next meeting would be of a more social nature. Then he said something in Spanish that I didn't understand, but I got the idea that it was maybe more towards creepy type one."

"Do you remember what he said? Even a close approximation?"

"Of course. I kept repeating it in my head so I could look it up later, but I just haven't had a chance yet. It was 'Estarías preciosa con mi collar alrededor del cuello.'"

I'm pretty sure my pronunciation is off, but Mono and Vince both seem to catch the meaning anyway. I see their gazes shoot to one another before focusing back on me.

Vince's voice is dark, low, and extremely controlled when he speaks, and I know at that moment that Casuelo's just dug his own grave.

"Repeat that for me, love?"

CHAPTER 26

I clear my throat and try again.

"Estarías preciosa con mi collar alrededor del cuello...?"

It comes out as more of a question this time, not because I'm not sure of the phrase, but because I'm certain that hearing it again is going to send Vince into a murderous rage.

"Well, look at the time. I think I have everything I need. Vince, buddy, call me if you need backup, and Liz, excellent work. We'll make a mafiosa out of you yet."

Mono shoots Vince a final concerned look and logs off without waiting for a reply. I raise my eyes to Vince's and ask the burning question, my curiosity outweighing my desire to quell the icy storm swirling in his gaze.

"It means," Vince grits through his teeth, "you'd look beautiful with my collar around your neck."

Oh shit. That bastard really is an idiot.

I get up and walk to stand in front of Vince's chair, raising his eyes to mine with a gentle finger.

"I'm fine. He's an asshole, but it's just bluster. He probably just gets off on the idea of being dominant, but from what I saw tonight, he's too lazy and dimwitted to do anything about it."

Vince rises from his seat then, hands coming up to cup my face as he steps into me.

"I don't care if he's a fucking quadriplegic. The mere fact that he thought of you that way at all, combined with the audacity to disrespect you by saying it to your face? I can't let that go, Venom. I mean, what if you read him wrong? What if he was putting on an act just the same as you? What if he had attacked you before you could leave? What if he was holding you captive in that restaurant right now with a fucking collar around your neck as he..."

His grip on my face is rigid, and his eyes clench shut as his words trail off. He's spiraling, concern for me making him lose his grip on

213

the cold and calculating demeanor he's so well known for. I do the only thing I can think of to break him out of it, to help him regain a sense of control over things, over me and my safety. I drop to my knees in front of him, hands on my lap, and look up with an open gaze.

My sudden movement snaps Vince out of his spiral, just as I'd hoped. His eyes shoot open and lock onto mine, questions and desires swirling within them. I keep my eyes on his as I make my intentions crystal clear.

"I've completed my mission, Sir. I'm reporting for my reward, as it was promised."

I watch his pupils blow out in real time as he realizes that I'm serious. *Did he honestly think I wasn't going to make good on my promise from last night? Well, this will teach him to doubt my word.*

His voice is rough when he speaks, and he has to clear his throat midway.

"You're ready for your reward, love?" Cough. "And what exactly would you like as a reward for doing so well?"

He runs a hand across my head and down to my cheek, cupping my face gently.

"Whatever you deem appropriate, Sir. I am at your command."

He sucks in a sharp breath, and his hand slides down toward my chin, gripping it firmly as he traps my gaze in place.

"Venom, what you're asking for..."

"I want it," I assert quickly. "I'm yours. And *you* are my reward. I need you. All of you. Don't hold back from me."

A fire lights in his eyes at my insistence, full of heat and promise that fully removes any lingering ice from his earlier rage. His hand moves from my chin to my throat, and he squeezes gently.

"Very well, love. I'll show you what it means to be truly at my command. But I warn you now, I don't have it in me to restrain myself tonight. If you agree to this, you'll need to be prepared for how rough it may get. Is this still what you want?"

I try to nod, but his grip on my throat prevents me from moving, so I manage to croak out a determined "yes" from my lust-fogged lungs. A dark smile crosses his face then, and I feel it straight to my core. *My attraction to terrifying men should be in a textbook somewhere.* He removes his hand to run a thumb along my lips, pulling away when I open them to invite him in. I pout, but he only chuckles.

"Excellent. Then listen closely. From this moment on, you do exactly as I say. Without question. Without hesitation. You place your trust in me, fully. Is that clear?"

I nod without breaking eye contact. Suddenly, his hand is in my hair, pulling my head back to look at him as he leans over me. My breathing speeds up, adrenaline rushing through my veins at the unexpected roughness in his grip, but I find myself only wanting more.

"Good girl. Here's your first rule. Don't ever nod at me again, not while we're like this. You will use your words, even if it's a simple yes or no. Understand?"

"Yes," I breathe the word, eager to please him and find out what he'll do next.

"Well done, but now it's time for the second rule. You will call me Sir, and you will use my title in every response, no matter how short. The only time you may call me something other than Sir is when you're screaming my name as you come. Am I clear?"

"Yes, Sir."

His answering smile is even darker, almost sadistic, and I shiver in response.

"You're doing so well already, love. Now the third rule is a big one. You will only speak or move when prompted by me. Unless I ask you a question, your mouth is for my use only. Unless I give you a command, your body is at my mercy. You don't even *swallow* without my permission. Do you understand?"

"Yes, Sir."

He groans at that, releasing my hair to trail his fingers down my jaw again.

"God, you have no idea what it does to me to hear you agree so willingly. You're intoxicating, Elizabeth. Are you ready for the final rule?"

I gulp, struggling to speak through the thick anticipation in my throat.

"Yes, Sir."

"Good girl. Listen closely because this is the most important rule of all. If ever things get to be too much, you are to yell 'red' immediately. If you say this, we are done for the night. I will stop right away and do whatever I can to take care of you. If your mouth is full, tap three times on any part of my body, and I will interpret it the same way. But be warned that I am dead serious when I say this..."

He trails off, his hand returning to my throat with a heavier grip as he pulls my face up closer to his own. His gaze is stony, his eyes penetrating as he continues.

"If you ever fail to use your word or signal when you need it, out of disregard for your well-being, we will never do this again. You are putting an incredible amount of trust in me, and I have to be able to trust you to stop things before they go too far with just as much certainty. Do you understand?"

"Yes, Sir," I say.

"Do you agree to all of these terms, knowing that punishment will be dealt swiftly for any infractions?"

"Yes, Sir. I agree."

He blows out a long breath and raises his eyes to the ceiling as if he hadn't been sure that I would agree. *As if.* This is the most thrilling thing I've ever experienced, and we haven't even started yet. I gasp when his eyes return to mine. They've grown somehow even darker, his expression hard and borderline terrifying. It's my first split-second glimpse of the man they call the Ice Demon, though his demeanor is still far warmer than I'm guessing is standard when he normally comes out to play. It's the sexiest fucking way he's ever looked at me. He smirks sadistically as he issues the first command, watching me closely.

"Open your mouth."

I shudder at his dark, possessive tone and obey immediately, lowering my jaw as far as I comfortably can.

"Good girl," he purrs, tightening his grip on my throat ever so slightly. I resist the urge to press my thighs together, my Type A personality still fully in control and demanding I follow his rules to a T.

"Now, stick out your tongue for me."

I comply and wait to see what he'll do next, anticipation thrumming through my veins as I try to guess for myself. Vince trails his hand up from my throat, bringing his thumb just beside my ear before trailing it down along my jawline toward my waiting mouth. He runs his thumb from the tip of my tongue back toward my throat, stopping midway. His remaining fingers grip the side of my jaw firmly.

"*Suck.*"

The authority in his voice is unmistakable and sexy as fuck. I close my lips around his thumb and suck, long and hard. My tongue swirls along the underside of his finger, and I feel a rush of feminine satisfaction when he groans. His reaction spurs me on, and I put everything I have into this simple act of foreplay, suddenly desperate to draw another moan from his lips. I look up at him and find his piercing gaze locked on my mouth, though his eyes find mine the moment he notices my attention.

"Venom, you're doing so fucking well. Look at the effect you're having on me with nothing more than my thumb in your mouth."

His free hand moves to palm his cock, the hard outline clear against his light grey slacks. I watch him and feel myself subconsciously suck even harder at the sight. He notices, of course he does, and he growls in response.

"Do you like that, Venom? Does it turn you on to see what you do to me? How badly I want you?"

I nod, my mouth still focused on teasing his thumb, but realize my mistake too late. His hand is in my hair in an instant, jerking my head back as his thumb leaves my mouth with a pop. He crouches low, his face only inches from mine, as he leans over me.

"Have you forgotten your rules already, Venom?"

"No, Sir," I say quickly, but he seems dissatisfied with that answer, his grip on my hair tightening even further. "It was just a momentary lapse, Sir. It won't happen again."

"I hope for your sake that's true, love. If not, your next punishment will be much more thorough than some pulled hair."

"Yes, Sir. I understand."

I look up at him, eager to pick back up where we left off, but he has other plans. He stands back up, the hand in my hair adjusting my gaze forward, but otherwise holding me in place. I'm eye level with his abs, and I watch the muscles flex beneath his white dress shirt as he moves his free hand to the buttons on it, popping them open one at a time until it's hanging loosely on his shoulders, his defined waist on clear display. I lick my lips and he smirks, moving a hand to his slacks.

He releases the outer buttons with practiced ease, even though his dominant hand is otherwise occupied, and frees the inner button just as quickly. He slides the zipper down slowly, then pauses. I swallow down my impatience, knowing that if I reach for him now, I'll only prolong the time it takes to finally get what I want.

"Kiss me, Venom."

I look up at him as best I can, expecting him to pull me to my feet, but when his hand presses my head forward instead, I realize what he actually meant. I place an open-mouthed kiss against his rigid cock, the taste of his zipper metallic on my tongue. He holds my head in place, so I continue to kiss him through his clothing, obedient but frustrated at the way he's teasing me.

"That's a good girl," he says after a while. "You can take my pants off now. *Only* my pants."

I move my hands to his waistband and pull down, discarding the slacks on the floor beside us once he steps free. I lean back and take in the way his cock is straining against the fall of his black boxer briefs before redirecting my gaze to him.

"Kiss me again, from base to tip."

I suppress a growl and lean my head down, tilting to the side to do as he's instructed. I kiss my way slowly and deliberately up his cock, lingering when I get to the head. His hand in my hair is kneading my scalp and pulling ever so slightly at my strands while I work. I get the impression that he's just as eager as I am to be past this toying stage, but some part of him is clearly enjoying the experience of me obeying him so readily, despite my frustration.

"Well done, Venom. Take them off. You've earned a reward."

I move quickly to free him, discarding his underwear in the vague direction of his pants. He removes his shirt while I work, leaving him fully naked in front of me. I bite my lip as his cock bounces in front of my face, hard and thick from our foreplay.

"Open your mouth again. Tongue out."

I moan as he slides his head over the tip of my waiting tongue and into my mouth. *Finally.* In my relief, I almost close my lips around him but stop just in time, realizing he hasn't given another command yet.

"Oh, that was a close one, Venom," he purrs threateningly. "It would have been a shame to lose your privileges when you've finally gotten so close."

I remain still, eyes focused on him as I wait to be released. His eyes are clear, confident, and borderline vicious, and his confidence reaffirms my own. He may be in control right now, but I take my own pleasure in knowing that I'm likely the only woman alive who could successfully handle the Marchetti family Ice Demon.

He slides himself over my tongue several times, his attitude that of a man out for a leisurely stroll. A low snarl escapes from the back of my throat, my impatience reaching a new peak.

A murmured, "Oh, really?" is the only warning I get before Vince pushes my head forward at the same time as he thrusts his hips, his cock reaching the back of my throat in a single fluid motion. I fight through my gag reflex, eyes watering, as he watches me through lidded eyes.

"Growl at me again, Venom."

It takes me a second to catch my breath, but after a deep inhale through my nose, I growl again, this one more feral than the last. His challenge has awakened my bratty side. *We can't let him forget who he's dealing with, after all.* My throat flutters around him, and I claim victory at the way his head lolls back as he bites out a curse.

"*Cazzo*[30]! You vicious beast," he groans. "Suck my cock, Veleno[31], while I tell you how filthy and dangerous you are."

I close my lips and begin to work him with gusto, his hand in my hair relaxing just enough to give me better range of motion along his length. I swirl my tongue along the underside of him, taking note of every reaction as I learn what he likes best. He begins a steady stream of vulgar praises, both for my current actions and for my performance earlier tonight.

"You're so fucking fearless, Venom. It's like you have no goddamn self-preservation instincts when you're so willing to jump into the snake pit alongside me. It terrifies me and thrills me all at the same

[30] Fuck

[31] Venom

time."

I bring a hand up to grip the base of him as I free my mouth and swirl my tongue around his leaking head. His grip on my hair tightens again, but he lets me continue to lead.

"God fucking dammit, and your mouth..." He's practically panting. "Whether you're using it as a window into your brilliant mind or showing me just how much of a slut you are for my cock, I can't get enough of it either way. *Fuuuckkk...*"

He presses forward again, and this time he takes over more fully, holding my head in place as he thrusts into my mouth at a steady pace. I'm able to keep up at first, but the longer he goes, the faster and deeper his thrusts become until I can barely breathe in between. Both of my hands come to his thighs to brace myself further, and I grip tightly.

"But you know my favorite thing about you, mia Veleno[32]?" His question seeps out through gritted teeth, his expression wild. "It's your godforsaken stubbornness. You never back down. You decided that I was worth your time, your attention, and even your affection. And it's like that was fucking that. You've never once flinched at how fucked up this world is, how depraved or sadistic I can be. Hell, I'm starting to think you *prefer* it..."

My grip on his thighs is so tight I'm sure that my fingernails are cutting into his skin, but neither one of us is willing to stop. With anyone else, I'd probably have tapped out by now. But hearing his words and being reminded of the way he sees me only makes me want to give him more, to *be* more for him. I let out another growl, this one in appreciation for how powerful he makes me feel, and it's enough to send him over the edge.

He roars, calling out my name like a plea and telling me to swallow every drop as his release shoots down my throat. I guide him through it

---

[32] my Venom

with my mouth, slowly and gently, until his cock finally stops pulsing.

When he comes back to himself, body shaking and fully spent, he places his hand on either side of my face and gently guides me off of him and to a standing position. One arm wraps around me to support my weight, my legs weak after so long on the floor. The other hand cups my jaw, his thumb running across my cheek as he pierces me with his honeyed gaze.

"And *that*, Venom, everything I just described and everything you just did? That's how I know Raphael doesn't stand a chance. You've set your sights on him. You are cunning, strong, and capable, and with both of our skill sets combined, nothing in this world can stop us from taking that bastard down."

I smile, my heart soaring, and he kisses me deeply for a long while. *I have never loved anyone as fiercely as I love this man.* The thought surprises me, but I don't shy away from it. Nor do I let guilt steal the beauty of what I'm feeling. It doesn't matter what happened to bring Vince and me together. There's nothing either of us can do to change it, and feeling guilty isn't going to redeem us from our VIP status in Hell, anyway. I just kiss him back and bask in the euphoria of being truly known and loved for who I am and having the opportunity to do the same in return.

Eventually, I feel goosebumps start to form on his skin, and I break away, prompting him to get dressed. I head toward the kitchen to rummage for a midnight snack, and as I return, I catch him on the phone with Mono.

"Two things, brother. First, export the last half hour of surveillance video from the living room and send me the encrypted file. Second, wipe it from the server once you've sent it my way. And don't you *dare* fucking open it, or I'll gouge your eyes out myself."

He chuckles at whatever Mono says in reply, then hangs up without so much as a goodbye. I continue into the room, arching a brow in his

review for an exact count, but it looks like maybe 20 or so, at least in this group."

I pinch the bridge of my nose, trying to breathe deeply. I feel like my demon is trying to physically break through my skin, ready to find Raphael right this instant and beat the ever-loving shit out of him. It takes me several long moments to bring myself under control. That would never work. I wouldn't get within 20 feet of him. No. I'll have my chance in a few more days. I just need to be patient.

"Alright. Try to figure out the pattern and when they're likely to bring in the next group. Hopefully, it's not before we've met with Raphael, but even if it is, those women do not leave this port. Am I clear?"

"As crystal, boss. I'll report back the moment I know more."

I turn to look around the rest of the warehouse. There are more shipping containers in a similar state, but I pause when I see a large wooden crate at the end of the row. Inside the crate, I find thousands of syringes, each filled with a clear substance. I'm willing to bet these are tranquilizers, but I pocket a few so I can have them tested. Plus, maybe I can make use of this with Raphael and give him a literal taste of his own medicine.

In the meantime, I can't leave this here for these assholes. I call Andre and give him instructions to have all of these replaced with identical saline syringes by tomorrow afternoon. Once I'm convinced there are no other fun surprises for me to find, I put everything back the way it was and head up to the roof. There's only one thing besides watching Raphael bleed out in front of me that can calm the storm that's raging through my veins, and she's only a few miles away, probably curled up on the couch watching some cheesy telenovela[33] at this very moment.

---

[33] soap opera

Chapter 28

Elizabeth

The Following Night

As I step out of the car in front of La Dolce, I marvel for a moment at just how much my life has changed in the last 12 months. At this time last year, I was probably in my pajamas, replacing fake monsters and pumpkins with Christmas lights on the balcony of the cheap, two-bedroom apartment that I rented for Sam and me after my divorce. Now I'm wearing designer clothes that my mafioso boyfriend bought me while I prepare to face off with real-life monsters in Spain.

Life really does feel like a simulation sometimes. I straighten my waistcoat, very similar to the one I wore when meeting Casuelo, but in charcoal now, and head for the main entrance as I hand my keys to the valet. I don't need to announce myself this time. The doorman greets me by name and immediately passes me off to the well-trimmed host.

"Welcome, Ms. Maizen. Mr. Colombo is ready for you. Please follow me."

After another bag and body scan, I'm shown to a booth in the very back of the restaurant. It's enclosed on three sides and looks out across the entire dining room, though there is a velvet curtain ready to drape across the front if more privacy is needed. Raphael is seated along the back wall, a confident smirk on his face as I approach. His eyes track my every step, and I don't miss the way he assesses every inch of me with his oily gaze.

"Mr. Colombo, it's an honor to meet you, sir," I say with a slight dip of my head, laying the fawning on thick, just the way I know he likes it.

Internally, I'm calling him every English curse word I know and some new ones in Italian that I've picked up from the Marchetti men. Raphael waves the host away and gestures to the seat at his left.

"Please, join me, Ms. Maizen. I've been looking forward to meeting Mr. Destino's formidable emissary ever since your interaction with Casuelo. I see he wasn't exaggerating at all with regard to your beauty, so now I'm eager to know if your brains are as enticing as the rest of you."

I slide into the booth as gracefully as I can manage, keeping a reasonable amount of space between us but not enough to appear meek or threatened by him.

"Thank you for the compliment," I say as I smile politely, holding back the disgusted grimace I'd rather display. "I've worked hard to ensure that I represent Mr. Destino well in all aspects. I look forward to hearing your assessment." *Ugh, gag me.*

As we place our orders, Raphael fills the air between us with empty talk about Valencia and how I like the Spanish coast. I'm careful to frame each answer I give through the lens of the fictional persona Mono's given me, that of a California girl with a law degree and family deep in the film industry who got bored with flashing lights and decided to dive into the dark underworld instead.

"I must say, Ms. Maizen," Raphael says in a low tone, still chewing his bite of steak as he speaks, "you are truly an exceptional woman. I'd be honored to show you around the finer side of Spain during your visit. Perhaps you might even consider staying on an indefinite basis to personally oversee this new partnership."

His hand moves to my knee as he speaks and the intent in his eyes is as clear as can be. I have to work to swallow my food and keep it from reappearing immediately. I take a sip of wine as I think of the best way to respond, then shoot him a demure glance.

"While that does sound...enticing, I'm afraid that your men may have failed to accurately relay my relationship with Mr. Destino. I don't just work for him. I *belong* to him, and he doesn't tend to be fond of sharing. That being said, you're welcome to broach the subject when you meet in person. If he's amenable, I'd love to see Spain through the eyes of a true local."

Thankfully, Raphael seems to respect the claim of another man, at least another relatively powerful man anyway, and he removes his hand from my knee in a gesture of surrender. He chuckles darkly as he speaks, his tone back to its original volume.

"Ah, I should have guessed. Any man would be hard-pressed to have a woman like you at his side every day and not stake his claim on her. And from what I've learned of your...*master*, he is not someone I care to be at war with just now. Hell, even the Russians seem indebted to him, and that is not something I've ever witnessed them admit freely before."

I aim for a natural chuckle of my own, nodding my head at your assessment.

"Ah, you've spoken with Mischa, I take it," I say, watching Raphael's eyes widen as I refer to the bratva boss by his first name. "Truly a charming man, once you get a few shots of vodka in him. Though, what truly bonded him and Mr. Destino, beyond our assistance with a 'problem' his men were having in the States, was their shared love of interrogation. I swear they were like children, swapping techniques and victories like trading cards. Less charming, for sure, but oh so interesting when you get into the mechanics of everything."

Raphael's expression has grown more and more stoic the longer I talk, and I know he's fighting for his life to avoid revealing how much that information concerns him. It's clear that he knew his newest business

230

partner was not a man to be trifled with, but it's only just now occurring to him how royally fucked he is if this deal goes south for any reason. *Oh, if he only knew just how quickly he'll get the chance to see that happen.*

"Well, Ms. Maizen, I look forward to meeting Mr. Destino soon. Perhaps he and I will find that we share some similar affinities as well. I always love learning new tricks."

Those words are exactly the opening I need to lay the final piece of the trap, though my skin crawls as I open my mouth to speak.

"Actually, Mr. Destino asked me to inquire specifically about your 'pet project', as he called it. He's particularly interested in acquiring a few new pets for the men he'll be stationing here in town to support the partnership. Would you be open to meeting him in person to discuss the details, preferably this week? He'd like to finalize that bit of business before the first shipment arrives."

The way Raphael's eyes light up at the mention of his human trafficking operation makes me want to punch him right in the groin.

"I see," he purrs. "I'd be happy to discuss things with Mr. Destino. I happen to have a fresh litter of kittens that will be ready to be adopted by the end of the week. If he's free in two night's time we could get together at my club to discuss his preferences and perhaps even find some suitable pets in the current group."

I nod, the movement clipped as I pour all of my energy into holding my tongue.

"I believe that time should work well, but I'll contact you to confirm after I've spoken with Mr. Destino."

Finishing the rest of our meal is absolute torture, and I'm more proud of myself for doing so without breaking character than I am for any of the other achievements I've earned since I started working with MI and the family. The exact moment that our dessert plates are whisked away, Raphael having insisted on us "sharing something sweet to commemorate many sweet profits to come," I gather my bag and issue a polite but irrefutable farewell.

My walk back to the car is filled with thoughts of exactly how I'll use the time Vince has promised me once we have Raphael secured. I've wanted to be the warm-up act ever since I saw the scars on Vince's body, but now I have even more reasons to make sure it's a performance worthy of such a vile and inhuman piece of shit. I make it back to the villa in record time, eager to debrief and pick Vince's brain for worthwhile ideas.

Chapter 29

Vincenzo

Two Days Later

I rest my arms on the side of the pool, breathless and panting. It's all happening tonight: the final meeting with Raphael, our revenge, and releasing the latest group of women he's trying to traffic. I'm fucking tense. This is so much bigger than our normal business. It means so much *more*. And a part of me is terrified that all the emotions tied to this operation, both in the case of Raphael and the emotions that I feel for Liz, will cloud my judgment.

Liz has been incredible on this trip. She's played her part flawlessly, making the road to this point so smooth that it's felt suspicious how well things have gone. But the other night, knowing that she was meeting with Raphael alone, knowing what I know about him, from his past and his current operations, I was practically feral while I waited for her to return.

I couldn't focus, couldn't think straight. All I could do was picture the absolute worst-case scenarios: her trembling inside one of those shipping containers or fighting him off as he forced himself on her. It drove me insane, so much so that I punched an actual hole into the sparring pad I was trying to release my frustrations on.

And to top it all off, I felt like a chauvinistic asshole the entire time. She has proven time and time again that she can handle herself. But because she's a woman...well, no, because she's *my* woman, I let doubt and fear get the better of me. So when I woke up this morning with everything we've worked for on the horizon, I resolved to keep my distance from her today. I need to shut down my emotions, as much as possible anyway, so that I can make the right calls tonight.

That's why I've spent the day making up excuses to stay out of the house. When I ran out of ideas, I thought it would be helpful to work out to release some of my nervous energy. I've spent the past hour doing calisthenics and swimming laps, but now I'm spent, and it's almost time for us to start getting ready.

I climb out of the pool and check the villa security system to see that Liz is working on her computer in the office. The coast is clear, so I head to the bedroom to shower and change.

As I exit the dressing room some time later wearing my slacks and a black undershirt, I see Liz perched on the edge of the bed, very obviously waiting for me. I stop in my tracks, leaving several feet of space between us and she smirks knowingly.

"Let me guess. You've suddenly recalled a very important package that needs picking up? Or wait, no, maybe you need to check in personally with your men, and a phone call just won't cut it?"

Her jab gets under my skin, and the simmering frustration that I've been caging in all day seeps out into my tone.

"Oh, I'm sorry. Has my handling of fucking business offended you? Did you get confused into thinking this was some sort of vacation? I had shit to do, doll."

Liz's eyes go wide at my response, and for a second, I think I see a glimmer of hurt on her face, but it's quickly replaced by a narrow glare and a pissed-off set to her mouth.

"Don't you fucking dare," she grits out, rising from the bed to stalk toward me.

One hand raises to poke me in the chest as she gets close, tilting her face up to mine with determination.

"I get that you're nervous about tonight. I am, too. But you do *not* get to deal with it by being an asshole and pushing me away. That's not going to solve anything, and you know it."

I grab the finger that's stabbing me in the chest and hold it away from me, my glare just as fierce in the face of her ire. I'm furious, mostly with myself, for being such a dick, but also because I know she's not going to back down easily, and I'll probably end up hurting her more just to get her to leave me be. I don't know what else to do. I have to go into this with a clear head. She can't be *my woman* on this mission. But that concept feels so fucking unnatural that I'm spiraling as I try to grasp onto any solution that might give me the space I need.

"All I *know*," I growl, "is that you should be getting ready to leave, but instead, you're in here harassing me because you feel neglected. This isn't playtime, Elizabeth. The smallest slip-up tonight and one or both of us could wind up dead, so you'll *excuse me* if I'd rather spend my time preparing and not playing house with you while pretending like I'm not a complete and total monster."

Her eyes flame, and she rips her finger out of my grasp, pushing at my chest with both hands.

"Oh, fuck *off*, Vincenzo. You have never once had to pretend like you're not a monster, even while we've been 'playing house,' as you so dickishly put it. I *know*. I've known since long before you and I were ever a thing. So please, bring the monster out to play. Let me talk to *him*. Maybe he'll be more prepared to deal with things in a mature, rational way instead of hiding like a scared child."

The viciousness in her words cuts right through the chains of my restraint, and my hand snaps out to grab her by the throat before I even process that I've done it. I feel the familiar, numbing adrenaline in my veins, and I can tell by the look in her eyes that my demon has made his appearance, deadening my eyes and turning my expression truly cold.

"There he is," she purrs triumphantly, a sinister smile spreading on her face. "Glad you could finally join us."

I use my grip on her neck to pull her face to mine, feeling her toes scramble to support her weight on the ground.

"You don't know what you're asking for, Venom. This is not the time to test me."

She stares back at me, challenge lighting her eyes, but says nothing. I set her back down, maintaining my grip on her throat while I consider my next move. I should probably just let her go and stalk off to start applying all those damn prosthetics, but even my demon seems entranced by her and far too curious to see what she intends to do next.

My curiosity is rewarded when she does the absolute last thing that I expect: her hands move to her top and undo the buttons until the entire shirt falls away. I watch her fingers intently as they move lower, popping the button on her shorts and shifting to the waistband to slide the fabric down her legs.

"Venom," I hiss, "what the actual fuck are you doing?"

She shushes me, her voice a low murmur.

"I'm going to fuck you while you're like this, icy and untethered. I'm going to let you dominate me, let you own me. And when we're done, we're going to walk into that club together with clear heads and the sort of vicious confidence that only the Ice Demon can inspire."

For all of my legendary willpower and unflappability, it's not enough to refuse her when she's talking to me like that, when she's demanding that I take her, even in my altered mental state. The things this woman does to me are...they should be fucking studied. It's supernatural, the hold that she has over me, despite all my best efforts to fuck it up.

I pull her back up to me, my hand still wrapped around her throat, and crush a bruising kiss to her lips. Sliding my other arm beneath her ass, I lift her from the ground and stalk toward the bed, throwing her roughly onto the middle of it. My shirt is off my body in one smooth gesture, and I free the buttons of my slacks in record time. Shedding the last of my clothes, I prowl towards her on the bed, only one thought running through my brain. *Mine.*

I grab her ankles and pull her towards me, her arms slipping out from beneath her so that she's flat on her back. I nip and bite my way up her calves to the soft, succulent flesh of her inner thighs, pressing her legs apart and firmly onto the mattress. Every bite earns me another gasp, another breath, another whimper, and they only serve to fuel the electricity in my veins.

Liz brings her hands down, wrapping her fingers in my hair in an attempt to guide my mouth to where she wants it. I surge forward, grabbing her wrists and pinning them above her head while I hold her in place with my hips. Running my nose along the pulse at her neck, I growl as I remind her what she's gotten herself into.

"You're confused, Venom. I make the decisions here. But since I know you're too fucking stubborn to obey orders, I'll make sure you have no other choice."

I hold both wrists in one hand while the other reaches toward my nightstand. I feel around for what I need, then flick my wrist sharply, unfolding the knife's blade directly in her line of sight. I watch as her eyes widen, but it's thrill and not fear that fills her gaze. *This woman is a monster all her own, I swear.*

I bring the blade to her ribs and trail it lightly down her skin, enjoying the way she shivers beneath me. I remember the first time I had a knife pressed to her skin, the way she ground herself against my thigh to assuage her desire, and decide to test the limits of this fear kink of hers. I press the knife more firmly against her as I continue, still shy of drawing blood but enough to ratchet up her body's instinctive response. Her shivers turn to a powerful shudder, and the moan that leaves her lips is positively sinful, the sound racing straight to my cock.

"You are always so full of surprises, Venom. Lo adoro, mia ragazza viziosa[34]."

I drag the knife to the space between her breasts, tracing circles on her sternum as I watch her squirming beneath me, eyes flashing with challenge and lust. *Hmm, wire-free. Excellent.* With a flick of my wrist, I pop her bra open, licking my lips hungrily as her breasts bounce into a more natural position. I slide the bra up her arms and off, maintaining my grip on her wrists lest she get cocky and try to reclaim control. That only gets us halfway there, though.

Resetting my grip on the knife, I trail the tip agonizingly slowly down her arms, over her breasts, and across her rib cage. As my blade reaches her underwear, I slip it beneath the fabric and slice upwards quickly, tearing it from her body. I shift to repeat the action on her other hip, then slide the material out from between us. I can feel the evidence of her arousal in the damp fabric, and I shoot her a knowing look as I dangle it in the air.

"Someone's desperate for me, isn't she?"

Her eyes flare at my taunt, but she doesn't speak. *Interesting.* Perhaps she wants to see just how far I'll go without her goading. I smirk and begin binding her wrists together with her shredded panties, knotting them tightly enough that there's no chance of her wriggling free, even if the fabric stretches. Grabbing her bra, I use the shoulder straps to create a loop between her wrists, then reach up to secure the other strap around the bedpost, sliding it down to the mattress.

I watch with amusement as she tests her binds, then bark out a laugh as she shoots me an approving look when she finds them unbreakable. I drop my head in mock prayer. *Lucifer, grant me mercy. This woman is likely to be the death of me...*

Raising my eyes back to hers, I send a serpentine smile her way and slide my head back to the sensitive skin of her thighs.

---

[34] I love it, my vicious girl.

"Now, where was I?" I taunt just before pressing a generous and punishing bite to her right leg.

She cries out and I release her to study my handiwork, running my tongue over the defined teeth marks in her skin. I do the same to her other thigh, then return to small nips and open-mouthed kisses as I travel up her body, leaving a trail of red marks and future bruises in my wake.

"You want to be owned by the Ice Demon, Venom? Then, I'll gladly stake my claim over every inch of your perfect skin. You'll wear my marks proudly, and every man who sees you will know better than to even look at you for too long or risk facing my wrath. No one touches you. No one marks you. No one but *me*. Is that what you want, Venom? You want everyone to know who you belong to?"

I raise my face from her neck to wait for her reply, studying her expression closely. There's not even a hint of hesitation in her gaze, nothing aside from desire and quiet confidence.

"Yes, that's *exactly* what I want."

I kiss her fervently, pressing her into the mattress with the weight of my body as if I'm attempting to fuse us together. My tongue drives against hers, eager to taste her, eager to claim her in every way possible. I run my hands along her supple form, mapping and re-mapping every curve, every dip for the thousandth time. After a while, my fingers trail between her legs, sliding between her clit and her entrance, the path slick and welcoming.

She starts to shift her hips in sync with my movements, heightening the pressure and attempting to draw my fingers inside her with each new pass. Eventually, I give her what she's craving, dipping my index and middle fingers into her before sliding back out and up to her clit again. I continue the motion, pressing against her inner walls, sometimes curving my fingers slightly, as I feel the tension in her body build. My mouth leaves her battered lips and returns to her neck, sucking at the sensitive spot behind her ear.

She moans, the sounds growing louder and more desperate as she nears the edge. I lock in, maintaining that exact pace and pattern for several more passes. With one final swirl of my tongue behind her ear, I feel her release take over, her cunt clenching around my fingers and my name shouting from her lips. I slow my pace but keep up the motions, drawing out her pleasure for as long as possible. Once the last aftershock has passed, I withdraw my fingers fully and grip her hip as I kiss her again, deeply but briefly.

"Did you enjoy that, Venom?" I purr.

She nods eagerly, her face flushed and chest still heaving.

"Yes, Sir."

"Good," I say as I flash her a wicked grin. "Because now that you're nice and warmed up, it's my turn."

Leaning back, I grip her other hip and flip her onto her stomach, chuckling at her surprised yelp. I slide one hand beneath her ribs to lift her and move her toward the head of the bed, propping her knees beneath her. Removing the tether on her bound hands from the bedpost, I position her directly in the center of the bed, trusting that she'll obey my commands.

"Grab the headboard."

She hooks her hands over the edge of the headboard and grips on tightly.

"Good girl. Now, stay just like that unless I say otherwise. Understood?"

She nods back at me over her shoulder, and I arch a brow. A loud smack echoes through the room as my palm lands on her ass, the skin reddening instantly.

"What have I told you about nodding at me, Venom?"

"I–I'm sorry, Sir. Yes, I understand."

"Better. Now, hold on."

I drive my hips forward, sinking fully into her wet cunt with a groan. *Lucifer, she feels incredible.* I waste no time setting a furious pace, her body well-prepared to take everything that I have to give. I channel all of the restless energy and all of the doubt that remains in my subconscious into my movements, driving it all away with the force of my thrusts until my mind is completely clear. Liz is screaming and whimpering as I fuck her harder than I've ever dared before, her head buried on top of her hands, and the sound of our skin slapping together loud enough to be heard throughout the entire house. Despite the ecstasy flooding through my veins, my human side pushes through, concerned that it may be too much for her. Gathering her hair in my fist, I pull back gently, forcing her head up and to the side so that I can see her face.

"Still think you like being fucked by a demon, Venom, or should I stop? Tell me the truth."

I'm still pounding into her, watching for a wince or grimace as I take her in case she tries to be stubborn, but I see none.

"Don't you dare stop," she pants. "Fuck me like the monster you are, like the monster I need you to be tonight."

Cazzo[35]. My cock pulses at the sound of that on her lips, and my voice is a low, menacing purr when I speak again.

"Call me a monster one more time, Venom. You have no idea what that does to me, hearing you say that so confidently, without the slightest hint of fear in your voice."

"You're a monster, Vincenzo. You're *my* monster. And those bastards are all going to fear you by the end of the night."

After that, I forget everything, everything except the feel of her sliding around me and the rush of power coursing through my blood at her words. I release her hair and grab her hips with an iron grip, pulling

---

[35] Fuck

her back into me just as forcefully as I'm pressing forward. We groan and pant in unison as the sensations build, my muscles coiling tightly in anticipation of release. When I realize I'm close, I move one hand between her legs, swirling my fingers on her swollen clit to ensure that she follows me off the precipice.

"Come for me, Venom. Let me feel you clenching around me. Let me hear you screaming my name. Make it a battle cry that sets fear into the hearts of our enemies."

She complies, my name a guttural cry on her lips as she explodes around me, pulling me into oblivion alongside her. I come for what feels like ages, unaware I was even capable of such excess until this point. Once I'm finally spent, I drop my chest to her back, enfolding her into my arms as I lie boneless for a mere second before pulling her back up with me to give her tired arms a rest.

I kiss her cheek, her neck, her shoulder, each press of my lips reverent and full of wonder at the extraordinary woman she is. She hums contentedly, pressing her still-bound hands against my arms affectionately, seemingly happy to stay just like this for the foreseeable future. Unfortunately, both of our eyes land on the bedroom clock at the same time, and I realize that we've cut things awfully close if we still plan to arrive on time.

"Here, let me set you free, Venom," I say as I grab her hands and make quick work of the knots, rubbing at her wrists as the fabric falls away. Once free, she pulls away, but only to turn around and wrap her arms around my neck, both of us still kneeling on the bed.

"I know we need to hurry, but I just need to say one final thing before we go into business mode," she says, looking up at me with a satisfied smile.

She captures my eyes with hers, holding my gaze steadily for a moment. I can tell that whatever she wants to say is important, but I'm not even close to prepared for what comes out of her mouth.

"I love you."

My every muscle freezes, my body instinctively feeling like prey caught in a trap, not because I don't feel the same way, but because I'm not sure I deserve her love, or that I ever could. I mean, fuck, look at what just happened. But, of course, she knows that. She probably sees every doubt run across my face as plain as day, so she presses on.

"Vincenzo Caputo, I love you with every fiber of my being, and you *deserve every ounce of it.* I have never felt so worshiped, so respected, so free to be my true self as I do when I'm with you. You treat me as a partner. You make an effort to care about the things that matter to me. You never judge the weaker or darker parts of me as less than. And you make me feel so safe and secure that I feel like I could take on the entire world and win. You are no saint, but frankly, the last thing this harsh world needs is more saints. You protect those who can't protect themselves and clean up garbage that the rest of the men in power refuse to acknowledge even exists. You are worthy, and it's time you start to see that for yourself."

I'm at a complete loss for words, my mouth opening and closing like a suffocating fish while she just stares up at me, her expression patient but slightly guarded.

"I don't," I start, but she cuts me off.

"You don't have to say anything. I didn't tell you that to pressure you. I just wanted you to know."

I fix her with a stern look, her obvious assumption that her feelings are one-sided enough to kick my brain into gear.

"I was *going* to say that I don't know where to start, but I've sorted that out now, so may I continue, Venom?"

She nods, her face sheepish and hopeful. I look at her with the same steady, sincere gaze that she gave to me and prepare to bare my soul for the first time in my life.

"Elizabeth Greystone, you have been completely unexpected since the day we met. I'm pretty sure I haven't known a single moment's peace since. And yet, the times we've spent together have been the happiest of my entire life. You say that I make you feel worshiped, respected, and free to be yourself, but I could say the same things about you. I have never been able to be so vulnerable with another person before. Even Damien, who I spent more time with than anyone, never really saw *all* of me. But you? You barreled into my life with your emotional x-ray vision and snarky attitude and refused to let me hide behind my masks. You are cunning, fierce, and worthy of running this whole damn empire should you wish it, and yet, for some reason, you still think my sadistic, emotionally-stunted ass is worth your time. I love you more than I ever thought I'd be capable of loving anyone. I'm utterly *drowning* in love for you. And I have no desire to resurface for the rest of my life."

Her smile is beaming, her eyes glassy, and she's never looked at me with such unfiltered emotion before. I kiss her fiercely and desperately, trying to reiterate every word, to brand it into her lips. She breaks away first, laughing softly and wiping tears from her face. I chuckle alongside her, feeling like I could fly, and we climb off the bed together, fingers laced as she pulls me to the bathroom to get cleaned up and don our disguises for the night ahead.

Chapter 30

Vincenzo

Later That Night

My senses are on high alert as I guide Liz through the doors of Paraíso, my hand firm on her back. At the entrance, a short woman in a skintight red dress greets us from behind a gleaming counter.

"Bienvenido al Paraíso[36]," she purrs.

I give Liz's back a gentle pinch of silent reassurance and smile warmly at the hostess. My Spanish isn't perfect, but Italian is close enough to be able to fill in the gaps, and she seems to understand me well enough. At the woman's request, I hand over the gold metal card that Raphael sent over yesterday. She inserts the card into a reader, smiling when it displays a confirmation.

"Muchas gracias, Señor Destino. Espero que pase una noche agradable.[37]"

The stone-faced men flanking the inner doors come to life at her nod and open them wide, granting us access to the club itself. The space is dark, full of glossy black marble and gold accents, with sensual jazz piping through the speakers. There's a large stage dead ahead, with tables for two littering the viewing floor.

---

[36] Welcome to Paradise

[37] Thank you very much, Mr. Destino. I hope you have a pleasurable night.

On stage, a redheaded woman is lying naked atop a velvet chaise, facing the audience with her legs spread wide as a dark-haired man drips wax onto her skin. The couples watching the show are in various states of undress, some watching raptly while others seem more wrapped up in one another than the provided entertainment.

I pull Liz closer to my side, breaking her gaze away from the carnal pleasures of the club and up to me. It's all I can do not to find the nearest private room when I see the lust in her eyes. I'd never even considered bringing her to a sex club before, but it's clear from her expression that I should rethink that position once we're safely back home.

I lean down to murmur in her ear, my fingertips dancing along the cutouts of her dress to grip her ass firmly.

"See something you like, Venom?"

Her eyes flare, and she nods, a smirk dancing across her lips. I capture those lips with my own, kissing her sensually as I try to reign in my raging libido. Our kiss is a bit awkward thanks to the prosthetics of my disguise, not least of which is the mustache I'm sporting, but at least they remain in place while I devour her. After a moment, I break away. As much as I want her, neither one of us would truly be able to enjoy ourselves with Raphael roaming free somewhere in the same building.

As we part, a staff member approaches us to say that Mr. Colombo has requested that we join him in his private room. I straighten and give the man a nod to lead the way, squeezing Liz's hip as we both steel ourselves for the night ahead.

"Ah! Ms. Maizen!" Raphael booms as we step into the room. "Such a treasure to see you again. You look ravishing."

He stands, raising a hand in my direction as he reluctantly peels his lecherous eyes off my woman. I'm starting to regret dressing her up like my own personal sex toy, even if it does make our cover that much more believable in a place like this.

"Mr. Destino, it's a pleasure to finally meet in person. I'm looking forward to a long and fruitful partnership between our two organizations."

I shake his hand firmly, gripping just a bit harder than is necessary, and fix him with a charming smile.

"The pleasure is all mine, and please, call me Lucien. I have a feeling we'll be as close as family soon enough."

Raphael booms with laughter at my request, eagerly accepting my invitation and reciprocating in kind. He gestures for us to sit, and I choose a spot across from him. I settle into the cushioned bench that lines the wall before pulling Liz down onto my lap, my arm wrapping around her waist possessively.

There are two other women in the room, workers, if I'm guessing, and they're eyeing Liz with thinly veiled disgust. *Interesting.* I nuzzle into Liz's neck so that I can whisper in her ear.

"See if you can find out if they're here by choice or if they're part of Raphael's 'litter.' If they're willing to help us, I think I've found our way out of here."

Liz giggles and swats at me playfully, playing her role perfectly as she nods. While we'd talked through hundreds of possibilities, we couldn't be sure exactly where in the club this meeting would take place and how it would all go down, so our escape plan is being formed as we go. But seeing those women, I think we can help each other get out of this place alive and in one piece.

"Oh, don't be coy. You know you're a slut for me," I say, loud enough that Raphael can hear. "Now, go sit with the girls while Marco and I discuss business. We'll have plenty of time to play later."

Raphael watches with undisguised lust as Liz stands and saunters over to where the women are seated, choosing the far side so that they're forced to turn their backs on him to chat with her. I smirk, thanking the universe once again for giving me such a perceptive and capable partner.

"I have to say, Lucien, I'm extremely envious of your ability to tame your woman so completely. She seems like the type to give a man a run for his money."

I turn my gaze to him and find him watching me carefully. I settle back into my seat and reach for the glass of scotch Raphael set before me earlier.

"It certainly wasn't easy. She thought I was the devil incarnate for a while, but breaking a woman is similar to breaking a prisoner. You just have to show them how much simpler life would be if they'd just submit."

I take a sip of my drink, letting my words marinate.

"Though, I won't pretend that my ownership has done anything to stem the strength of her wrath toward anyone else. She's a force to be reckoned with when crossed."

Raphael laughs at that, his head thrown back in true enjoyment. *You won't be laughing later when you experience the truth of those words, pompinara*[38]. Once his mirth subsides, he fixes me with a curious look.

"So, I hear you're in the market for some new pets for your men."

"You heard right. I'm told you provide the finest quality in the area. Here's what I'm looking for..."

I lean forward and set my drink down, diving into the conversation. I sneer as I describe my requirements, making sure I'm lurid enough to keep Raphael's full attention so that Liz can recruit his women to our cause without suspicion. When her eyes finally catch mine, signaling that she's done and they're willing to help, I steer my conversation with Raphael to an end, telling him that I'll send a man over for the pickup tomorrow night.

"Now that business is settled, how about you show us around, Marco? We only made it as far as the main room earlier, and I know that Olivia

---

[38] cock sucker

would just *love* to see what happens in the playrooms, wouldn't you, pet?"

I gesture for her to rejoin me as I speak, standing up and pulling her back to me, my hand resting dangerously close to the juncture of her thighs. Marco agrees and stands up as well, gesturing for his girls to return to his sides. They position themselves under each arm and smile up at him, though I catch the sideways glance they send my way.

As Marco walks around the low table and toward the exit door, I fall in behind him and bring the stolen syringe to his neck, wrapping a firm hand around his mouth to keep him from calling out. He struggles for a few moments, but my grip is unyielding, and after a short while, the tranquilizers start to take effect. I'm able to release my grip, stepping back to see if the women will be able to support his weight.

In Spanish, I relay the full plan to them, telling them that he'll be loopy for a few minutes, but we need to be out of the club by the time he passes out completely. As far as anyone knows, he's drunk and we're going to have some fun back at the compound. I reassure them that I'll do all the talking, then whisper into Raphael's ear that the girls are taking him for some fun. The drug has taken effect enough for his addled mind to believe the idea. He starts blathering about how he's going to show them how it feels to bed a real man.

I gesture to the door for them to walk out first, shooting the guards a knowing look and acting a bit plastered myself as I stumble out the door behind him, Liz pretending to support my weight while I press a sloppy kiss to her cheek. The guards don't even flinch. It must not be uncommon for Raphael to let himself go while he's here. *Excellent.* The girls lead us toward a side exit that opens to the parking lot. They've just opened the door when Raphael goes completely limp, his added bulk too much for the women to carry. As he crumples to the floor, a nearby guard sounds the alarm and I spring into action, pressing the spare car key into Liz's palm as I push her toward Raphael's unconscious form.

"Get him into the car and get out of here," I command, my tone brooking no argument. "I'll hold them off until you leave, then I'll be right behind you."

I can see the fear in her eyes, but she doesn't hesitate, nodding with determination before running to help the girls pick up Raphael and drag him out the open door. I fight off the first wave of guards who ran over to check on Raphael, and I can practically feel the tension in the air thicken as his men realize this is not a simple case of overindulgence. The first gunshots ring out as the door closes, his men having been too cautious to fire while he was still in view, and I roll out of the way, unholstering my weapon to return fire.

I have no way of knowing if they've escaped. All I can do is hold off the men inside and hope that they're able to get away before the outer guards reach them. I flip a nearby table on its side, ducking behind it as I pick off two of the guards in front of me, more taking their places almost immediately.

I feel a breeze on my neck and spin, catching the arm of the man attempting to creep in behind me through the exit door. I break it and bend his arm back toward himself, using his own weapon to put a bullet through his heart. As he drops, a second man opens the door and I tackle him low out into the parking lot. We wrestle on the pavement for a few moments and he manages to land a solid head butt that knocks me off of him, but it only serves to give me the space I need to aim my gun at his head and fire.

I scramble to my feet, ducking low as I dart between the rows of vehicles. I don't see Liz or the SUV anywhere, so it seems they were able to get away in time. *Thank fuck.* I check my phone for a message from Liz, but find it smashed and the screen dark. Oh well. With a final visual sweep of the parking lot, I make myself scarce. I need to find a ride that's unlikely to have GPS ability so I can join the really party at the warehouse. I hear Raphael's men shouting as they search for me, and I chuckle as I put more space between us. *Happy hunting, dipshits.*

Chapter 31

Elizabeth

An Hour Later

My feet are kicking up dirt on the floor as I pace near the main door of the warehouse, trying to tune out the sound of Raphael bitching and moaning from his place within the stacks. He's gagged to keep him from making too much noise, so I can't tell exactly what he's saying, but I have a pretty good guess.

It's been a little over an hour since we left the club, and Vince still hasn't arrived. I'm alone. Andre has already left to take the workers we rescued over to the villa with the rest of the women Vince's men freed while we were at the club.

To say that I'm starting to panic would be an understatement. I've tried calling him, but his phone is going straight to voicemail. We made sure they were charged before we left, so that means it's either broken or was purposely turned off. Neither possibility makes me feel any better.

*Come on, Liz. This is Vincenzo we're talking about. He's fine. He's **always** fine.*

I repeat the mantra to myself several times, but it doesn't help. Eventually, the combination of fear and annoyance makes my temper snap, and I march back to the center of the stacks where Raphael struggles in vain against his binds. I have to admit, I did some nice work on those restraints. Neither his arms nor his legs have shifted from where I tied them around the metal chair that was bolted to the ground in preparation for tonight. Vince will be proud. *If he's even alive to see them.*

No! Stop that right fucking now. He probably just had trouble finding suitable transportation after he escaped. I'm sure he'll be here any minute.

In the meantime, I grab Raphael by the hair and pull his head back, leaning over him with a scowl.

"I swear to God, if you don't shut the hell up, I'm going to give you a real reason to scream, you disgusting sack of shit."

Raphael's gaze hardens and he jerks toward me, but only makes it half an inch at best. I pull my arm back to slap him, intending to release some of my nervous tension on his rage-inducing face, but a hand on my wrist stops me in midair.

"Woah, there, Venom. Easy, girl. There will be plenty of time for that later."

Vince!

I spin around, checking him for any signs of serious injury. There's dried blood on his face from a cut above his eye, and he's sporting a busted nose, but nothing concerning beyond that. I lock my eyes with his, silently asking for confirmation that he's alright. He smiles tenderly and gives me a succinct nod.

"I'm fine, Venom. Just a few scrapes, but frankly, Raphael's men were pretty pathetic sparring partners."

I hear a muffled sound of surprise from behind me, and Vince looks over my shoulder pointedly. Turning my head, I see Raphael staring him down intently, eyes narrowed in question at the use of his real name.

"Ah, whoops, I let the cat out of the bag a bit early, didn't I? Oh well, I suppose it's time you and I had a little chat anyway."

Vince gestures for me to remove the gag, and I do so, dropping

253

the rags to the floor and walking back around to stand next to Vince. Raphael wastes no time resuming his tirade, telling us that his men will find him, and we'll be food for the sharks. I smirk up at Vince, and he chuckles, which only pisses Raphael off more.

"You think this is funny?! You won't be laughing when you're strung up like livestock watching my men run through your girl."

That was the wrong thing to say. Vince's hand is around Raphael's throat in an instant, his expression murderous. His fingers are leaving deep imprints, and I can tell Raphael is already finding it hard to breathe.

"You still have no fucking idea who you're dealing with, do you? Threaten her again, and I'll feed you your own balls before I even start with what I had originally planned for you. Capito?[39]"

Raphael doesn't agree, but he also doesn't say anything else, so Vince releases him and steps back.

"Now, where was I?" Vince asks with an exaggerated hand on his chin, already starting to showboat a bit. "Oh, right! Your men won't be coming to save you, Raphael. After all, why would they bother to check your own warehouse, especially when the video feeds and security system show everything is locked up and empty? So, you may as well get comfortable. We're long overdue for a little...family reunion."

The intense stare is back on Raphael's face, and I can almost see the gears turning as he tries to piece together what exactly Vince means by that statement. I see suspicion enter his gaze, but he's clearly not sure yet. Vince must see it, too, because he raises his hands toward his face and starts to speak again.

"I can see you still don't know what I mean. That's fine. Allow me to demonstrate."

Slowly, he pulls away the silicone mask, his dark wig falling away as

---

[39] Understand?

well to reveal curly brown locks and a face that bears an unmistakable familial resemblance to Raphael's own. *Thankfully, those similarities are slight.* Raphael's eyes blow wide, and his mouth gapes for a second before he catches himself and shuts it firmly. Vince's eyes are cold but shining and fixed entirely on Raphael.

"Hiya, Dad. Did you miss me?"

Raphael opens his mouth again, probably to start begging for his life if he's been keeping up with his son's reputation, but Vince cuts him off.

"Actually, don't answer that. I don't give a fuck. All I care about right now is making sure you finally pay the price for Mom, Mrs. Marchetti, and every other woman you've hurt during your worthless life."

Vince prowls forward, placing his hands atop Raphael's wrists and leaning over him, his expression dark and his voice low and frigid.

"And I'm going to take my time extracting that payment, inch by excruciating inch."

He pauses for dramatic effect, Raphael's fear-stricken face providing exactly the reaction he predicted. I chuckle darkly at the sight, catching Vince's attention. He turns a wicked grin in my direction but still directs his words to Raphael.

"But first, I promised Venom here that she could warm you up for me. She's got her own vendetta to settle."

Vince calls me over with an outstretched hand, pulling me in front of him and wrapping around me with his chin on my shoulder.

"Still planning on doing some painting, love?" he asks as he kisses my neck. *Mmm.* My head tilts subconsciously to give him more space to work with as I confirm my intentions with a low hum.

"Help me unwrap the canvas?" I ask with mock innocence, playing along with his metaphor. Vince presses a final kiss to my neck and steps away, his eyes glittering.

"With *pleasure.*"

He flicks open his knife as he grabs Raphael by the shirt, slicing down the front roughly until the garment falls open. A few more strategic, but not gentle, flicks of his wrist, and the tattered clothing slides to the floor, leaving Raphael shirtless and bleeding faintly.

After slipping on two pairs of disposable gloves, I pick up a glass jar, pipette, and glass stir stick from the nearby table, walking with measured steps to avoid spilling the contents. I set them down on a stool I positioned earlier, close enough to reach without the risk of accidentally knocking into it. *High-school me would be shitting herself right now. Who knew that one day I'd be putting our intrusive thoughts from chemistry class to real-world use?*

"Alright, now I just need my model. Shirt off, love, and stand just to the side there. Back toward me."

This part of my plan is a surprise to Vince, and the flash of delight that dances across his expression tells me it's a welcome one. I send him a wink and mime a shooing motion to hurry him along. He complies, unbuttoning his shirt and turning his back to me as he sheds it. My mood loses its whimsy as I take in the evidence of Raphael's abuse once more. I reach down to grab the bastard's jaw and force his gaze toward Vince's exposed back.

"You see those scars?" I growl. "I'm going to give you a matching set, except instead of a belt or a knife, I'm going to use something rather more painful."

I point to the supplies I've gathered, turning his head so he can get a good look.

"That jar contains 98% sulfuric acid, and I'm going to use it to paint those scars onto your flesh. I might also take a few creative liberties. It's not every day I get to try out a new technique on such a deserving subject, after all. Shall we begin?"

I release his jaw and turn without waiting for a reaction, though he isn't shy about telling me just what he thinks of my plan. His vocabulary is fairly disappointing, though. I've learned far more creative terms just by quizzing Vince's men during slow days.

Grabbing the jar, I dip the glass stirrer inside and walk back over to Raphael's struggling form. Looking at Vince's back for reference, I start on the top left corner of his chest and draw a long slice diagonally toward his pec muscle. Raphel grits his teeth and hisses as the acid begins to work. I'm entranced by how it bubbles and sinks through his skin. There's no time for staring, though. I want to see how many strokes it takes to get him screaming.

It takes twelve. Too bad for him, I'm barely a third of the way done mapping the cuts he gave his adolescent son. His screams only become more guttural as I continue, and it gets harder to draw straight lines with the force of his trembling. I decide to forgo the glass stirrer entirely and pick up the pipette instead. If the lines are going to be crooked anyway, might as well explore with some drip work.

I fill the tube and run it horizontally along his stomach as I squeeze, watching as it runs down his skin, corroding everything in its path. Vince approaches from behind, having realized that I've gone off-map, and he whistles as he leans in close.

"Whooo, that's *glorious*, Venom. You really hit a home run with this idea. I may have to add it to my regular rotation. Just *listen* to the sounds he's making."

I turn my head to his and steal a kiss from his lips. The high of revenge and his murmured praises shift my focus away from Raphael and onto the terrifyingly sexy, shirtless demon at my back.

"Hmmm, I'm glad you enjoyed it. I think he's nice and warmed up for you now."

Vince kisses me again, this one more heated than the last, and carefully takes the jar from my grip to set it on the stool without breaking the contact of our lips. I rip off my gloves and bring my hands to his chest, digging my fingers into the hard planes of muscle as he brings his hands up to cup my face and pulls me further into him. I moan, completely forgetting where we are or what we were doing just moments ago until Raphael finally regains the power of speech.

"You're fucking demented, the both of you!" he spits. "You're sick, twisted, fucking psychopaths!"

Vince breaks our kiss slowly, keeping his face close to mine, and I shudder with dark excitement as I watch his face shift from heated and hungry to frigid and terrifying. He turns toward Raphael with sinister slowness and fixes him with a hollow smile.

"Oh, Raphael," he purrs. "You haven't seen the half of it yet."

I spend the next two hours being continually surprised by the creativity of Vincenzo's methods as well as impressed at the clinical precision with which he employs them. Though I enjoy every second of watching Raphael get his due, I can't help but flinch at some of the more grotesque and brutish techniques. I know that Vince notices because I catch his eyes darting to me every time, so I make sure to keep up a steady stream of commentary and flirtatious dialogue to reassure him.

Watching him work for the first time is certainly intense, but it changes nothing. It's the *why* behind it that matters to me. If he were doing this to innocent civilians just to get his rocks off, that would be different. But he's not. He's not a sociopath just trying to feel something. He's a dark guardian, protecting those same civilians from the real monsters.

Eventually, Raphael passes out entirely from the blood loss or the pain, or most likely a combination of the two. Vince looks over at me, kicking Raphael's limp foot with a put-out expression, like a kid whose favorite toy just broke. I stand and walk over to stand in front of him, wrapping my arms around his neck and tilting my head to meet his gaze.

"I think you've done more than enough justice by Damien and everyone else this bastard hurt, Rattles. What do you say we wrap this up and head home where I can reward you for such a remarkable performance?"

Vince's expression turns wicked, eyes heating instantly as he tightens his arms around my waist and runs his tongue along his back teeth as he makes a show of considering my offer. He kisses me deeply, practically sucking me in, before letting go and stepping over to grab another syringe from his work table. He jabs the needle into Raphael's heart, and the next moment, Raphael gasps awake, delirious and confused.

"Glad you could rejoin us," Vince tells him, standing tall so that Raphael has to crane his neck to look up at him. "I want to be able to watch the life leave your eyes when I put a bullet in your head."

I'm not sure if Raphael is even capable of processing Vince's words at this point, and in the end, it doesn't seem to matter to Vince either way. He raises his pistol and fires, the sound ringing loudly through the metal warehouse. He stands there for a moment, just staring at Raphael's limp form. But then the moment is over. He casually returns his gun to its holster and steps back over to me, looping an arm around my neck.

"Let's go home, love."

Chapter 32

Elizabeth

Four Months Later

I'm seated at the bar at Hank's as I answer emails. The old haunt brings back a flood of memories, both heartwarming and bittersweet. Vince is in Spain yet again. He's been there for the past month with Adrian Nuñez as they continue expanding the Marchetti and Saltero footprint in the area. I know it's important that he be there to oversee this transition himself, but I still hate being away from him for so long.

In the months since we returned, he's moved into the penthouse with Sam and me, keeping his loft around solely for the purpose of handling family business so Sam can stay far away from it all. Sam's adjusted better than I expected. It almost feels like I have to fight for Vince's attention at times with how close those two have become. Though I can tell, we only have a few years at most before we'll have to tell Sam the truth. The kid is already too observant for his own good.

Even so, things have been amazing lately and I wouldn't trade any of it for the world. But having Vince so entwined in our lives only makes times like this more difficult. Even with plenty of work at MI and helping Luca run the family operations here in town, I feel his absence acutely. I suppose I was hoping that spending time back in the place we first met would help me miss him a little bit less.

I'm writing a particularly lengthy email response, getting frustrated when autocorrect keeps censoring my words as I tell an erstwhile supplier exactly what will happen if he continues to fuck with my timeline. I feel a presence at my back, and my muscles tense on instinct, but a low voice in my ear sets them at ease instantly.

"Want me to beat him up for you?"

My phone clatters to the bar, and I spin in my chair, throwing myself into Vince's arms. He chuckles at my enthusiastic welcome and wraps his strong arms around me, nuzzling his cheek onto the top of my head.

"When did you get back? I thought you weren't coming home until next week!"

"Andre has things well in hand, and Adrian's going to stay on for a few more weeks, so I decided to surprise you. It seems it was fated timing, me finding you here of all places."

I look up at him and beam, my world securely back on its axis now that he's next to me. I might even cut that vendor a bit of slack. *Ha, as if.*

Vince gestures for me to return to my seat and snags the chair next to me, flagging the bartender over. He tells me about how he left things in Spain, and I fill him in on the latest with everything here at home. We've talked every single day, so the updates don't take long, and I catch him watching me with an unreadable expression on his face as I finish.

"What?" I question, eyes narrowing in suspicion. "Why are you looking at me like that? What's running through that terrifying brain of yours?"

"Just ruminating on an idea I had, another expansion of sorts, if you will."

"*Another* expansion? Jesus, Rattles, is your kingdom not wide enough yet? What could it possibly be lacking at this point?"

Vince slides a slow hand toward me on the bar, eyes gleaming as he holds my gaze in his and replies.

"A queen to reign alongside me."

My eyes are drawn to his hand as he lifts it away from the bar, and I gasp at the sight of a marquise-cut emerald ring shining up at me from a black velvet box. My eyes shoot back to him, but he's no longer sitting next to me. He's kneeling on the floor before me, one hand coming up to grasp mine as the other reaches out to grab the ring box.

"Elizabeth Greystone, you breathed life back into my soul when I was all but dead. Your empathy, your fire, your perspective, and your refusal to take my shit have shaped me into a version of myself I never thought I could be. I love you more than my own life, and if you would do me the honor of agreeing to be my wife, I will spend every day I have left endeavoring to be worthy of you. So, will you marry me? Will you tie your soul to mine, now and for eternity?"

The entire restaurant is silent, everyone within earshot waiting with bated breath as the legendary Vincenzo Caputo bares his heart, publicly and unapologetically. I move my hands from where they're covering my mouth to wipe away the tears on my cheeks and nod enthusiastically.

"Yes. Yes, I'll marry you, Vincenzo. And you'll never be rid of me from here on out."

Vince is on his feet in a millisecond, wrapping me up in a celebratory kiss as he slides the emerald ring onto my finger. We're both laughing in between kisses, and I swear if he wasn't holding me, I'd float right up to the ceiling. The entire restaurant is applauding and whistling. I even see Hank himself in the back corner, discreetly wiping at his face.

After a minute or so, Vince sets me down, smoothing his countenance and his suit before turning around to face our audience.

"Drinks are on me tonight, everyone! Feel free to spread the word that the Marchetti empire has a new queen."

Vince turns back to me, as the other diners cheer even louder, his expression heated and his voice low.

"As for you, Venom. Let's go home so I can show you how it feels to be worshiped as a queen."

He slides a warm hand around my waist and leads me through the front door and toward the rest of our lives.

Made in the USA
Monee, IL
08 January 2025

76178547R00163